D1391594

ADVENTURE STORIES FROM BLACK PONY INN

ADVENTURE STORIES FROM BLACK PONY INN

by Christine Pullein-Thompson

illustrated by Glenn Steward

AWARD PUBLICATIONS LIMITED

ISBN 0-86163-847-6

Text copyright © Christine Pullein-Thompson 1976, 1978
Illustrations copyright © Award Publications Limited 1998

Strange Riders at Black Pony Inn and *Mystery at Black Pony Inn*
first published 1976
Secrets at Black Pony Inn first published 1978

This omnibus edition first published 1998 by
Award Publications Limited,
27 Longford Street, London NW1 3DZ

Printed in India

CONTENTS

Strange Riders at Black Pony Inn

CONTENTS

One

Taking the plunge

Dad had summoned us all to the dining-room. It was
spring, one of those bright sunlit days which seem so full
of hope that you can almost feel the sap rising in the
trees. We could see the lawns stretching away in front of
us and the daffodils tall and yellow under the apple
trees. Beyond the lawns were the stables and the
straight-railed paddocks, where the first tips of grass
were appearing at last through the winter mud.

We knew it was serious. Things had been going
wrong for a long time. Creditors had telephoned demanding money, while more and more men had been
laid off at the factory. Our house and the paddocks and
everything we loved were up for sale. Soon our ponies
might be going too. It wasn't anybody's fault. Dad had
made a lot of money. He had bought the house and realised a dream he had had for years; now no one wanted
his products any more and the dream was over.

Dad had a pile of letters in front of him. I was feeling
sick. I had the feeling that this was the end of a chapter
in our lives.

I was just twelve, with nut-brown hair and blue eyes.
Lisa, who was nine, was sitting with Twinkle, our black
cat, on her lap. Ben was reading a Western, pretending
he didn't care, his fair hair flopping over his eyes, his
outgrown trousers barely covering his ankles. James

paced the room. Mummy sat with her hands curled round a mug of hot coffee.

"The house isn't selling. The deal has fallen through," said Dad, putting on his glasses. "The Arab company doesn't want it after all, and who else will pay £500,000 for a place like this."

It was almost a relief to know that the house wasn't sold after all, that we could go on living here with all the last demands in red still coming through the letter box.

"What now, then?" asked Ben, putting down his book. "What did they want it for anyway?"

"A guest house for Arab businessmen. I suppose they've found somewhere more convenient, nearer London," Dad answered.

"We needn't move then?" cried Lisa with hope in her voice. "We can stay, can't we? And the ponies can stay too?"

Dad looked at the letters in front of him. "We can't stay as we are. It isn't possible. I can't go on paying the heating bills and lighting bills and . . ." he began.

"And the shoeing and the hay bills," continued James.

"I'll do the mowing," said Ben. "And the ponies can live on straw and . . ."

"Can't we run it as something?" suggested Mummy. "Run it as a guest house and keep everything just the same? Then the ponies can give rides and pay for themselves."

"A children's guest house where children can come when their parents want a change," I cried.

"We can do up the attic," Mummy added.

"And teach riding," cried Lisa.

Suddenly we were all talking at once.

"I can be hall porter and run reception. I can leave school in the autumn," cried James.

"Old ladies would be more profitable," said Dad.

"We'll have to charge less for children," replied Mummy quickly.

"Old ladies eat less than children."

"We can have both," said Mummy, pushing her short dark hair behind her ears. "We can say children over eight are accepted on their own."

"And the old ladies will look after the children," cried Lisa, beginning to laugh.

I was feeling excited now. For months life had been difficult, with rows over lights being left on, rows over hay bills, oat bills and the cost of petrol for the Land Rover and trailer. For months we had been living beyond our means. Now we would all be helping to pay the bills. I saw hordes of children arriving with suitcases. I saw myself taking them up to the newly painted attic, escorting them for rides. I thought of the house full of laughter with twenty to dinner in the long dining-room and a log fire burning in the huge fireplace. I had been wanting a job for ages, but there was nothing but the local paper round which James had bagged years ago. Now we all had jobs. Our lean days were over.

We made plans. We rushed from room to room counting how many beds would go in each. The attic was full of cobwebs and old suitcases. There were three rooms up there and we reckoned each would take six children.

"Eighteen children! That will bring in hundreds of pounds," cried Ben.

"But they will have to be fed," said Dad.

"But we can charge for riding," argued Ben.

"But they will need someone to cook and sweep up after them," said Mummy.

"Perhaps they will bring their own ponies," suggested Lisa. "I don't want my darling Jigsaw worked to death."

"We don't need to make a lot of money, just enough to go on living here," said Mummy quietly.

"And employ a gardener, three grooms and a butler," added Ben, who has disgusting ideas of grandeur.

Later we wandered round to the stables, which had once known better days. We had turned our ponies out earlier, but they came across the field when they saw us, hoping for a second breakfast. James doesn't ride. He's tall and dark and rather vague and just sixteen. He had stayed behind to help Mummy count the sheets in the airing cupboard.

"I hope they don't mind being ridden by strangers," said Ben, patting his dark brown, part-bred Welsh cob, Solitaire.

Jigsaw was small and piebald with a clever face and a crooked patch of black above his left eye. He had a quick trot which had won Lisa a host of trotting races. He had spring, too, and could jump almost anything. He was the apple of Lisa's eye. If she could, she would have taken him to bed with her like a teddy bear.

Then there was Limpet, the little black which we had all grown out of in turn. Once he had been our only pony and we had fought over him, fallen off him and generally mismanaged him. My mare was a grey with a head which pulled at your heartstrings. She was dappled like an old-fashioned rocking horse and I had called her Lorraine after the poem by Charles Kingsley.

"Four ponies won't go far with eighteen children," I said.

"So we may have to buy some more," suggested Ben optimistically.

"From the horse sanctuary or the market," added Lisa. I saw the yard full of horses, greys and bays, blacks, chestnuts and roans.

"They must be safe," I said. "We don't want any accidents."

"What shall we call the place?" asked Ben. "The Great Ranch Guest House?"

"Don't be mad," I answered. "It's going to be a guest house, not a ranch."

"Can't we call it The Little Pony Guest House?" Lisa asked.

"No, that's pathetic. It makes it sound little, and it isn't," replied Ben.

We sat on the rail fence trying to think of a name. There was sunlight everywhere and life seemed lit with hope. None of us stopped to consider the trials and tribulations which might lie ahead, the piles of washing up, horrible children, unmanageable ponies, unpleasant or fussy old ladies, heaps of dirty clothes.

"We must have 'horse' or 'pony' in it," Ben said. "Then even if we get bags of old ladies, they will be nice horsy ones, you know, old experts who can teach us lots about horses, titled ladies."

"Titled ladies! Honestly, you get worse every day," I replied.

"I think 'Inn' sounds much more old-world than 'guest house'," Ben said. "'Guest house' is genteel."

"Let's call it Black Pony Inn after Limpet. After all, he taught us everything," I said.

"Great," cried Lisa.

"Brilliant," said Ben.

We rushed indoors with the suggestion, but Mummy had a pile of silver in front of her and Dad was going through the demands in red. They seemed preoccupied. Dad just said, "Go away."

Mummy said, "Tell your father I'm going to sell all the silver. There's no point in keeping it. Nasty children will nick it."

"Nasty children!" I cried.

"Yes, we will have some for sure," replied Mummy.

"But what will we eat with when all the silver's gone?" asked Ben.

"Cheaper cutlery."

I remembered that Mummy had come from a well-off family and had inherited the silver. Dad had made his way by hard work and enterprise. Ben had turned quite pale. He loved things like the silver.

"The money from the silver will buy sheets and blankets, and we'll need a big deep-freeze and bags of food from the supermarket," she said. "We are lucky to have it to sell. The sheets and blankets will cost a fortune."

I went upstairs to see what I could sell. My bedroom looked towards the stables. It was large, with an armchair and a desk as well as a bed and lots of cupboards. I had an idea it wouldn't be mine much longer. I found some outgrown clothes, and a pile of books which I had meant to keep for my children if I had any. They might buy a bag of pony cubes, I thought without much hope, and heaven knows the ponies need more food. It had been a disastrous year, the price of hay and oats had soared. Now we had no hay left, only oat straw and a bit of hard feed, and the Easter holidays were just beginning.

I put my books into a suitcase and thought how lovely it would be to be rich again, to be able to buy bags and bags of pony cubes and tons of oats; to buy bran and linseed again and to have our ponies shod when they needed it instead of waiting until their shoes were dropping off. I was ready to work myself to death for it if necessary. We needed new clothes too. Ben's jacket was halfway up his arms. Lisa's crash-cap was frayed in front and I had grown out of my riding-coat six months ago. As for James, he had taken to buying his clothes from the Oxfam shop.

The next few days we worked almost non-stop, clearing out the attic, painting the rooms, spring-cleaning the

whole house. Our arms and legs ached. At night we slept like logs, too tired even to dream. Yet in a strange way we were happy, happier than we had been for months. We seemed to be doing something concrete at last. We were no longer sitting on the fence watching our lives crumbling about us. We were fighting back at last. We were certain that the awful days were over, that we were going to save ourselves, and would never have to ask Dad for money again. We were convinced that in a few weeks money would be flowing into our house like gold in a gold rush.

We hardly rode at all because we had no time and because our ponies looked so awful with deep marks round their quarters and their coats falling out.

Mummy received enough money from the silver to buy a deep-freeze, two new beds with first-class mattresses for the old ladies and some cheaper second-hand beds for the children, and a pile of sheets, pillowcases and duvets.

My clothes and my books fetched enough to buy a whole hundredweight of oats and a few pony cubes. Ben sold his radio-cassette recorder and bought himself a jacket because he said he must look smart if he was to wait on old ladies.

By the middle of April we were ready, and Dad suggested we should advertise in the local paper which was bought over a wide area and wouldn't cost as much as advertising in the national press. He was still gloomy. More men had been laid off at the factory and he was now working on the floor himself instead of supervising from his office. He came home late every night with a case full of work. The lines had deepened on his face and he looked much older. None of us dared ask him for anything.

The spring grass had really come and at least the

ponies were beginning to look fatter. Ben and I drew up the advertisement on the kitchen table because James and Mummy were out stocking up with food. It went like this:

GET AWAY FROM IT ALL AT THE BLACK PONY INN Middle Hampton. Sumptuous weekends in the country at moderate rates. Long-term guests. Unaccompanied children over eight accepted. Full board. RIDING. Ring Middle Hampton 2222 for details.

We looked at it for a long time before we posted it in the little red post-box near the village shop. In three days it would be printed. The house was polished, the tack was clean; we had even brushed our shoes and clothes.

"We've taken the plunge," said Ben as we walked home together. "For better or for worse."

"Like marriage," said Lisa, catching us up.

"It's the only way. Whatever happens afterwards we must remember that there was no other way," replied Ben.

19

Middle Hampton is small with cottages built of brick and flint. Our house was once the Manor House. It stands a little way away from the other houses, looking towards distant hills.

"We need a sign now," Ben said. "I'll make one straight away. Otherwise no one will find us."

"And an arrow," I added.

I couldn't believe it was happening, that we had reached this stage at last. Ben was running towards home; we were all running.

"I know where there's a bit of suitable wood," he cried. "I wish I could draw."

"James can," I yelled. "Ask James."

"We must put 'guest house' somewhere, or people will think we sell drinks," Ben replied, slowing to a jog.

"Like a pub?" I asked.

"Yes, we can put BLACK PONY INN, and then under the picture of Limpet's head, *Unlicensed Guest House* in smaller letters. James can do the head and I will do the lettering," said Ben.

"And we can have a wooden arrow further up pointing the way," cried Lisa. "Or a hand. What about a hand?"

"Yes, a hand," cried Ben. We started running again as though success and happiness were running ahead of us, waiting to be caught.

Two

I'm crazy about horses

After the advertisement came out, we waited a whole day for something to happen. The house seemed to be waiting, too.

Dad said, "I knew it wouldn't work."

Mummy said, "Give it time."

"I'm frightened," cried Lisa. "Supposing I hate the children."

"There aren't going to be any children," replied Ben.

I thought of the sheets and the quilts, of the deep-freeze stocked with food which we would never eat on our own. Then there was a knock on the door and we all jumped, thinking that it must be a prospective guest. But it was only old Colonel Jones from the village come to tell us that we needed permission before we could erect a sign.

"To the devil with permission," replied Dad. "You know it takes months to get a decision; and we can't afford to wait."

"You'll be made to take it down. I'm on the Parish Council. I know what's going on," replied Colonel Jones.

Mummy offered him a cup of tea or a drink but he said that it would look like bribery if he accepted.

Outside it was raining, and no one had written or telephoned and the day was nearly gone.

"They'll make you take it down," muttered Colonel Jones, going out the way he had come.

"Who's 'they'?" asked Lisa, chewing a pencil.

"The District Council," replied Dad.

"If they touch my sign I'll kill them," said Ben.

The next day the telephone rang. We were eating breakfast at the time. Ben answered. He stood holding the phone and smiling.

"It's lots of children," said Lisa hopefully.

"It's the District Council demanding immediate removal of the sign," replied James.

"It's someone demanding to be paid," I said gloomily. After ages of suspense, Ben put down the telephone.

"It's about an old lady," he said, his voice thick with disappointment. "Her daughter wants us to have her for

three months while she's with her husband in South Africa. She keeps on talking."

Mummy went to the phone.

"I knew it would be like this," said Ben gloomily.

"I feel sick with excitement," Lisa said.

"We'll have to wait on her, and she'll hate us," continued Ben. "She'll criticise our clothes, everything."

"She'll want breakfast in bed," said James. "And Harriet will have to take her out in a wheelchair."

"She's eighty," Ben told us.

"That's terribly old," cried Lisa.

"She'll be senile," said James.

"What's senile?" asked Lisa.

"They are all coming round to look in half an hour," said Mummy, putting down the phone. "The old lady sounds a dear, she does really. She says she likes a full house, and she wants to do the garden. Think of that at eighty!"

We began to feel better.

"One old lady, just one old lady," said Ben.

"I like old ladies," exclaimed James. "I've always wanted lots of grannies."

But now the telephone was ringing again. We fell over each other trying to reach it. James got there first.

"It's a mother this time. She's got a terribly bossy voice and her daughter rides," he said, handing the phone to Mummy again while the person at the other end went on talking.

"It's a success, it's going to be a success," shrieked Lisa.

"Don't count your chickens before they're hatched," warned James.

"Well, there is a bus service but it only runs twice a day," Mummy was saying. "No, there's no station. Yes, it's quite isolated."

23

"Perhaps she's bringing dogs," suggested Ben.

"We'll do our best of course, but it's not a prison," Mummy continued.

"A convict, we're going to have a convict," muttered James.

"Yes, four ponies, two are quite large. Yes, almost unlimited riding," Mummy said.

"A riding maniac," said Ben.

"Are you sure you don't want to see the place first? I mean, Mary might not like us," Mummy continued.

"We are going to have a difficult girl. She must not be allowed to disappear alone," Mummy said, when she had put down the receiver. "We must hide the car keys. Do you think we'll manage?"

"What's the matter with her?" asked Ben.

"She's in love with an impossible boy. And her mother thinks riding will take her mind off him."

"Oh no!" cried Ben.

"How old is she?" I wanted to know.

"Thirteen. She's coming tonight complete with luggage. Her mother seems in a great hurry to be rid of her. She's paying extra for special care."

"Can she ride?" I asked.

"Yes. She's very keen. She used to have a pony of her own."

"Bags I take her riding then," I said.

The telephone rang once more, a bit later on. This time I answered it. The voice at the other end was decidedly American. I fetched Mummy. We had made up the old lady's bed and Mary's by this time and put the kettle on and had tea cups ready for our prospective customers. Mummy talked for ages.

At last she stopped. "We have a boy coming too, with an Anglo-Arab called Apollo which cost two thousand pounds. Can you have a loose box ready?" she asked.

"Yes, of course," I said.

"His parents are going back to an apartment in the States, in Washington, and he won't go without his horse. So they want him to stay till they have things sorted out. He'll go to boarding school and they are paying in advance." She sounded tired, as though now suddenly she saw the problems which lay ahead. Lisa put her arms round her.

"Don't worry, it's going to be all right," she said. "Mary will fall in love with Ben or James and Harriet can look after the American boy. Don't worry, Mummy darling. Just keep calm."

Ben and I bedded down a loose box. We didn't talk much.

"There's going to be a lot of strange people around here," Ben said at last. "I hope we can cope."

"So do I," I replied, shaking up the straw.

Later we heard the front doorbell. "Which one is it?" I asked.

"The old lady, I expect," replied Ben.

Presently we saw her walking round the garden with Mummy and James, admiring everything. She was small, like people were years ago, and looked incredibly old. We could hear her say, "I love gardening. I shall soon have things straight. And if you want the spuds done, I'll do them."

"But you're paying," Mummy replied. "You mustn't work all the time."

She came to look at the horses and admired them, too. "And what a lovely stable-yard!" she exclaimed. "When I have time I'll weed it for you."

"She's sweet," said James later. "A really nice old lady. She won't be any trouble."

Mary came later with a tall, thin-lipped mother in tweeds. Mary wore nail varnish and was slim and tall

25

for her age. She didn't say much, though I saw her looking hard at James and Ben.

Ben hardly spoke three words to her, but her mother
never stopped talking. "You will like it here, Mary," she
said. "You'll be able to get up early every morning and
go riding just as you did when you had Trixie. And you
can help with the mucking out, too. You'll never have a
dull moment, will you dear?"

Mary remained aloof and detached. I felt that she despised us all and would hate every moment of life with
us. I prayed that she would not stay, but after a time I

heard Mummy saying, "We'll do our best then, Mrs Harris. But I'm not making any promises." And Mary looked round and smiled, a nasty, secret smile.

Later we had tea together in the kitchen. The old lady, who was called Mrs Mills, poured out. "I'll have a mug," she offered. "I hate cups and saucers."

She was deaf and kept shouting "What?" and "Oh dear, I must get a deaf aid; you all mutter so."

Mary said, "Whatever do you do all day here buried in the country, miles from everywhere? I should go mad."

"We ride," replied Ben. "And if you don't, I should beat it because you'll be bored stiff."

And then there was a knock on the back door and a voice said, "May we come in?" The accent was unmistakably American.

"Yes, of course," cried Mummy. "But you should have come the front way."

Mrs Mills got out some more cups and started to fill them with tea.

"It sure is a cute place here. What do you say, Paul?"

The father was large, with success written all over him. The mother was square-shaped, with short, greying hair cut in a fringe. Paul was large, like his father, with a scrubbed look about him. His hair was short and curly and he was wearing grey trousers and a blazer with a crest on it.

"Sure, great," he answered. "But it's the stables I really want to see. Have you got a box ready for my chestnut yet?"

I nodded.

"The name's Armstrong. We're sure glad to meet you," announced the father.

We shook hands. "Show Paul the stables," Mummy said.

27

The box was ready. We had even filled a bucket of water and a haynet. And Ben had spent ages banking up the straw round the sides. It really did look lovely.

Paul breathed a sigh of relief. "It sure looks great. Can I pin his name on the door?" he asked.

"If you like," I said, "but you'll have to take down Limpet's name."

"I've got a chart here saying what he needs to eat. Can I pin it up somewhere, too?"

"Yes, in the tack room," I said, thinking that he was certainly keen on pinning things up.

"Have you got him outside?" Ben asked.

"No, we've still got to fetch him. Can I see your horses? This place is sure okay," Paul continued. "I couldn't stand going back to an apartment in the States. I'm crazy about horses. How about you?"

"Us too," I said.

"You wait till you see Apollo, he's some horse," he said.

His parents were approaching. They walked round talking, saying, "This will be great for Paul. Now about his school, can you take him back and fetch him at half-term?"

"Yes, we'll do that," Mummy answered, looking dazed, as though too much had happened too quickly and she was still trying to get things straight in her mind. "He's having your bedroom, Harriet," she said, "because yours has a washbasin and he wants a room facing the stables, so that he can see Apollo."

It was my first sacrifice for our paying guests. I tried not to feel resentful. Mrs Mills had one spare room and Mary had the other. The attic rooms were still empty. I supposed I would be sent there to sleep alone. "Sure you don't mind?" asked Mrs Armstrong. "You're not upset, dear?"

"No," I said. "Not at all."

"Okay then, all set," said Mr Armstrong. "Paul, you're going to be real happy here, aren't you? You're sure?"

Paul nodded, looking at me, then to Ben and back again.

"It will be great," he said. "I feel it in my bones."

I wanted to say "Touch wood," but I didn't.

Afterwards I wished I had. It might have altered things, saved us the horrible moments which lay ahead, unknown to any of us.

Mr Armstrong wrote Mummy a cheque in the large sitting-room which has deep armchairs and lots of re-production furniture and an expensive carpet. It is the only smart room in the house and we had decided to keep it for occasions like this.

"That's three months in advance – plus extra to cover Apollo's keep and more for petrol. I want you to give Paul his pocket money too – that's ten pounds a week," he said, putting his gold pen back into his pocket.

Mummy looked at the cheque, then folded it up. "Right you are," she said.

The Armstrongs left by the front door and somehow the house seemed smaller and more humdrum when they had gone. I can't explain why – they just made everything seem bigger, greater, more important.

Twilight had come and it was too late to ride. We could hear Dad returning. Mrs Mills had washed up and was peeling potatoes for supper.

Mary was sitting in the study, watching television.

I set the table for the supper. I was upset at losing my bedroom. It was full of my things. But it would be even worse when the guests started riding Lorraine. I wished that Mary was different. She was old for her age and smart and I had wanted a girl of my own age in faded jeans and an old sweater. I couldn't imagine Mary mucking out even if she had once had a pony called Trixie. I supposed Ben and I would muck out Apollo's box, taking it in turns. We would probably have to groom him too, and Paul might expect his tack cleaned as well.

Supper was laid at last. Mummy appeared and put her arms around me. "I hope you don't mind losing your room. We've got two more guests coming, two little girls. I want you to share the attic with them. Their mother has gone into hospital and their father's had a car crash. Their grandparents are desperate. They like riding. They can ride Limpet . . ." she said, looking into my face. "You don't mind, do you? The money Mr Armstrong gave us for Apollo's keep is to go to you and Ben to spend on horse food, and so will any riding money. Okay?"

"Okay," I said. "But what are the girls called?"

"Phillipa and Georgie. They sound sweet. Their grannie's bringing them. They're only here for two weeks, that's all. Do cheer up."

"When's Apollo coming?" I wanted to know.

"Tomorrow morning. I want you to take Mary out early. She'll have to ride Solitaire, won't she?" Mummy asked.

"Yes."

Ben was beating the gong, which had always stood in the hall but had never been used before. Mary wanted her supper by the television and James took it to her on a tray. I think we were all tired, though Lisa kept talking, saying that Paul was handsome and Mary nasty and that the two new girls would be her friends and that she would teach them to ride whatever Ben said.

Later I lay in bed, trying to imagine the future, thinking that it was my last night in my own bed, wondering

whether it would ever be my room again. Lisa slept in the little room next to Mummy and Daddy. Ben and James slept at the back of the house in two rooms which looked towards the village.

Then Ben knocked on the door and came in. He sat on my bed and said, "Think, all that money to spend on what we like. We can buy oats, and a martingale for Solitaire and the type of rug you've always wanted for Lorraine. We're going to be rich, you realise that, don't you? – rich! And it won't be Dad's money this time. It will belong to all of us."

"Yes, but money isn't everything," I said.

Ben stared at me. "It's a heck of a lot," he said. "Did you want to leave here? To go back to living in a street, in a row of houses . . .? We are making a success. Everything's going like we dreamed it would. What more do you want?"

"Nothing," I answered. "I just wish Mary was nice, that's all."

"Well, I love money," said Ben, going out without shutting the door.

We will go on taking in these desperate cases because Mummy is so generous, I thought, and the house will soon be full of selfish Marys and decrepit old ladies, and it won't be any fun at all. I could hear Ben arguing with James on the stairs, and Dad letting Twinkle out.

I shouted, "You didn't shut my door!" but no one paid the least attention.

Trying to sleep, I decided that when I was grown up I would school horses, turning four-hundred-pound animals into jumpers worth thousands of pounds. I shall have a big house with lots of paddocks, I thought, and a proper jumping saddle with a spring tree, and my own bedroom with photographs of horses all over the walls, and no one will turn me out of it. And if I marry, it will

be to someone horsy, so that we can go to shows together and perhaps to America and then the Olympics.
And when I fell asleep at last, it was with imagined
cheers ringing in my ears, and with the Union Jack being
raised in a great arena and my name in all the papers of
the world.

Three

A quarrel

I got up at half past seven in the morning. The sky was full of mad, scurrying clouds blowing hither and thither, like scraps of torn paper.

Mummy was getting breakfast in the dining-room, putting out packets of cereals, spoons, sugar and milk. Mrs Mills had already had her breakfast. We soon learned that she never waited for anyone but got her own – a vast mug of coffee, toast and marmalade. Already she was more like a relation than a guest. James was still in bed and so was Mary. The rest of us went down to the stables.

We had left the ponies out last night for the first time since October. There were four loose boxes and six old-fashioned stalls with Staffordshire brick floors, iron mangers and hay-racks, and partitions with brass knobs on them like old bedsteads. There were still cobbles in part of the yard, dating back years. They made me imagine the horses which might have trodden them down – the proud carriage-horses, the master's hunters, a little pony which pulled a governess cart. Everything felt lovely in the early morning, completely fresh and new and spring-like.

Ben put clean water in Apollo's box. "Everything must be perfect," he said.

I loved the yard, the lovely smells of straw and hay

and horse. I sat on the fence and looked at it and thought how lucky we were to be here in the spring sunlight with our ponies grazing in the paddock and the whole summer before us.

Ben was looking at the garden. "Next year we will have a swimming-pool; heated, of course," he said.

He was always optimistic. He made everything seem possible, even the wildest dreams. Lisa had her arms round Jigsaw's thick black and white neck, her face buried in his mane.

For a moment everything was still and beautiful and I thought: If only everything could stay like this for ever, if only we never grew older, just stayed the same.

Then we heard a lorry coming along the road and a minute later Ben was shouting "Horse box!" and opening the yard gate. Then we could see Paul Armstrong's clean, scrubbed face looking at us through the cab window. It was a beautiful horse box, all varnished wood and padded partitions; the sort which costs pounds and pounds to hire. Apollo had a race and snip and three white socks and a flaxen mane and tail. He was almost a palomino with thin legs and small hoofs and the carriage of an Arab. He wasn't my sort of horse, but you could see that Paul worshipped him. His legs were bandaged, his tail covered with a tail guard. His elegant rug had Paul's initials in gold on one corner – P L A.

Apollo walked down the ramp and into his loose box like a prince.

"You're early," Ben said.

"My cases are in the cab, wait a sec." Paul was dressed in breeches and boots and a tweed jacket. He had brought three cases, all with his initials on them in gold lettering, too. Once I had thought we were rich, but we had never had gold initials or a two-thousand pound pony. Paul tipped the driver five pounds.

Apollo started eating his hay as we stood and looked at him over the door.

"He's some horse, isn't he?" asked Paul. "You understand now why I couldn't go back to the States without him?"

I took off his leg bandages and tail guard while Ben held him. Paul watched. You could see he was used to being waited on. I wanted to say, "Why don't you give a hand?" But I remembered that we were being paid to look after his pony.

Apollo was very well behaved and stood with his eyes half closed meanwhile.

"He's certainly no trouble," commented Ben. "He's far quieter than any of ours."

"He's sure good-natured. He's the same to ride," replied Paul.

Mary was up when we wandered indoors for breakfast a bit later.

"I got her up," James said. "I just went on banging on the door until she couldn't stand it any more."

She was wearing jeans and a sweater. "I never get up before twelve at home," she said.

"We must have some rules here," Mummy replied. "Even the best hotels don't go on serving breakfast for ever."

"I never eat breakfast at home," answered Mary, "so I shan't eat it here."

We looked at one another, hating her, knowing she was going to spoil the rest of the holidays.

"I want to ride this morning," she continued. "Can I take which horse I like?"

"No. Harriet will ride with you," Mummy said.

Daddy had left for the factory. I wished he was here to manage Mary. I didn't want to ride alone with her. I could see her galloping along roads, ignoring me, saying, "You're only a kid," and, "So what!"

It was nine o'clock now. Mrs Mills was cleaning saucepans just as though she was our help, not a guest. I took the dirty plates out and stacked them in the dishwasher. Paul hurried down to the stables to look at Apollo again.

"Is he afraid he'll melt or something?" James asked.

"He loves him, that's all," I said.

Lisa ran after him shrieking, "Wait for me."

Mummy said, "I'm going to advertise for some help. I can't cope alone."

"Let me do the beds," offered Mrs Mills. "I love making beds."

I said, "Coming?" to Mary and we went down to the stables together. Ben had caught Solitaire and was grooming him. He looked at Mary with dislike.

"If she hurts Solitaire, I'll kill her," he muttered.

He didn't mean it, of course. But I knew how he felt. It's one thing to let someone you know ride your pony, quite another to let someone you hate.

Lorraine was clean. I tacked her up and waited. Paul was talking to Apollo. "He needs a day to settle down, doesn't he?" he asked. "He's still half asleep from the journey."

Ben nodded. "You can't be too careful with a horse like him," he said, with laughter behind his eyes.

Ben held the stirrup while Mary mounted. "He goes best on a loose rein," he said.

"I don't need your advice. I can ride. I won a Best Rider class when I was eight," she said.

Ben looked as though he was praying as I led the way out of the yard.

We rode across the common and down into the beech-woods where everything was bright and green and new. Spring seemed everywhere. Birds were singing in trees, new calves lay by their mothers in green fields. We didn't talk much, but I could see that Mary could ride. She rode easily on a loose rein and Solitaire strode out, his ears pricked, his eyes shining.

Finally I asked her where she lived and she replied, "In Surrey, in a ghastly place full of rich people's houses."

And then I said, "What happened to Trixie?" and for a long time she didn't answer, just looked straight ahead into the distance.

"Mother sold her," she said finally. "She was a grey like yours – a wonderful pony. But I would rather not talk about it. Can we canter?"

"Okay," I said, and saw with a twinge of envy that she rode better than I did, far better.

When we drew rein, I asked her if she missed her boyfriend, but she said that she would rather not talk about that, either. "You're only a kid," she continued. "You wouldn't understand."

"I'm nearly as old as you," I replied.

"In years perhaps, but in other ways you're much younger. You still dress like a child, don't you? And talk like one. You're years and years behind me," she said.

I knew it was true, but I didn't want to grow up. I wanted to stay eleven or twelve for ever. I didn't want the responsibilities, the discos, the agonies of being a teenager. I couldn't explain it. But I just wanted to go on as I was. I looked at her superior, made-up face and hated her.

We were nearly home again now. We didn't talk. She was probably hating me, too. I noticed that she wore a cross round her neck and her ears were pierced for earrings. I still envied her the way she rode.

When we reached the stable-yard, she threw her reins to Ben, "I like your horse, but he's too much on the forehand. He needs more balancing exercises," she said. "I'll school him for nothing if you like."

"No, thank you," replied Ben, running up the stirrups, hating her as much as I did.

As she walked away, we looked at each other and tried to laugh. "She rides beautifully, you needn't have worried," I said.

"She's a horrible little madam," said Ben. "And there's something odd about her. I'm sure she's horrible on purpose."

"She's hating everyone," I answered. "I don't believe she's really that bad."

"She's a sadist then," said Ben.

The weather was changing. It was almost too hot for spring and yet the sky was filling with clouds, and there were flies already buzzing round the ponies' heads.

"She's going to spoil the whole holidays, I feel it in my bones," I said.

The two little girls had arrived when we went indoors. They were playing with Lisa. They both had long hair tied back behind their ears and small faces. They laughed and chattered and I could see that everybody was going to like them. Mrs Mills had already found a game of ludo and they all planned to play together after lunch.

Mummy looked relaxed and happy. Paul was reading a book of Ben's called *Stable Management and How to Cope*.

Nobody talked much at lunch. Mummy said, "What about this afternoon, Mary? Have you any plans? How about a walk? Or are you going to ride again?"

"I shall write letters," Mary said. "And my hair needs washing; I have plenty to do."

"I'll take Georgie and Phillipa riding later if they like," I offered.

They bobbed up and down in their chairs shrieking "Hurray" and "Yes, please", while Paul put his hands over his ears and Mary said "Excuse me" and left the table.

"You had better go soon, before the storm breaks," suggested Mummy.

We all cleared the table. I went outside to catch

Limpet. The dark skies seemed nearer. It was as though everything was waiting for something. I wondered how long we would be able to stand Mary. Paul was irritating, but Mary seemed out to annoy everyone. No one had mucked out Apollo so I fetched a barrow and tools and cleaned out his box. Then I caught Limpet and groomed her. After that I went indoors to find Georgie and Phillipa, and found Ben having a row with Mary in the hall.

He had bumped into her on the stairs, and she had called him a stupid fat lout. It was one of those rows which start over nothing and go on and on.

Ben should have held his tongue, but he isn't like that – it's blow for blow as far as he's concerned and no holds barred.

"Well, you're a stupid old cow," he cried. "And a sadist, and if you think you're going to ride my pony again, you're not."

"I pay to be here," shrieked Mary, "and I will do what I like. It's a pretty crabby place anyway and you're the most boring people I've ever met."

Mummy came into the hall at that moment. "Go to your room at once, Ben," she said.

He stood – glaring at her, defying both of them.

"I always get the blame, don't I?" he said at last, going back upstairs.

"I think you had better leave tomorrow, Mary. I don't think we can cope with you. I'll talk to your mother again tonight," Mummy said.

There was a horrible silence while Mary turned pale. "But he bumped into me," she said. "He should have apologised."

"You were screaming like a fishwife," Mummy retorted, "and we don't want fishwives here."

"I can't go home."

"You will have to go somewhere else then."

Mummy went back into the kitchen, shutting the door after her.

Mary looked at me as though she wanted to say something, but I was too angry to speak, for she had spoilt the whole day as far as I was concerned and had called my brother a fat lout. I didn't want to be her friend, not now or ever.

"My mother pays extra for special care," she said. "And I'm not getting it."

"What do you expect?" I asked. "Breakfast in bed?"

"Extras," she muttered.

"You're mad," I said. "Goodbye."

I slammed the hall door after me and found Phillipa and Georgie playing ludo with Mrs Mills in what used to be called the nursery. They found their crash-caps and boots and ran ahead to the stables. Limpet loves small children and he behaved beautifully. I took them each in

turn and we did bending and I made a practice garden path out of sticks and they rode down it. Then we practised potato race and reining back. And nothing awful happened in spite of distant rolls of thunder and Paul watching over the gate.

After that we cleaned the tack together and they told me about their guinea-pigs which were called Spick and Span.

I didn't want to go back into the house, but James came down to the stables and said that it was tea and what had I done to Mary: she was crying her eyes out.

"What have *I* done? I like that," I answered.

Mary had tea in her bedroom. I suppose she didn't want anyone to see that she had been crying. Later, Dad came home and talked to her for a long time and it was finally agreed she could stay on.

"She's just a mixed-up kid," Dad said. "Basically there's nothing wrong with her. It's just a difficult age."

"She's just a sadist, that's all," said Ben.

"And thoroughly unpleasant," I added.

"And mean and vain and horrible," shrieked Lisa.

We were in the sitting-room all together for once without a single guest in sight. Then Mary came in quickly and stared at us and said, "I heard what you said just now, every word. I was listening at the door." And then she rushed out again.

Dad went after her and I went red and Ben said several words which we are definitely not allowed to use. And Mummy said, "That's that then."

Then the telephone started to ring. It was for Paul. I fetched him from where he was watching television and he talked for ages.

"They rang up to say goodbye," he said, hanging up at last. "They wanted to know if Apollo was okay. They said something funny too; they said, look out for letter bombs and don't accept lifts from strange men. What do you think they meant?"

"They were just being funny, that's all," Mummy answered.

"They've never said it before."

Outside, the storm was breaking at last. Lightning lit up the room, crash after crash of thunder followed. Lisa screamed and hid her face.

Dad came back. "I've calmed her down. She doesn't want to leave. You must all try to be kinder to her," he said. "Her parents are separated. She's in her own private hell and very mixed-up."

"She'll have us all mixed-up soon," said Ben. "You know insanity can be catching."

"Shut up," replied Dad. "She's paying extra. She's entitled to extra treatment. She's asked for steak tonight and she should have it."

"But we haven't got any," Mummy said.

In the end we had braised steak. We talked about gymkhanas all through supper and suddenly another day had gone. I played with Georgie and Phillipa before they went to bed. The three of us slept together in the first room, which had pale-blue walls and curtains with prancing horses on them. It looked out at the back of the house on big oak-trees where squirrels played and grey wood pigeons nested. Phillipa and Georgie loved it. They kept saying, "It's tons better than our rooms in our horrid little doll's-house."

Before I went to bed I wandered down to the stables and everything looked new and clear and sparkling after the storm. The ponies came across the field to me in the dusk and nuzzled my pockets and Apollo whinnied from his loose box. The storm was still lingering. Dark clouds lay on the horizon and there was the occasional distant rumble. Ben came down and filled up Apollo's bucket and said, "Everything all right?"

"I think so," He was being nicer than usual. Usually we quarrelled a good deal, but having guests has somehow made us better friends.

"I wish I could sleep here," I said.

"Same here," he agreed.

Apollo looked sleepy but otherwise well. We went inside his box and ran our hands down his legs and checked that his haynet was full. Ben said, "Except for Mary I think we are making a success of it, don't you?"

I said, "We've only just started. Sometimes I'm frightened. Supposing burglars came to stay, or murderers?"

"Why should they?"

"Or Apollo got colic and died."

"Don't be silly and neurotic. Everything is going marvellously. Why spoil it?" asked Ben.

"I don't know what we will do when Mrs Mills leaves," I said next.

"Get another old lady to pay and do all the work," replied Ben, laughing.

I didn't want to go indoors. I had the feeling that disaster lay just round the corner. I checked that the field gate was shut. Apollo was lying down now and I checked that his door was bolted top and bottom and shut the yard gate.

"Crikey, you are nervous tonight," Ben said.

"I'm afraid we're going to be struck by lightning," I replied. "Listen, the storm is just waiting to come back."

The air felt tense and humid and the horses in the field were restless. We went indoors together. "I shan't sleep," I said. "I feel upset. I suppose it's Mary."

Lisa was playing in the attic. I chased her downstairs to her own room. Georgie and Phillipa wouldn't stop talking. I heard Dad putting Twinkle out, locking up. I heard the rumble of distant thunder and dogs barking down in the village. When I fell asleep I dreamed that I was riding towards a precipice with Mary, and as we drew near she tried to push me over. I woke up to find I was sweating and that my bedclothes were on the floor. The thunder was still rumbling. The gods are angry, I thought, and fell asleep again.

Four

The field's empty

It was daylight when I wakened again with Lisa in the room screaming at me, "They've gone. All of them. The field's empty." My eyes were full of sleep, my hair a tangled mess.

"Who? What?"

I saw that Paul was standing behind her.

"Apollo's gone too," he said.

I leaped out of bed. I could feel my heart banging inside me, my pulse racing. "I checked everything. Where's Ben?" I yelled.

"Getting up."

Phillipa and Georgie woke up and started asking questions which no one had time to answer.

I pulled clothes on over my pyjamas, tore downstairs, found my boots. Ben was just ahead of me, still in his dressing-gown.

Apollo's door was open, the field gate was open, the gate into the road was open. I wanted to scream or cry, but no sound came and no tears.

"Look at the tyre marks," shouted Ben. "Look!"

"It could be thieves, rustlers," I said. My voice came out small and croaky. We knew about horse and cattle rustlers. In March they had carted away whole fields of cattle and half a dozen horses from a village just five miles away.

Lisa was standing and screaming, "Jigsaw, Jigsaw, where are you?"

Paul said, "That won't do any good, stupid. They're taken away, gone, dead." He looked frozen to where he stood.

"Let's look outside," said Ben. "Come on, standing won't get us anywhere."

There were hoof-marks across the common.

"So some of them got away," he said.

Everyone was in the yard now, except for Mary and, of course, Dad, who had gone to work hours ago.

"I'll ring the police," James said.

"I'm going to be sick," Paul said. "My father will sue you for this. Apollo cost him two thousand pounds. You didn't shut his door."

Mummy and Mrs Mills took him inside.

Ben found his bike. Mine had a puncture, so I ran across the common on foot with Lisa just behind me. There were plenty of hoof-marks on the common, but whether they were last night's or yesterday's or from the day before we didn't know.

Ben shouted, "I'm doing a broad sweep. See you in half an hour."

I walked on, imagining the ponies dead already, stripped of their skins, meat for dogs or humans. I could feel the tears coming, an endless, stupid flow.

Lisa took my hand. "Poor little Jigsaw," she said. "Poor darling Jigsaw."

"He may not be dead. We mustn't give up hope," I said.

The sky was clearing, but it was still a dank, dreary day. We are doomed, I thought. I felt it last night. Why didn't I stay up?

Ben looked mad, bicycling through the village in his Paisley dressing-gown. The church clock struck eight.

"We've forgotten to bring any halters. So we can't do much even if we do find them. We had better go home and get dressed properly. Perhaps the police know something by now, perhaps they've even found them," I said, without much hope.

"This is the third thing. First we didn't sell the house, then Mary came and now the ponies have gone," Lisa said. She was wearing trousers and plimsolls which were soaked through, and an old grey jersey which had once been mine.

"Some of them got away. Ben saw the hoof-marks," I said.

"But where are they, then?" cried Lisa.

"In a lovely field eating lovely grass," I replied quickly but without conviction.

Ben was coming back. "Old Mr Baker thinks he heard hoofs in the night. He said a stranger rode through the village," he cried.

"You know he's dotty," I answered. "What strange rider, anyway? It's obvious what happened. There was a cattle truck parked outside. Can't you see? They drove the ponies into it. All of them. It's as plain as plain. They've been taken away for their skins and their flesh and poor hoofs and . . ." I could go no further. I was thinking that I would never see Lorraine again, never, never. I was remembering the wonderful hours I had spent on Limpet. Now Ben was crying too and I hadn't seen him do that for years. He looked too big and silly and pitiful all at once.

"We are going to find them," he said. "And if I do I shall shoot the men, all of them." We looked the other way when we passed the empty field and Apollo's box. The yard seemed quiet, empty, impossibly lonely. We found Mummy cooking breakfast in the kitchen. "Paul won't eat a thing," she said. "He keeps being sick. He's back in bed. Mrs Mills is sitting with him."

"Thank heavens for Mrs Mills," replied Ben, sniffing.

"The police have all the details," said James, tall and businesslike. "I'll go out in the Land Rover in a minute. I don't care if I am only a learner or about to be. I can still drive it."

"No you can't," Mummy said.

Georgie and Phillipa sat without speaking, their little faces looking pinched with worry. I thought: They're not having much of a stay – we ought to do something for them, but how can we?

I didn't want any breakfast, but Mummy made me eat a bowl of cereal. Then I rushed upstairs and took off my pyjamas and dressed properly, thinking all the time that it couldn't be true. They can't all be gone. Life can't be that awful. Sooner or later they must come back, wandering into the yard, looking hopefully into empty buckets, whinnying when they see us. It just can't be the end of Lorraine for ever and ever. I haven't jumped her in a ring yet. She hasn't won anything. She was going so well. I had such plans . . .

Ben met me in the passage. "The police will never find them. I'm going out on my bike," he said. "I'll take the halters and some string. You have the headcollars."

"You can't lead all of them," I answered.

"They won't all be there," he said.

"What about Apollo? What about Paul?" I asked. "What about him suing us?"

"Forget it. James is ringing up the horse abattoirs at Bristol and Abergavenny. There's Reading market to-morrow, so he's on to them too. He's being marvellous. Mummy's been on to Dad. Keep hoping. We'll beat the swines yet," Ben said.

I could hear Paul sobbing as I went downstairs.

Lisa was talking to Phillipa and Georgie. She had been told to amuse them but she couldn't stop crying. James was on the telephone again and Mrs Mills was making beds.

Mummy said, "I suppose Mary doesn't want any breakfast again. Really, she'll wither away if she doesn't eat more. Do you think you can wake her up, Harriet? It's half past nine."

I went back upstairs and knocked on her door. I waited, listened, knocked again.

"She isn't there," said Mrs Mills, scurrying along the passage with a dustpan in her hand just like a little Miss Tittlemouse. "I've done all the rooms. I've made her bed. You look for yourself."

I didn't look. I rushed down the stairs shouting, "Mummy, Mary's gone! She's run away or something. Gone where she wasn't meant to go."

Mummy looked as though she couldn't take any more. She said, "I wish your father was here. I wish he wasn't at the factory. What are we going to do?"

Ben stared at us with his mouth open. "She could have let the ponies out, just for spite," he said. "And stolen the others. She's capable of it."

"She can't be," Mummy answered quickly. "I shall have to telephone her mother right away. Where did I put the number?"

"Goodness knows!"

"We had better go on looking anyway," said Ben. "There's no point in staying here."

"I'll search the woods," I said.

"I'll meet you on the far side by the Dog and Duck. Okay?" Ben asked.

Lisa wanted to come. "You can't lead five ponies," she cried. "You'll need me."

"We'll come too," said Georgie.

"No," shouted Mummy. "I don't want anyone else disappearing. Harriet must go alone. Do you hear?"

I put lots of 10p pieces in my pocket for telephone calls, and a penknife and some string and bits of bread and pony nuts. I put three headcollars round my neck. Ben had already left with a bucket over his handlebars, a map, and our three old hemp halters plus string. It was still raining.

I went through the village first and an old man called, "Found them yet?"

"No," I shouted.

He said, "They'll be in tins of dog meat by now, you'll see," which made me start crying again. Then I remembered Mary.

"We've lost a guest, too," I shouted. "A tall girl with long hair."

"Well I never," he said.

Then I noticed that Ben's sign had been chopped in half. I don't want to go on with the inn if the ponies have gone for ever, I thought, because we'll never be able to afford new ones.

It was a long way to the woods down a farm track deep in mud which oozed through the hole in my boot and clung to my sock.

Heifers stared at me with large, wondering eyes. I looked for hoof-marks and found plenty, but whether they belonged to our ponies or not, I didn't know. I started to run and to call the ponies by name each in turn, but without hope.

The woods were damp and dark when I reached them. There were tracks leading in all directions. I took the one on the left which led to a clearing where apple-trees grew and there were ant hills lying like sand castles in the wiry grass. It was very quiet, with no sound but the rain falling through the trees. I was soaked through by this time and the head-collars had left greasy marks round my neck. I walked on thinking about Mary, wondering where she was now and when she had left and why. She hated us and we were horrid back, I thought. We should have been nice. We should have turned the other cheek but we didn't, and now we are being paid back.

I started to run again. The woods were full of fungi here and new damp primroses. I ran and ran until I could see light ahead and knew I had reached the wheat fields beyond the wood. Miraculously the sun was shining on the new green wheat and there was a rainbow in the sky. Then I saw our ponies grazing in the distance on the headland. I started to shout "Found! Found!" and to leap into the air with unbelievable joy. Then I was running again, my feet leaving footmarks in the new wheat, my spirits soaring. They raised their heads and looked at me. We'll ride again, I thought happily.

There were no hoof-marks in the wheat the way I walked, but when Solitaire saw me he started to trot in a circle, round and round, leaving deep hoof-marks with his large cob feet. Lorraine whinnied and walked towards me, while Limpet watched, his dark eyes alert, his black coat shining wet like patent leather. Then, with a sickening lurch of my stomach, I realised that Apollo wasn't there.

I unwound the headcollars from round my neck and, wishing that the Dog and Duck was nearer, I started to wonder how I was to get the four ponies home. Everything was very still and green and the rain had stopped completely. I could hear a pigeon cooing in an oak-tree. I made a halter for Limpet out of string and tied him to a tree, then I caught Lorraine and Jigsaw. Solitaire was still trotting his wheat-destroying circles, wanting me to follow him as he always did, proving his point that *he* would decide at which moment he should be caught, not me. I heard a tractor in the distance and wondered whether it would come our way and the driver see the trampled wheat. I thought of Mary lost and Apollo probably in a knacker's yard by now, and Paul crying his eyes out at home. I thought how pleased Lisa would be to see Jigsaw again and how awful it would be for Paul. Then Solitaire came up to me and announced that he was ready to be caught.

I tied Limpet and Jigsaw together and prayed that they would behave, then I vaulted on to Lorraine and, leading Solitaire on the other side, started riding along the headland of the wheat field.

It wasn't easy because there just wasn't room for four

horses on the headland and, whatever I did, Solitaire's great hoofs churned up the wheat. I wondered how I would manage when I reached the road, and whether the ponies had eaten anything they shouldn't and would die of colic.

My moment of triumph suddenly vanished and as I rode I started to shout, "Ben, I've got them, got them, got them," until all my words became jumbled together. Finally I reached a gap into the road and I knew the way home.

The ponies pricked their ears and hurried. Jigsaw and Limpet pulled. Solitaire dragged. Cars hooted. The sun came out. Then I saw Ben coming down the road, pedalling his pathetic old bike as though his life depended on it.

"Gosh, well done!" he yelled before he saw that Apollo was missing. He got off his bike then and stood waiting for me. "I'll leave it in the hedge," he said, flinging it down. "We can come back later for it in the Land Rover."

"Aren't you pleased?" I asked.

"Yes, but where's Apollo?"

"Search me."

He took Solitaire and untied Limpet. "Can you manage him in a headcollar?" I asked.

"I'll have to," he said.

We were both worried about Apollo. I dreaded meeting Paul. "Perhaps the police have found him," I said at last.

"And perhaps they haven't," replied Ben.

We rode through the village and the old man shouted, "Well done!"

"If only Mary hadn't gone as well," said Ben.

We started to trot. I thought: There may be news, we may find Apollo returned, standing in his loose box unscathed. Mary may be back with her mother by now. Everything may be all right.

"I could cry over my sign," said Ben. "It took me ages to make it."

"Mary must have chopped it up," I answered.

"And let out all the ponies too," Ben cried.

"Yes, out of spite," I said. "But what about Apollo?"

"I don't know. It doesn't fit."

"Nor do the tyre marks if it was Mary."

The yard was empty when we reached it.

We turned out the ponies. Apollo's empty box reproached us.

"Everything's too quiet," Ben said ominously as we walked towards the house.

Five

A long ride

Everybody was standing in the kitchen.

"We've got the ponies," I said.

And they started to shout, "Hurray! Well done!"

I wanted to say, "Except Apollo," but Lisa wouldn't stop shouting and leaping over chairs and generally making a fool of herself.

"Except for Apollo," yelled Ben. "We must go on looking for him. We are *not* giving up."

"I want to look too," said Paul, with his eyes full of tears. "I thought you had found him . . . I thought . . ." but he couldn't go on. He ran from the room in floods of tears.

"Why not Apollo?" asked Mummy.

"I don't know. That's the mystery," Ben answered.

"Somebody look after Paul," Mummy said.

Mrs Mills went. I wondered how we would ever manage without her. She was the kindest, nicest, most unselfish old lady I had ever met.

Mummy put the kettle on. I could smell lunch cooking in the oven. Life was going on as usual. Then the telephone rang.

"That will be Mary's mother," Mummy said.

"We haven't told the police yet about Mary," James explained. "Her mother doesn't want to start an official search unless it's absolutely necessary." He paused.

"Where did you find the ponies?"

I started to explain, then Mummy came back. "She's furious. She's going to stop her cheque and sue us. Isn't life awful?" she said. "She's going to speak to Mary's boyfriend and ring back. She says she's thoroughly upset and humiliated. She sounds a thoroughly neurotic woman," continued Mummy.

Lisa had disappeared with Georgie and Phillipa to see the ponies. Paul was still upstairs with Mrs Mills. Mummy handed us each a mug of coffee.

"What about Apollo?" I asked.

"We had better go on looking for him. He may have got separated from the others somehow," Ben suggested. "We can go out on the ponies now."

"There goes the telephone again." Mummy ran through into the hall. I looked at the electric clock above the cooker in the kitchen and saw that it was nearly one o'clock.

"Mary isn't with her boyfriend," said Mummy, returning. "Mrs Harris is coming to conduct the search herself. She doesn't want the police informed. She wants us to look for a note."

"Mrs Mills swept up her room, any note is probably in the dustbin now," I said.

"Oh no! Come on, we had better have lunch," said Mummy. "Call everybody. We can't think properly on empty stomachs."

It was a dismal meal. Paul hardly ate a thing and Lisa was convinced that Jigsaw had colic. Mrs Mills kept on and on about there not being a note in Mary's bedroom. "I wouldn't have swept it up. I'm very careful. I am really," she said half a dozen times. Phillipa and Georgie remained silent.

"I guess he's dead," said Paul suddenly. "Either run down by a lorry or slaughtered."

Mummy put her arm round him. "Don't despair," she said. "We will find him, I promise."

"We're going to look for him now. We don't want any pudding. Come on, Harriet," cried Ben.

I couldn't bear to look at Paul's face any longer. I know what it's like to love a horse. I couldn't blame him for crying even though he was ten and boys aren't supposed to cry as much as girls.

"Poor devil," said Ben as we ran towards the stables. We found Jigsaw rolling. We stood and stared in dismay.

"Not that!" cried Ben. "Oh no, get a headcollar, for heaven's sake."

"Lisa was right," I shouted. "She's no fool after all."
I grabbed a headcollar and thrust it over Jigsaw's ears.
Ben slapped his quarters. I hauled. He stood up, shaking
and sweating.

"He must have eaten lots of the wheat," I said.

"Or something worse. Can you hold him while I telephone the vet?" asked Ben.

"All right."

"I'll send Lisa to help." But Lisa didn't need sending.
She was there already, saying, "I told you so. He's probably twisted his guts by now."

It was a struggle to keep Jigsaw on his feet. Supposing they all have it, I thought, and then remembered that
the vet's bill was the one which had been coming in red
for many months.

"I got him on his mobile. He's on his way," said Ben
returning. "I'll catch the others and tack them up. Lisa
can manage once he's here, can't you, Lisa?"

"I don't know," moaned Lisa.

"You will have to. You're nine now. You're not a
baby any more," said Ben, brushing Solitaire.

"I will help her," said Mrs Mills, appearing suddenly
from nowhere. "Don't worry yourselves. I used to hunt
once, side-saddle of course. I know about horses,
though we had grooms in those days. Give me the halter
rope, Lisa, and let your brother and sister go in search
of Paul's pony. He could be hung up somewhere, and it
will be dark soon, and just look at the sky – there's acres
of rain in it."

"Thanks a million," said Ben gratefully.

I caught Lorraine and tacked her up. Jigsaw was a bit
calmer and Limpet looked all right. I could hear a car
coming along the road.

"Perhaps Apollo has gone back to where he came
from," suggested Mrs Mills. "Horses do sometimes.

They get homesick. Shall I ask Paul where he lived before and get James to telephone for me?"

I shouted "Yes," nodding at the same time for fear she wouldn't hear. She's no fool, I thought. I wish she was our real grannie and could live here for ever.

Our vet, Roy Smart, is fortyish and not smart at all, he usually wears old jeans with gumboots turned down at the top and a riding mackintosh. Today he didn't waste any time but said at once, "Which one is it? How long has he been like this? And what's he been eating?"

"He's been out in the woods," I said.

"And on new wheat," added Ben.

"He's as tight as a drum," said Roy, feeling Jigsaw's stomach.

"You two had better go," said Mrs Mills, "or it will be dark before you get back. Lisa and I can manage, can't we, Lisa?" Lisa nodded.

"Mrs Mills is one of our guests, Roy," Ben explained, sounding a bit embarrassed. "She really is a wizard at everything."

Mrs Mills was wearing an old skirt, thick stockings, lace-up shoes, a cardigan and, tied firmly round her waist, a large apron.

Roy bent down to shake her hand. "I shall need a bucket of warm water and some soap," he began. "What about the others, are they all right?"

"We hope so," replied Ben, mounting.

"We've had enough tragedy for one day," I said.

"How's that?"

"It's a long story – ponies out, guests lost – we must go," said Ben, looking at the sky.

Lisa had gone to the house for water and soap. Mrs Mills was still holding Jigsaw as we went to get our boots and hats. He lifted his head and whinnied and then whirled round and round, but Mrs Mills held on to

him, looking small, tough and indomitable. I hoped that I would be like her when I was eighty.

The church clock struck two when we left. The common was misty and empty and glistening wet. Our ponies were tired from their night out; we were tired too.

"Let's go a different way this time," suggested Ben.

"We are looking for Apollo, okay?" I asked.

"Yes, that's right. Mary's probably in London by now, lost for ever," replied Ben.

"Is James going for your bike?" I asked.

"I forgot to tell him about it," replied Ben.

We were cantering now. We each had a headcollar round our waist and pockets full of pony nuts.

"Mummy's going to ring Paul's parents later. They're in Washington," Ben said.

"That will cost a pretty penny, and supposing everything gets in the papers?" I asked.

"We're finished then," replied Ben.

"If only we knew the answers," I said. "Why Mary went? Who let the horses out and why? Nothing makes much sense, does it?"

"There must be an answer. It's probably quite simple really," Ben replied.

We rode down a long, stony lane and into a dark wood of conifers. We stopped to look for hoof-marks. We called, "Anyone about?"

The trees were close together and the wood was dark and wet. We were both glad when we reached the other side. We rode up a chalky hill which smelled of thyme. We stood at the top and stared across three counties, and saw trains and small neat farms and great, round cooling towers looking as though they were built out of sand, and a village with a church, and cows looking like toy animals in the distance. But no Apollo.

"We should have brought Dad's binoculars," Ben said.

We rode down the other side, our ponies slipping on the chalky ground, and approached the motorway, weaving like a snake through the hills. Lorraine neighed and we stopped and stared until our eyes ached, but there was no answering neigh, only rabbits fleeing to their burrows at our approach, and the same wonderful smell of herbs and wild grasses.

There was a huge bridge sweeping across the motorway, looking proud and alien and lonely. We halted and sat hating it for slicing across the valley and the motorway for cutting the valley in half.

"If Apollo got on to the motorway, he's dead, because you don't think any of those speed merchants could or would stop for a pony, do you?" Ben asked with hate in his voice.

"No, I don't, but if there was a crash surely there

would be some sign of it?" I asked.

Ben shook his head. "No, it would have been swept up clean and forgotten ages ago – just another accident, don't you know!"

"But the police would know. Someone would have mentioned a horse," I replied.

We couldn't cross the motorway except by the terrifying bridge. "He wouldn't have crossed that anyway,"

said Ben, turning Solitaire. "Let's go through Hangars Wood and on to Wadlington and back over Chalk Hill."

"Back through the woods where the others went?"

Ben nodded. We rode down a grassy track which had once been a railway line. I imagined all the people who had gone along it for fifty years or more in a little train pulled by a steam engine, clutching their suitcases or shopping bags – old ladies, children, men on their way to work. We passed the remains of a station. A young couple had converted it into a house. We stopped and called, "Seen a pony?"

They came out on to the track and said, "What sort of pony? There was one came past a couple of hours ago." Our hopes rose.

"A chestnut?" cried Ben.

"That's right. With a girl in plaits riding it. Is that the one?" The woman was clutching a baby. The man had a haversack over one shoulder and looked like an artist. We shook our heads and rode on.

Wadlington was full of shoppers. The bank was shut. We stopped and asked people if they had seen a loose pony. They looked at us as though we were mad.

"What, in the town?" they asked.

"Yes." Ben even went into the post office to ask. Then he remembered the riding-school on the other side.

"We had better try there," he said. "It's only half a mile further on." So we clattered through the town, Lorraine shying at the pedestrian crossing. Someone shouted, "Ride him, cowboy!"

Solitaire slipped and slid and nearly fell. Then we were on the other side of the town riding down a quiet road.

"It's getting late," Ben said. "We had better hurry."

The riding-school had thirty ponies. It was run by an

elderly lady called Miss Jackson. She had given us our first riding lessons. She was old and weather-beaten and charged too little for her lessons. She drove an old car and people laughed at her, but I think she was happy.

We found her cleaning tack. We dismounted to rest our ponies and Ben told her in great detail what had happened. Once he had been devoted to her. It had been, "Well, Miss Jackson says this," and, "Miss Jackson says that," until Mummy had screamed, "If you say 'Miss Jackson' again, I shall go mad."

Today she looked even older, but she was just as nice and kind as usual. "I should try the abattoirs," she said, when Ben stopped talking. "There's one at Bristol and one at Abergavenny."

"We have," I said.

"And why would the thieves leave the others?" asked Ben.

"Perhaps they got away. Or perhaps they only had room for one, or perhaps they were disturbed," suggested Miss Jackson.

"But there's much more flesh on Solitaire," argued Ben.

"Perhaps he's difficult to catch and box."

"Yes he is, you're dead right," said Ben.

"And Lorraine hates men," I said.

"And Jigsaw and Limpet are small and both still a bit thin," suggested Ben.

Some children were filling up buckets and everything smelled wonderful, a glorious mixture of saddle soap, horse dung and hay. I wished we could stay. But Ben was already mounting, saying, "Well goodbye then, and thank you very much."

"I will ring you up if I hear or see anything," promised Miss Jackson. "You have told the police, haven't you?"

Ben nodded. Lorraine snatched at her reins and jogged. The children filling buckets stopped to stare at us.

"Coming here makes me feel old," exclaimed Ben.

It was ten miles home. "I wonder how Jigsaw is," I said.

"Do you think Mrs Harris will have arrived yet?" Ben asked.

"I expect so."

"Poor Mummy!"

"I expect Dad will be home by now."

The shops were shutting in Wadlington. The motorway was crowded with cars looking like toy cars in the distance, racing, jockeying for position. The railway track was quiet and peaceful. The young couple waved to us from the old waiting-room and called, "Any luck?"

We shook our heads and I was suddenly filled with a sense of doom. Everything is going wrong – Mary has gone, Paul is in tears, Apollo is lost, probably dead, I thought, we've failed everybody.

Our ponies were tired and there was evening in the air already, a damp, cloudy evening to match our spirits. There were rabbits on Chalk Hill, hiding behind bushes, and a few sheep.

"What Miss Jackson said made sense, didn't it?" asked Ben. "The thieves could have taken Apollo and let the others out, either on purpose or by mistake."

"But what about Mary?"

"That could be pure coincidence. After all, she was hating us all evening and there was thunder in the air – that always makes temperamental people worse," replied Ben.

"So she walked away in her nightie?"

"Nobody has thought of looking at her clothes, have

they? So we don't know what she took," Ben answered.

"No. Nor did we look in the larder to see what food she may have taken," I said. "She could have hitched a ride and been murdered," said Ben in a worried voice, starting to trot. "You know – strangled by some awful man."

We hadn't thought of that before. I started to feel sick. Neither of us spoke again for some time.

"She was just an unhappy person," said Ben at last. "And wouldn't you be with her mother?"

"I don't know. She was probably awful to her mother too," I answered.

Suddenly I didn't want to get home, to face our exhausted parents and Paul and Mrs Harris. I felt like riding for ever. I wanted peace and there wasn't any anywhere. We could see the woods now which I had run through in the morning. That seemed an age away already.

"I don't want to go home," I said.

"Nor I," said Ben. "But we have to. We can't run away."

"Paul's parents will make us pay two thousand pounds for Apollo," I said. "And Mary's parents will sue us for losing their daughter."

"They can't," Ben said.

"Mummy accepted extra money for extra care, don't you remember?" I asked. "Isn't that legally binding?"

"It could be, but I doubt it."

I thought of Mummy, of how we had meant to help our parents, of how we had thought we would make a lot of money. We have been very naïve, I decided. Very gullible.

"Mrs Mills, Phillipa and Georgie are a success so far, aren't they?" asked Ben.

"They may be."

"Let's face it, our parents haven't got good business heads," said Ben.

"Dad had once."

We had reached the beech-woods by now, where some trees grew straight and splendid while others were crowded and twisted with trying to reach the sunlight. It was nearly dark in the woods and rain started to fall, dampening our already damp spirits still further.

We've wasted hours and hours and achieved nothing, I thought, as we started to canter along a track winding between trees.

The ponies knew they were going home – they lengthened their strides and fairly flew. The rain was in our faces. In places the track was deep in mud, but we were past caring about our ponies' legs; all we wanted now was to reach home as soon as possible and learn the worst. And then suddenly Ben stopped.

"Listen. I heard something," he said. "Sounded like someone calling."

For a long time all we could hear was the rain falling

through the trees and the creak of our saddles and Lorraine restlessly chewing her bit.

Ben kept saying. "Shush, will you. Listen, for goodness sake."

Lorraine turned round and round, longing to get home. And then we heard a faint call. It could have been "Hi" or "Help" or just someone calling their dog, but suddenly we were both filled with indescribable hope.

Ben shouted, "It came from over there. Come on!" We hurtled through the woods like maniacs, praying and laughing at the same time, having no idea of what we expected to find, but filled with hope just the same.

Six

Why didn't you get help?

For a time we seemed to be riding in circles. We stopped to listen but there were no more cries for help, just the dripping trees and the approaching darkness.

"We imagined it," I said, drawing rein. "You know how easy it is to imagine things you want to hear, like hoofbeats on the road, or the back door opening and Mummy home when she isn't at all."

"It wasn't imagination," replied Ben firmly. "It was someone calling."

"But who?"

"I don't know."

We were both soaking by this time and our ponies were covered with mud and sweat.

"I want to hear how Jigsaw is. It seems years since we left home," I said.

"Let's try calling," suggested Ben. He started to shout, "Where are you? It's Ben." His voice echoed and came back.

"Why should they know who Ben is?" I asked.

"Shut up," he said. "Just listen!" We listened and listened.

"Let's go back via the Dog and Duck," Ben said finally. "I know it's longer, but we haven't been that way yet today."

"Today, is it still today?" I asked, turning a reluctant

Lorraine away from the track which led straight home. I knew how she felt, we had been riding hard for five hours and now we were asking her to go somewhere else. She kept stopping and trying to go back, she must have thought we were lost or mad. Wet branches brushed against us, making us wetter than we were already; water trickled down our necks. In the distance we could see where the woods ended by the light coming through the trees. Few people walked or rode this way and the path was narrow and winding. Once we saw some deer and there were birds everywhere, settling in the trees for the night. And then suddenly our ponies stopped, their heads raised, their ears pricked.

"There's something ahead. Can you see anything?" shouted Ben.

I was leading. I could feel Lorraine trembling with excitement. Then she whinnied and went on with Solitaire snorting behind. And then we saw what we had been looking for all day long – Apollo, but he was lying on his side among the trees.

"Oh God, he's dead," said Ben.

"He can't be. Why? How?" I said.

The ponies stood and looked and snorted. "Here, hold them," shouted Ben. "There's someone else." We slid to the ground. I held the ponies and was glad that Ben had come, that I wasn't alone in the woods trying to cope. He ran forward. I tied the ponies to trees with string, forgetting the headcollars we carried, and went after him.

"It's Mary," he said.

She was sitting up. Her hair lay wet across her face. "I've been calling," she said in a vague voice. "Calling and calling."

"You've killed Apollo. He's dead," shouted Ben. "Dead!"

74

I had never seen a dead horse before. I started to shake all over.

"And you let the others out," I yelled. "You pig, you swine!"

She tried to speak again, but we wouldn't listen, for suddenly we were overcome with uncontrollable rage. Ben kept shouting, "He's dead, and what will Paul do? He loved him. Can't you understand? No, of course not, you wouldn't, would you?"

"You might have killed ours, too," I shouted. "Jigsaw is ill with colic because of you."

"You aren't fit to live," yelled Ben.

"No wonder you need extra care. You'll start killing children next," I shouted. And then, as suddenly as we shouted, our tempers evaporated. We looked at Mary and saw that she was crying silently, like someone who

has reached the end of a long road and can't go any further.

"How did he die? Why didn't you get help?" asked Ben. Apollo was wearing his tack, and his reins were broken and his saddle crushed.

"He's lying on my leg. It's broken, I think," Mary said in a whisper. She was shivering and even in the dusk I could see that there was no colour in her face. I was concerned for her now. She was obviously in pain and her leg could be crushed. I had learned some first-aid years ago in the Brownies; I put my coat round her.

"I'll get some wood and lever poor Apollo off," Ben said.

Solitaire was leaping about and in another second he had broken his string and was gone. "Oh no!" I shrieked.

"It can't be helped," said Ben, coming back with a branch. "Just hang on to Lorraine."

Mary was groaning now. "I want to die," she moaned. "I don't want to go on any more. Please, just let me die."

Ben wiped his brow with the back of his hand. Lorraine neighed.

The first piece of wood was rotten and broken. Lorraine started whirling round and round. And, in the gathering darkness, the wood was full of eerie sounds, strange rustles and great, menacing trees. I found myself praying, "God, make everything all right. God, make Mary live and Paul not too upset. Please, God."

Ben swore and tried to break a young sapling. Apollo seemed very still and Mary was quite silent now, so that she could have been dead, too.

"Why don't you help?" Ben shouted at me.

"How?"

"By pulling this," he shouted.

He was uprooting a young tree, struggling and pulling, with sweat running down his face and his hands scratched and bleeding. I seized the tree lower down and pulled, too; then something snapped and we both fell back on to soft earth. Ben was up first.

"Come on," he shouted. "I can't do it on my own. You will have to help."

"I can't touch Apollo – he's dead," I said.

"We know that. But you can help lever him off Mary's leg, can't you? Or do you want her to die?" he asked.

"I think we should go for help," I said. "It's too much for us. Injured people should never be moved except by experts – doctors or ambulancemen, or trained nurses."

But Ben wouldn't listen. He wedged the broken sapling under poor dead Apollo and Mary opened her eyes and asked, "What's happening?"

"Get ready to move," yelled Ben in reply. "Come on, Harriet, pull, will you, pull!"

I dug my feet into the soft, peaty earth and thought of Mummy waiting at home, wondering where we were.

The sapling bent because it was young and green. "Hold it," yelled Ben. "Hold it still."

"I can't," I screamed, straining and pulling, feeling the wood slipping through my hands.

But Ben was on the ground now, pushing Apollo off Mary, saying, "Pull back. What's the matter? Can't you move?" Then the sapling sprang back like a catapult and we were back where we were, with Mary moaning and the darkness descending above the treetops.

"Let's go for help," I suggested. "We need strong men."

"We'll try again, we'll get it further under this time. Ready, Mary?" asked Ben.

"I want to stay here," she answered. "I don't want to begin again."

"Begin what?" I asked.

"Don't listen, she's delirious," shouted Ben.

Mary started to moan. It was a strange, animal sound, not human at all.

"We need a doctor and an ambulance. Please, Ben," I pleaded. "I can go for them on Lorraine. You can stay with Mary."

"I won't give in. It's only her leg. She can move her back," argued Ben. "It's not broken."

His face was set and determined. I had never seen him like this before. It was as though he had suddenly grown up and become a man.

We set to work again without speaking and this time we felt Apollo shift. Then Mary gave another long moan and suddenly she was free, saying, "My leg doesn't work. It's numb. I can't feel my toes at all. I can't feel

78

anything." Ben put an arm round her. He was still pant-
ing from his exertions.

"You're going to be all right," he said.

Mary looked ghastly, worse than I had ever seen anyone look before.

"How long have you been here?" I asked.

"Since last night. Or is it another day?"

"Almost," I answered.

She was wearing trousers and a pullover on top of
pink pyjamas; and wellington boots.

Between us we managed to heave her on to Lorraine.
Ben gave me his coat. It was still raining. I led Lorraine
while Ben held Mary in position. She was very quiet, too
quiet. She looked in agony.

"Your mother is probably waiting for you at our
place. You'll be all right," I said.

"I didn't let them out," she said, through chattering
teeth. "I swear I didn't."

"But you stole Apollo. He was worth two thousand pounds. We'll have to pay compensation. We'll be ruined. And no one will come to Black Pony Inn any more. The whole idea is finished," said Ben bitterly.

We waited for an answer but she had drifted into sleep or unconsciousness, we didn't know which.

Ben and I didn't talk any more because suddenly everything seemed too bad for words. I wondered how we would tell Paul that Apollo was dead, and about his parents and what they would say. I prayed that Solitaire had reached home safely. And I wondered whether Mrs Harris was in the kitchen yet, yelling at Mummy.

I wished we hadn't shouted at Mary and called her names. Dad says that you should never judge anyone until you've heard all the facts, but we had judged Mary without hesitation and said things she would never forget. I felt very tired suddenly, but now in the distance we could see lights, the lights of the village and home.

"Our parents must be beside themselves with worry," Ben said. "They've probably sent out a search party for us."

"At least we've got Mary," I replied.

"We will have to send the horse slaughterers for Apollo," Ben said.

"Why did he die?"

"We'll soon know. She'll have to explain," Ben said.

The village was wet and silent. Lights shone out from cottage windows. A dog barked. The common was empty.

We found Solitaire in the yard, his reins broken. Jigsaw was still in Apollo's box. We left Solitaire as he was and led Lorraine to the house. Then Ben called, "Open the door. We've got Mary. Open up." Mummy came out, looking all in pieces, followed by Dad.

"She's unconscious," Ben said.

"Telephone for a doctor," shouted Dad, picking her up in his arms. Mummy ran back indoors.

Mrs Mills looked out of a window. "I'll put some hot-water bottles in her bed," she called.

I stood holding Lorraine, feeling numb, exhausted inside and out, while Ben ran back to the yard to see to Solitaire. Presently I put Lorraine in a box and bedded her down. I didn't want to go inside and run into Paul, I didn't want to explain. Ben put Solitaire in another loose box. We rubbed them down and left them with water and feeds and their rugs inside out with straw under them. I felt stiff all over.

"We had better go in; we can't stay out here for ever," Ben said.

We put our tack in the tack room. It looked sodden and broken and I remembered Paul's tack lying in the wood with Apollo.

"We had better go in and explain," Ben said.

I followed him up to the house, my feet squelching inside my wet boots.

Seven

I just love that horse

James was sitting in the kitchen with his head in his hands. "Paul has gone," he said.

"Gone?" I cried. "Him too?"

Ben collapsed into a chair. "No. It's impossible. It's like ten green bottles hanging on the wall. You know, the song," he said, trying to laugh, trying to make us all laugh, but failing utterly.

"We were out," continued James, raising his head to look at us. "Mrs Mills was with Georgie and Phillipa. She says she heard a car come up the drive; then someone banged on the door; but by the time she got downstairs the car was gone and she found a note in the hall saying: *I can't stay any longer. Paul.* The police have the note now. Mummy tried to get his parents on the telephone, but they weren't there. It's been awful here – awful – Mummy crying, Dad shouting, Mrs Mills putting on the kettle and saying the same things over and over again, and never hearing anybody's answers."

"We had a bad time too – Apollo's dead," said Ben.

"Oh no, not that too!" cried James. "How did he die?"

"We don't know yet," Ben answered.

Mummy came into the room then. She had lines on her face I had never seen before. "Thank heavens you're back," she said.

"Are you ready for some more bad news?" asked Ben.

"I don't know. What is it?" she asked, pushing her hair back.

"Apollo's dead," Ben said.

"Dead!" she cried. "But how?"

At that moment Dr Hobbs pushed open the back door, saying, "May I come in? Where's the patient?"

"Upstairs. She looks awful," Mummy said in a distracted voice. "Follow me."

He smiled at us as he rushed through the kitchen clutching a bag. "Cheer up," he said. "Every cloud has a silver lining."

"Our clouds seem to grow blacker every moment," I muttered.

"You've said it," agreed Ben.

James handed us mugs of steaming coffee which we accepted gratefully.

"Is Mrs Harris still coming?" Ben asked.

"Yes, she's on her way. She wasn't much perturbed by the news. There was no panic, no screams. I really don't think she cares much for Mary; I think she would like her out of the way just as long as she could put the blame on someone else," replied James.

"Charming," said Ben.

"Poor Mary. But what about Jigsaw?" I asked. "Is he all right?"

"You had better ask Lisa," replied James.

I wondered what Dr Hobbs was doing upstairs. I hoped Mary's leg would be all right, that she hadn't broken anything else. I was very tired in spite of the coffee and when you're tired everything seems worse. Supposing she never walks again, and we're sued for damages, I thought, and Dad has to pay a hundred thousand pounds; we'll be ruined for life.

And the clock went on ticking as though nothing had happened, ticking our lives away.

James fetched bread and cheese from the larder. "Why did Apollo die?" he asked.

"We don't know. We reckon Mary killed him and smashed her own leg in the process," replied Ben.

"She looked awful when Dad carried her in. I thought she was dying," James said.

"Shouldn't we be looking for Paul?" I asked, standing up ready for action.

"The police are looking. They have panda cars touring the countryside," replied James, making himself another mug of coffee.

"I think he's searching for Apollo," said Lisa, coming into the kitchen. "It was still daylight when he went and he had been crying ever since lunch. Is Apollo really dead?"

I nodded. "Dead as a doornail," said Ben.

She started to cry. "It's so awful for Paul," she said.

"How is Jigsaw?" I asked.

"Okay. We were just in time. Roy thinks he must have eaten a lot of young wheat," she said.

We could hear Dr Hobbs coming down the stairs. We heard him say, "I will arrange for the ambulance to be here at ten in the morning. I've given her a sedative. If she wakes up, give her warm fluids with plenty of sugar, but nothing after 5 a.m. as she will probably be having an anaesthetic."

Mummy showed him out the front way. "Thank you for coming," she said, and shut the door after him.

"It could be worse," she said, coming into the kitchen. "It's a simple fracture of the femur and she's suffering from exposure and exhaustion, but there's no complications at the moment, like pneumonia or bronchitis."

84

"No broken neck?" I asked.

"Of course not, silly," replied Mummy.

"I hear a car," cried Ben.

"That will be Mrs Harris," said Mummy.

"Let Dad deal with her – you've had enough misery for one day," suggested James.

"He's out looking for Paul."

Mrs Harris rushed into the kitchen like a hurricane, leaving the back door open. "Well, have you found her?" she cried in a high-pitched voice.

If she had been a dog she would have been yapping, with her hackles up, spoiling for a fight. It was obvious that she hadn't shed a tear for Mary for she was perfectly made up and smelling of expensive perfume, whereas we all looked grey with fatigue and Mummy hadn't a spot of make-up on her face and was still wearing the disreputable pinny she had put on at lunch-time.

"Yes. She's upstairs with a broken leg," Mummy replied.

"So she is hurt! I knew it," said Mrs Harris.

"She's sedated. Everything is under control and the doctor's been," continued Mummy. "She's going into hospital in the morning. Would you like a drink?"

"No. I must see her at once. I must know what's happened," cried Mrs Harris.

"She won't tell you because she's asleep," replied Mummy, leading the way upstairs.

Ben and I went outside to put our ponies' rugs the right way in. The ponies were very tired and rather cross. We topped up their water and gave them the last of the oat straw. Then we returned indoors and presently Mrs Mills, Georgie and Phillipa appeared, wanting supper, but there wasn't any prepared so James started opening tins.

"We must do something about Apollo," said Ben. "We can't leave him in the wood and there must be a post-mortem. I think I will ring Roy."

His energy had come back, whereas I felt like a damp rag. I longed to go to bed and sleep and sleep and then to wake up and find that everything was all right.

I started to lay the table, missing out Paul's and Mary's places.

James decided to cook curry, which he loves. I opened a tin of mince and we found some rice. James already had a saucepan of tomato soup heating on the cooker. "Spoons for curry," said James. "Don't forget."

I didn't agree with spoons, but I was too tired to argue about it.

"Mary was out all night in all that rain," I said.

"Roy is coming here to pick me up first thing in the morning, as soon as it's light," Ben said, returning. "He wants us to question Mary."

86

"She won't be awake by then," I replied.

"She'll have to be."

We ate supper too worried and too tired for conversation. It was very late. Dad was still out looking for Paul. The police hadn't telephoned, nor had Paul's parents. It was awful sitting and eating and all the time not knowing where Paul was.

"He was such a nice boy," said Lisa, helping to clear the table.

"*Was!*" cried Ben. "You're making him dead already."

Mrs Harris had decided to stay the night. Mummy made up a bed for her in the room next to Mary's, which had once been her sewing-room. Mrs Harris didn't speak a word to me or Ben. She fetched a small case from her car and disappeared upstairs.

I took Georgie and Phillipa up to bed. They said, "Need we wash and clean our teeth?"

I said, "No, just forget it."

"Do you think Paul's dead?" asked Georgie.

I shook my head.

"But where is he then?"

"The police will find him. They always find people." But I didn't believe what I said because I know there are lots of people who are never found.

"Will they put his photograph outside police stations?" Phillipa asked.

"I don't know."

"What will his parents do?"

"Sue us, I expect."

"That won't find Paul. Will they send out the army?" asked Georgie.

"And drag rivers?" asked Phillipa.

"We'll see," I replied, suddenly too weary for words, too weary for anything. They looked small and sweet in bed. I tucked them up. "You'll soon be home," I said.

"Have you heard from Mummy yet?"

"Yes, we got postcards. She's all right."

I could see they wouldn't sleep. I remembered things Mummy had said to me when I was little. "Think of something nice, think about Christmas," I whispered, tiptoeing from the room.

It was nearly ten o'clock. "Have a hot bath and go to bed," Mummy told me when I appeared downstairs. "Your father and I are taking it in turns to stay up in case the call comes through from Washington. Their time is different from ours. And the police may telephone about Paul, but you needn't stay up."

I looked out of the passage window and everything was bathed in moonlight. I could see the ponies looking over their loose box doors. Was Paul out there somewhere in the moonlight? I wondered. Ben came and stood beside me.

"I think he's lost," he said.

"I think he's kidnapped," I replied.

"We can't do any more now but I want you to help me tomorrow," he said. "You know Mary."

"I ought to."

"I must question her before I go out with Roy. He wants to know what happened before Apollo died. He may have eaten yew. She may have ridden him to death, or tried to kill him in a fit of madness. I'm going to set my clock. Roy plans to be here some time after six; we'll have to wake up Mary and talk to her. I need you."

"She may not wake up whatever we do," I said.

"I'll call you at five forty-five. Okay? We'll slap her with wet towels if necessary," replied Ben.

"Okay."

I went upstairs to the attic. Georgie and Phillipa were asleep, cuddling a variety of stuffed animals. The moonlight cast strange shadows across the room. I climbed into my humble iron bed. I wanted to pray for Paul, to ask God to bring him back at once, but I fell asleep before I got further than "Please, God."

It seemed but a minute later that Ben was shaking me by the shoulder, saying, "Wake up. We've got to question Mary – remember?" He drew back the curtain. In the distance cocks were crowing. Outside everything was still and misty, waiting for the day to begin in earnest.

"Don't be long," he whispered. "There isn't much time."

"Any news in the night?" I whispered, madly rubbing my eyes.

"I don't know yet," he said.

"Any telephone calls?" I insisted.

"I didn't hear any, but you know me, I sleep like a log." He was dressed in a big sweater, corduroys and thick socks. He tiptoed from the room.

I thought: Supposing she screams and wakes the whole house? Her mother is in the next room. She will go crazy. But I knew it was a risk we had to take because somehow we had to know why Apollo had died.

Phillipa stirred and muttered "Mummy" as I put on my dressing-gown, which I had had since I was nine and now only reached to my knees.

Ben was waiting outside my door. He had brushed his hair.

"We must be friendly this time," he said. "No nasty names."

"You called her names, too," I answered.

"I know and I bitterly regret it," he said.

We crept down the attic stairs. "We can't knock or her mother will hear. You go first," whispered Ben.

Mary was lying partly curled up with one leg awkwardly alone under the blankets as though it were detached from the rest of her body. She was heavily asleep. Her hair lay sprawled across the pillow and she was snoring. I was afraid to touch her.

I said, "Mary, wake up. It's me, Harriet."

"Don't say your name, you know she hates us," whispered Ben. "Touch her, gently, don't shake her."

"I'm not a fool," I retorted.

I touched her shoulder and whispered, "Mary, wake up. Please wake up." She wasn't cold any more and the room smelled of antiseptic. She stirred and groaned and muttered something. I shook her gently. "What happened to Apollo?" I said. "Please, you must tell us, it's vital, please."

"I didn't kill him. I went after the others. He bolted. He went mad, it was awful." Tears ran down her cheeks.

"Isn't that enough?" I asked.

"Who let them out?" said Ben.

"I was trying to help," she answered, opening her eyes. "I swear to God I was. What are you doing here anyway. Get out of my room."

"The vet has to know. He's doing a post-mortem," said Ben.

Her eyes were shutting again. "It wasn't my fault. He went mad. He went on and on, mile after mile. Then he died," she muttered. We crept from the room. The passage outside was full of sunlight.

"Do you think she's speaking the truth?" I asked.

"Yes."

We went downstairs and made ourselves mugs of tea in the kitchen, heaping spoonfuls of sugar into them to give us energy.

"But why did he go mad?" I asked.

"He may have had a fright and died of heart failure."

"But he looked all right when he came."

We drew back the curtains.

Dad appeared from the sitting-room. His clothes were crumpled. "No call from Washington. Pour me a mug of tea, please," he said.

"What about Paul?" I asked.

"The police brought him back. They found him wandering along the B20, completely lost," Dad said.

"He wasn't kidnapped then?" asked Ben.

"No, Lisa was right. He was looking for Apollo. Mrs Mills must have dreamed up the car or else it was some potential guests having a look at the place," replied Dad.

"Did you tell Paul that Apollo was dead?" asked Ben.

"No."

So that awful moment had still to come. "I thought you could tell him, Harriet," Dad said.

91

"Me? I can't. Ben, you're the nearest him in years. I wouldn't know how to begin," I cried.

"Just try," said Dad wearily. "You must know exactly how he feels about that horse."

We heard a car horn. "That's Roy," Ben said, slipping out of the back door.

"I'm going back to bed," I said. "Thank goodness Paul came back before his parents telephoned."

"Yes. We only have to tell them about their horse now," Dad answered. "Let's hope he was insured. Be gentle with Paul when you tell him, Harriet. Take him out for a ride. He can ride Jigsaw, can't he?"

"If Lisa doesn't mind, but it will be a bit of a come-down after Apollo, won't it?" I asked.

I went back to bed, but I couldn't sleep and presently Phillipa and Georgie woke up and wanted to know whether Paul was back. They were pleased when I told them that he was safe asleep in bed.

"Does he know about Apollo?" Georgie asked, sitting up.

"Not yet. Please don't tell him. I'm going to tell him on a ride," I said.

"Okay. Can we ride?"

"Yes, afterwards," I said.

I wanted to get the awful task over with, but it was hours before Paul got up and there was still no sign of Ben, nor had the call from Washington come through.

But then at ten o'clock the ambulance came and Mrs Harris escorted the men upstairs, her lips tight and disagreeable. They carried Mary down on a stretcher, still half asleep.

"I'm going with her," said Mrs Harris. "I don't suppose you'll see either of us ever again. I've stopped the cheque."

We'll never know what really happened then, I

thought. How sad. And she'll never be grateful for us finding her and bringing her home. And we'll never know why she behaves as she does. It was like getting halfway through a crossword puzzle and having to stop, only much worse because it was real life. Perhaps I can write to her, I thought.

James was helping Mrs Harris with her suitcase. One of the ambulancemen tucked a blanket round Mary's legs. She lay looking at the roof of the ambulance. I wanted to scream, "What really happened? Tell us, please, so we can tell Paul." But I knew it would only cause a scene. She was going away and I would never know her any better, or apologise for calling her names. It was life.

Paul was behind me now. He said, "Where's Apollo? I must know."

"He's hurt," I answered, hating myself for lying. "Will you come out for a ride now? I think you could do with it."

There were dark circles under his eyes. "Okay. I'll just get kitted out," he said.

I felt cornered and terribly alone waiting in the yard for Paul. It was a lovely morning. Everything was suddenly sparkling and the trees were still at last, basking in the sunlight. Jigsaw was sleepy. Lorraine stood with her head up looking for further adventure. It isn't fair, I thought, why should I tell him?

It wasn't a morning for bad news. It was a morning for silver cups and red rosettes and great hopes being realised.

I wondered how Ben and Roy were getting on in the wood. They had been away a long time already. Perhaps Mary had ridden Apollo into a tree. Perhaps she had gone mad, not Apollo. Would we ever know the truth? I wondered.

Paul came at last, smiling. "I hear the vet has been. Has he taken Apollo to hospital to make him better?"

"No, not really," I answered quickly and with a choke in my voice, thinking of the horse slaughterer's truck which had HORSE AMBULANCE written across the front when it should have had DEATH CELL or MORTUARY, and how it was probably in the wood by now taking away Apollo. I could feel tears running down my cheeks and I hid my face in Lorraine's mane saying, "Are you ready to get up?"

Paul nodded.

I tightened Jigsaw's girth, and Paul said, "You're crying, why?"

I didn't answer. I ran down his stirrups and said, "Jigsaw is lovely to ride. Not like Apollo, but nice and kind, and very brisk. He trots very fast, too," but my words got mixed up with my misery and came out shaky.

"I can take bad news," replied Paul, mounting. "Don't worry about me. If Apollo's broken a leg, I don't mind waiting until it's mended. I don't mind waiting years. I just love that horse."

I mounted Lorraine. Her neck in front of me gave me comfort, her pricked ears gave me courage. I'll wait a bit and then tell him after a canter, I thought. I'll break it gently, bit by bit. "We'll go across the fields. I'm sick of the woods," I said. "Are you okay? Are your stirrups right?"

Paul was smiling again now. "I remember the first time I saw Apollo," he began. "I saw him, and knew he had to be mine. Has that ever happened to you?"

I shook my head. "Lorraine was dead cheap," I said. "She was skin and bone in the market."

"He'll mend, won't he? Broken legs mend nowadays?" asked Paul.

"Some," I said. "Shall we canter?"

Paul wasn't much of a rider. I wondered how he had ever managed Apollo. We drew rein and he said, "Hi. Look. There's the horse ambulance. It must be bringing Apollo home. Let's go back. I want to see him."

And my silly tears came back and I said, "No, you can't, you'll never see Apollo again. He's dead."

But Paul didn't believe me. He said, "Sure," and "No kidding," and "Thanks a lot."

I looked at him and said, "I'm sorry. We don't know why he died. The vet is doing a post-mortem on him now. It's just one of those things." And my tears fell into Lorraine's mane and I wished that Ben were there to explain things better than I could.

Then Paul said, "I want to go back anyway. I want to speak to my parents back home."

I've made a muck of it I thought, I make a muck of everything. And we turned round and rode back.

We found Mummy opening letters in the kitchen. "All these people want to come and live with us; isn't it extraordinary?" she asked.

"We can't have them," I said. "We can't have any more. It's too awful."

"He knows then?" asked Mummy looking at Paul, going to him, putting her arms round him.

He pushed her away and said, "I don't want sympathy. I want to talk to my parents now."

"We've been waiting for them to call since yesterday evening," explained Mummy, "and we're still waiting."

"Can we ride now?" shrieked Georgie and Phillipa, coming into the kitchen. "We've been waiting for ages."

"Put on hard hats," said Mummy. "I'll look after Paul, Harriet. You've had enough misery for one day."

"By the way, the sign's gone," I said.

"I know. Colonel Jones chopped it down on behalf of the parish," Mummy answered.

"Just one more blow," I said.

"When things are better we'll put up another one," Mummy said. "Your father's getting permission."

"Who are we riding?" shrieked Georgie and Phillipa, dancing downstairs. "Do we need whips?"

Eight
A call from Washington

I tacked up Limpet for them. I had left Jigsaw waiting
with his tack on. I took them to the smallest field by the
stables, which we call the paddock, and I pretended we
were preparing for a dressage test. I made them enter the
arena at a trot and halt at X (which was a cross made
out of sticks) and salute and then ride forward straight.
Limpet dawdled, but Jigsaw trotted straight as a die. I
made them change ponies and back straight between
poles on the ground, but all the time my mind was else-
where with Ben and Roy in the dark damp wood, or
with Paul, heartbroken in the house. I made them ride
without stirrups and then take them back and have a
walk and trot race. I wondered how Mary was in hospital and whether we would ever see her again. The sun
was shining and there were flies round the ponies' heads
and Phillipa and Georgie decided to take off their coats.
I put up little jumps for them and a grid.

"Hold on to the mane if you feel unsteady," I
shouted. "Not too long a run. Don't start till the pony
in front is over." And all the time I was wondering
where we would live if we decided to give up the inn.
And what I would do with Lorraine. We had some more
races and then an hour was up and we untacked the
ponies together and turned them out, and Georgie in a
rush of affection held my hand and Phillipa told me how

her father always shouted at breakfast. "Fathers always shout at breakfast," I said. "It must be almost lunchtime by now. Race you to the house," and they rushed after me screaming. All the way back I was wondering whether the call had come through from Washington and what Paul's parents had said.

Georgie and Phillipa wouldn't stop talking now. "I suppose the inn is named after Limpet?" asked Georgie.

"That's right," I answered, opening the back door.

"Did you learn to ride on him?"

"Yes, that's right."

"He's a super pony. Has he won many rosettes?" asked Georgie.

"About a hundred all told," I said.

"What about Jigsaw?"

"We haven't had him long. He's won about fifty."

"You must be terribly good riders," gasped Georgie.

"No, just lucky."

There was no sign of anyone. I stood in the kitchen listening, praying that nothing else had gone wrong.

Then the telephone rang and I ran through into the hall and picked up the receiver. A voice said, "I have your personal call to Washington. Can you take it?" Suddenly I felt sick.

"Hang on," I replied and rushed through the house shouting, "It's the Washington call."

Mummy and Paul came hurtling down the stairs together, but Paul got to the phone first. "Mom?" he cried. "Something terrible's happened. Apollo's dead."

"Hold on a minute," said the voice at the other end, "you're not through yet."

"I wanted to speak first, to explain," said Mummy.

Georgie and Phillipa disappeared in search of Lisa. The sun sent dusty shafts of light across the hall. Time seemed to stand still.

"Heaven knows what they'll do," said Mummy. She looked haggard. I wanted to put my arms round her and say, "Everything's going to be all right," but I couldn't because I didn't believe it myself. At this moment, I saw only failure ahead – the house up for sale again, being sold for next to nothing, the end of our dream.

"It's me, Paul. Is that you, Mom?"

We heard his father's voice loud and clear saying, "No, it's me, Paul, what's biting you? We've been at the cabin in the mountains."

"It's Apollo. He's dead."

I wanted to shut my ears but I couldn't. I tried not to listen, but I could hear the anger vibrating along the line and Mummy seemed to shrink as she listened. I wished that Ben or James or Dad were there to comfort Mummy.

"No, I don't know how he died. The girl took him . . . no, a house guest," Paul said. "Yes, stole him, stole my horse, Dad . . . Yes . . . She killed him. Rode him to death."

I thought of the minutes passing, adding pounds to our bill. I thought, there is no end to it, no way out – he's dead, and death can't be bypassed or excused or conveniently exchanged for something, or forgotten.

I went and stood by Mummy and said, "It will pass. Time is a great healer," which she had said to me once a long, long time ago when I had done something idiotic and killed a friendship for ever.

"Sure. He wants to speak to you," Paul said, holding out the receiver.

Mummy took it. "I can't say how sorry I am," she began but Mr Armstrong cut in on her, shouting that we weren't fit to look after guests or animals. I wanted to snatch the phone away and try to explain, to say, "Leave Mummy out of it, it wasn't her fault."

But now I could hear Ben shouting, "Anyone at home?" and then, "Do you want a cup of coffee, Roy?" I rushed into the kitchen and Ben put his thumbs up and said, "It's okay." He was carrying Apollo's tack and it started me crying again.

"Mr Armstrong is on the telephone, he's shouting at Mummy," I cried. "He's being awful about Apollo. He says it's all her fault. It's awful."

Roy was in his usual clothes, his boots were covered with mud and his hair had leaves in it. "He is, is he? Well, let me speak to him," he said.

He strode into the hall and took hold of the phone and we heard him say, "Excuse me, I'm a veterinary surgeon. . . yes, a horse doctor if you like, and I've just done a post-mortem on your pony and you're lucky he is dead."

Ben whispered, "It's all right, Harriet. Stop crying."

"Yes. He had a tumour. He could have gone mad with your boy on top and killed him. It was pressing on his brain. Didn't you have him vetted when you bought him? . . . Oh I see, what a pity. I expect he was pretty quiet for such a well-bred pony – well, sleepy."

We could hear Mr Armstrong arguing but Roy said firmly, "I will be mailing the lab report and the results of all the tests to you during the next few days. Show them to any veterinary college in the world if you want a second opinion. I can send you the tumour, too, if you want it. He really died just in time, another day and your boy would have been on top and he might be lying in hospital with a fractured skull or worse."

"Good old Roy," whispered Ben.

"The call will cost a fortune," I said.

"Never mind, we're saved," replied Ben.

"Well, I should ask the people here to choose your next pony. They're no fools and I will vet it for you personally, for nothing if you like . . . Yes, of course."

He handed the receiver back to Paul, who said, "Well, I like Jigsaw and I'd like to stay on as arranged as a house guest, sure I would."

And Ben pretended to faint and Mummy said, "Well I never. What a surprise."

Then Roy said, "I must be off," and Mummy shook him warmly by the hand. "I can never thank you enough," she said.

Roy replied, "You don't have to, it's all in a day's work."

Ben showed him out and when he returned we saw for the first time how filthy he was. "Take your boots off at once!" shouted Mummy. "Just look at my clean floor."

But Ben only laughed, saying, "I'm going to be a vet when I'm grown up, I've decided at last. We went to the

102

lab at the veterinary college. I helped him all the way."

Paul put down the receiver and said, "Dad says I'm to tell you I'm real sorry and so is he. And I want to stay on if I may and I want Harriet to teach me to ride properly and help me buy a pony. Okay?"

"Okay," said Ben and I together.

He held out his hand and we all shook it in turn and Mummy said, "This calls for a drink. How about some cider?"

Lisa came tearing downstairs shouting, "Cider, yes please." James and Dad appeared five minutes later and we all sat together drinking cider.

Paul said, "I'm real sorry about everything."

"It was natural," I replied. "I would have felt the same if Lorraine had died."

"I want a cute pony next time, something like Jigsaw," he said. "What we call an apache pony back home."

"You'll need something of fourteen hands because you're going to grow," advised Ben. "Not like Lisa."

"I'm not the smallest in my class any more, Angie is," retorted Lisa.

We all started to feel drunk quite soon, not with drink but with relief.

There was hotpot in the oven for supper and Mrs Mills came down and had a tot of whisky with Dad. Paul was still rather quiet, but not bitter any more and after a time I found *Horse and Hound* and we read it together, searching for a suitable pony for him.

"I'll sure have it vetted this time," he said. "We trusted the people who sold us Apollo and they were real cheats, no kidding."

"He must be quiet and sensible and a good jumper," I said.

"And quiet in traffic," said Ben.

"With a kind eye," said Lisa.

"I don't want another chestnut. If I can't have a pinto, I would like a black," said Paul.

" 'A good horse is never a bad colour'," quoted Ben.

"There's the telephone again," said James.

"More disaster," exclaimed Ben.

"We should leave it off the hook," said Dad, going to the telephone, then coming back to say, "It's Mrs Harris, it's for you, Harriet."

"For me?" I cried. "It can't be. It must be Mummy she wants."

"She said you," replied Dad, sitting down again.

I went through to the hall shaking with trepidation. "Hello, it's Harriet here," I said. Then I saw that my hand was trembling which was something it had never done before.

"Mary wants to see you and Ben. She insists," said Mrs Harris with disagreeable reluctance, as though it was the most unsavoury request she had ever made.

"What for?" I answered.

"For a chat."

"For a chat?" I replied, unbelieving. "Are you sure?"

"Yes. And Ben. Any time after ten o'clock in the morning and before lunch. Don't forget to bring your brother," said Mrs Harris.

I thought: She can't harm us in a hospital or pay us back for what we said, and we may learn what really happened at last. Suddenly I felt my spirits rising.

"Okay, we'll be there, I promise," I said. "Even if we have to walk."

"Goodbye then," said Mrs Harris, sounding even more disagreeable.

I put down the receiver. "It's fantastic, absolutely fantastic," I cried, going back to the kitchen. "Mary wants me and Ben to visit her in hospital tomorrow."

"What for?" cried Ben.

"To make her peace. She's a good kid really," said Dad, giving her the benefit of the doubt again.

I sat down.

Dad told Lisa, Georgie and Phillipa to go to bed. Paul was still reading *Horse and Hound*.

"We must go," I said. "I promised we would."

"I'll take you," offered Dad, "because I think she needs help."

"Don't we all?" asked James.

"Exactly," agreed Mummy.

"She probably wants to say she's sorry," said Ben.

"Or to tell her side of the story, and it had better be good," I answered. "Because she's caused plenty of misery one way and another."

"We all make mistakes," replied Dad.

"I want to hear her story anyway, and I want to say I'm sorry, too," I answered.

Outside it was dark. It had been a long day. The morning seemed already to belong to another life. Soon we'll be back at school, I thought, and I don't remember anything from last term, not a word of French nor a line of English. It all seems so small compared to life. What does the French for 'horse' matter compared with Apollo dead in a wood – or Mary with her leg broken? I shall never cope, I thought, never concentrate again, and Miss Pitts will be furious and I shall be hauled before the headmaster.

I struggled to my feet. My legs felt heavy and suddenly I was tired beyond words. "I'm going to bed," I said.

Mummy was telling Ben to clean his nails and wash his hair. "They don't like dirty people in hospital," she said. "They won't let you in."

James was making himself yet another cup of coffee.

"I'm going to bed, too," Paul said. He had dark circles under his eyes, but he wasn't crying any more.

"Sleep well," said Mrs Mills. "I'm on my way as well. I'm just going to fill my hot-water bottle first."

Phillipa and Georgie had put themselves to bed, leaving a note on my pillow which read: *We hate Mary and love you. P and G.* I thought that I didn't deserve it, that I didn't help anyone enough and had made a mess of telling Paul about Apollo. In fact, one way and another,

I was a bit of a failure. There was a moon outside now, looking wild and free in the sky, and the village looked shadowy and romantic like something in a film.

The hours in the wood and finding Apollo dead seemed impossible as I undressed and got into bed. Whatever happens tomorrow can't be worse than today or yesterday, I thought.

Nine

Mary tells her story

The next morning was wild and windy. I had slept badly, dreaming of Mary throwing bricks at Ben. There was a pile of letters on the hall mat when I wandered downstairs still half asleep. Mrs Mills appeared and held out a hand. She was always hoping for a letter from her daughter, which never came.

"Sorry. Nothing," I said now, saddened by her disappointed face.

It was like any other morning except for our impending visit to the hospital hanging over everything. I dressed and ran round to the stables. It was still early and everything smelled lovely, full of hope and rising sap, new leaves, growing grass; there seemed no room for sorrow or regrets. I found Paul already there, leaning on the field gate.

"You're early," I said. "Couldn't you sleep?"

"No, not a wink," he answered. "Say, there's a sale of horses next week. How about going? It's in the same county as here." He had *Horse and Hound* in his pocket and he unfolded it now and read: '300 horses and ponies; 150 lots of saddlery and harness, etc.' There's sure to be something suitable and I don't want to wait," he added.

I knew how he felt, how he hated waiting, how we seemed to be doing nothing though Apollo had been dead for two days. I could understand his impatience, but buying a horse in a hurry is apt to lead to disaster, or so the experts say.

"It's in three days' time," he continued, "and some of them are warranted, so we needn't get another one like Apollo."

"Buying a horse in a sale is always a risk," I said, feeling mean. "I know Lorraine came from one, but we knew her history."

I ran my eye over our ponies without really seeing them, but I knew they were all right, without strains or sprains or colic or anything else.

"Can we look at some anyway?" insisted Paul.

"Okay, if there's any transport. But I want to improve your riding first; otherwise we'll have to get something solid and quiet because we don't want any more accidents," I said.

We went back to the house together, and I set the table for breakfast and woke my parents with a cup of tea.

Dad didn't go to the factory every day. He had paid his workers large sums of money to compensate them for losing their jobs, but no one had paid him anything. Once he had risen before any of us, but this morning he wasn't up till nine and then he sat for ages simply sipping coffee.

Paul read *Horse and Hound* all through breakfast, marking advertisements with a pen.

"I want to call up Dad later to ask how much we can spend," he said, looking round the breakfast table.

"I'm afraid we can't advance you a thousand pounds," replied Dad quickly. "But call up your dad by all means. James will put you through."

"I'm just checking your clothes for school. You've only got five more days here," Mummy said.

109

The holidays were almost over. I went away to get ready for hospital. I was longing to hear Mary's side of the story, to know what had really happened. But would she tell us the truth?

The hospital smelled of antiseptic. Ben had put on his new jacket and brushed his hair until it lay like polished, flattened straw across his forehead. I had put on jodhpurs because my trousers were either dirty or frayed or far too short. I had put on jodhpur boots, too, and my best polo-necked jersey.

Mary lay in a long ward full of old ladies with broken limbs. She sat propped up with pillows, looking young and fragile.

A nurse said, "Now don't stay long, and don't upset Mary, she's still suffering from exposure and shock."

"Okay," said Ben grinning.

The old ladies stared at us as though we were strangers from outer space. I felt hideously self-conscious in my riding-clothes.

Mary waved a hand in our direction. "Come and sit down," she called. We found two chairs and sat on them.

"Are you getting better?" asked Ben.

"How do you feel?" I inquired at the same moment.

"All right. But what about Apollo? Mummy didn't say a thing. Why did he die? What did the vet say? Was it my fault?"

Ben shook his head. "He died of a tumour; that's why he was so sleepy when he came. We should have realised, but we didn't. He didn't look round or neigh or anything – remember? He was going to die anyway. Roy says he must have been seized by a frenzy, that's why he galloped and wouldn't stop," continued Ben.

"Shhh, you're keeping the ward awake," said a nurse. "It's rest time, you know, talk softly."

"Sorry. He must have gone on till he hit that tree and then had a fit. That's what Roy says. Is that right?" continued Ben, lowering his voice.

Mary nodded. "I thought it was my fault," she whispered. "I've done so many awful things. I thought that it was just one more: I've been so miserable. I just wanted to die."

"What really happened?" I asked.

"Begin at the beginning," suggested Ben. "Why did you get up in the middle of the night?"

"I heard the horses neighing. I wasn't really asleep. I was dreaming about Trixie. She was lost and I was looking for her and for a time I thought it was Trixie and then suddenly I knew where I was. I leaped out of bed and pulled on some trousers and a pullover. There was

111

a horse box by the gate with its lights on, and men in the yard. I shouted, 'Get out, clear off, I've called the police.' All the gates were open. I was terribly scared really. My knees were knocking. I heard someone throw up a ramp, the roar of an engine, and then suddenly the box was gone."

"And the ponies?" asked Ben, leaning forward in his chair. "Where were they?"

"All the gates were open. The box must have been backed up to the yard entrance," continued Mary. "And by the time I got there the ponies were thundering away across the common. Of course I should have gone back to the house then and raised the alarm, but I didn't. I wanted to show you I was all right really, to make amends. So I tacked up Apollo and went in pursuit and that's when it happened – he went mad. I pulled and pulled, I even yelled. He went round and round in circles and then suddenly straight for the woods like something possessed. I tried to steer him into the trees to stop him but he just went on until he fell . . ."

"And had a fit," finished Ben. "That's how Roy said it would have happened."

"I wanted to make a good impression by saving the ponies," said Mary wearily, wiping a tear from her eye. "You won't believe it, but I did. I know I'm objectionable. I don't like being the way I am, but I can't stop myself."

"We're all like that sometimes," Ben said, in a voice I had never heard before.

"But what about Paul?" asked Mary. "Is he very upset? Are his parents blaming you?"

"Roy, our vet, did a post-mortem. Everything is all right. Don't worry," Ben replied, in a soothing voice which made me feel out on a limb all of a sudden.

"You don't understand, I love horses. I always have

and I always will. It's my mother who doesn't like them. She says she's allergic to them. I think it's just an excuse to keep away. She doesn't like me either," continued Mary.

"She must," I said, "she's your mother."

"It doesn't follow. Don't be a fool, Harriet. Not all mothers love their children," replied Ben.

"Most do," I said, "it's natural."

"It was all right until Trixie went," continued Mary. "I was quite a nice person until that happened. Nothing has been the same since then. When she went I wanted to die."

"What happened?" I asked.

Mary looked away. Ben frowned at me and I knew he was thinking that I was tactless, but I wanted to know now, before Mary was gone for ever.

"It's a long story," she began. "Dad bought her for me on my ninth birthday. I remember when she came. It was so lovely. He brought her right into the kitchen and she ate oats off the kitchen table. She was grey like Lorraine, but smaller, and she was the first pony I had ever had."

The bossy nurse came back. "Only five more minutes," she hissed.

Ben made a face at her back. "Go on," he said.

"Then a year later Mummy and Daddy broke up. They had been quarrelling for years. Daddy simply got fed up and went off with someone else, right away to South Africa."

"How awful," I said.

"It was such a long way, I knew it was final. I blamed Mummy. I couldn't forgive her. She sent me away to a boarding school. I remember it so well. I was all dressed up in some ghastly uniform –" Mary was crying openly now "– and the last thing I said was, 'Look after Trix, won't you? Two full haynets a day and two feeds, don't forget.' I wanted to say goodbye to Trixie once more, but Mummy wouldn't wait, she said we were late already. She said, 'Don't worry, I'll look after her, I promise.' Then when I came back Trixie was gone. Mummy had sent her to the market, she said she couldn't afford the food for her now that Daddy had deserted us and I should blame him, but the cocktail cupboard was full of drink and the deep freeze was full of steak and you know what that costs," finished Mary.

I tried to think of something to say.

Ben said, "Why didn't she find her a nice home or lend her to someone?"

"She couldn't be bothered, that's why," replied Mary bitterly. "It would have meant seeing people, explaining, and she doesn't know the first thing about ponies. So you see I hate both my parents. Daddy for going away and leaving me, and Mummy for selling Trix. And I hated you too," she continued, "because you had all the things I had lost – two parents, ponies, the lot."

"Perhaps we could find Trixie," I replied, feeling hopelessly inadequate to the situation.

"She went for meat. They all did that month, there was a hay shortage and a meat shortage and it was halfway through the winter, the worst time to sell a pony. And Trixie was only entered as 'Grey pony' in the catalogue, nothing about being good or kind or a lovely ride. Mummy was too lazy or too ignorant to put anything else. That's my mother for you," finished Mary.

Most of the old ladies in the ward were asleep by this time.

I imagined Mary coming home from boarding school, finding the paddock empty, running to the house, shouting, "Where's Trixie?" How I would have felt?

"Then I met Ted. Here, I've got a photograph of

him," said Mary, putting a hand under her pillow. "His parents are separated too. We discuss our situations. He's the only person I can really talk to – you see he knows what it feels like to be me. I didn't really run away, Mummy invented that. She knows I talk about her to Ted, that's why."

I looked at the photograph. Ted was dark-haired with a kind, square-shaped face. He looked like a person you could trust. "He looks nice," I said. "And good-tempered too," I added, passing the photograph to Ben.

Suddenly two or three nurses rushed into the ward and started straightening bedclothes. The old ladies sat up, dazed, and one asked, "What is it, nurse? What's happening?"

"It's the consultant, he's come," replied a nurse.

We knew we would have to go in a minute and we hadn't said half the things we wanted to say. A nurse started straightening Mary's bed. "How do you feel, dear?" she asked.

"Better, much better."

"You two must go now," the nurse said. "The doctors are on their way. It's the consultant's morning."

116

"Just one more minute," pleaded Mary.

"Just one then, but keep your voices down," replied the nurse.

"I don't want to go home," announced Mary, looking straight at Ben. "Will you have me back? I will help, I promise. I will be like Mrs Mills. I'll make the beds and wash up, and groom the ponies and muck out. Mummy's going to marry someone I hate and they won't want me around – please."

I couldn't imagine Mary making beds or washing up or being like Mrs Mills.

I looked at Ben. We could see people coming into the ward. Ben looked as though he wanted to say yes, but he didn't dare speak for our parents, he had to ask first. Mary grabbed his hand. "Please . . ." she said, as though that one word could melt a heart of stone.

"Can't you wait a few hours?" asked Ben.

Mary shook her head. "Mummy's bringing my clothes this afternoon. They want the bed. I've told everyone I'm going to you. I was sure you would say yes, when you knew the truth."

I thought of her lying upstairs, being waited on, getting better. She might change and become nasty again. How could we tell? But Ben was on his feet now. "I'll go and ask Dad, he's outside waiting for us," he said. "I can't say yes on my own."

And I knew what Dad's answer would be for he couldn't turn a wounded fly away, much less Mary. He simply wasn't tough enough.

"You don't mind, do you? I don't mind where I sleep. And Mummy will keep on paying, she gets loads of alimony," Mary continued, as though it was settled already.

"I'm sorry about Trixie. It must have been awful," I said. "And I'm sorry we called you such awful names."

117

"It doesn't matter. I can go to the local school, can't I?" I nodded. I wondered what Mummy would say when we told her. The doctors were coming nearer every moment. I stood up. Ben came back smiling, followed by three nurses buzzing round him like angry bees.

"It's all fixed up," he said.

"Out," said one of the nurses. "Out at once."

Mary smiled at us.

"See you later," Ben said.

"Mummy's going to un-stop the cheque. I made her," Mary said.

"Out," hissed the nurse. "You shouldn't be in here, the consultant's here."

Outside the air was fresh and free and sunlit. Dad was smiling in the car. "I knew she was a good kid," he said. "Just a bit mixed-up."

"We don't seem to have lost a single guest after all," I said. "I just hope she doesn't change back to how she was before."

"Change back?"

"To how she was three days ago," I answered.

We told Dad what Mary had said on the way home.

The house looked peaceful when we reached it. Mrs Mills was weeding a border and Mummy's new help had come and was shaking mats. James was practising driving the Land Rover and Lisa was jumping Jigsaw, watched by Paul, Phillipa and Georgie.

"She meant well," said Ben, getting out of the car. "And she was jolly brave going out alone to face horse thieves." I thought that he was like Dad, always willing to give anyone the benefit of the doubt. "She probably saved the ponies too," he added.

"I'll break it to your mother. I'm sure she'll be pleased," Dad said.

We had been through a kind of hell and yet nothing

was really changed. The house looked the same, and the stables; only Apollo was missing and Mary's leg would have to mend, otherwise all was the same – the flowers were still growing, the trees still stood where they had always stood.

I could hear Mummy laughing as I went inside.

"So she's coming back after all," she said. "And we have all these other people who want to come. Let's go through the letters together. We can pick and choose our guests now. Isn't it fantastic?"

"No more neurotic girls, please," said James, coming in with the sun behind him.

"No more sick horses," I added. "I can't bear another death."

"There's a colonel," began Mummy, "who wants to look after the garden for a small reduction. He's ninety-two. And there's a strange man who calls himself Commander Cooley; and a family of five with Mum expecting another who want a rest. They want reductions because all the children are under ten and Dad knows about horses and can drive."

"They all sound strange," I said. "And we've had enough of strangers already. No one could have been stranger than Mary was."

"Or poor sick Apollo," added Ben.

"Or the Armstrongs paying all that money for a dying horse," said Dad.

"And then there's one from a social worker who wants us to take on a delinquent boy who loves horses; and there're three children who need a foster mother. And five horses who need a home for six months," continued Mummy.

"We'll take the horses," cried Ben.

Mummy put down the letters. "I have been writing up a guests' charter," she said. "Two in fact – one to hang in the hall, the other to be signed by adults when they leave their charges here. We should have thought of it before. Listen."

She started to read and it took me back to my infancy when she used to read aloud to us before we lived in our present house.

ALL GUESTS TO HAVE BREAKFAST BY 9.30 AM
ALL CHILDREN UNDER FOURTEEN TO BE IN BED BY 9.30 PM

"That's too early," yelled Ben.

ALL CHILDREN TO WEAR SUITABLE HARD HATS WHEN RIDING
ALL RIDERS TO LEAVE WRITTEN NOTICE OF WHERE THEY ARE
    GOING WHEN HACKING
ALL PONIES TO BE BROUGHT HOME COOL
ALL DIRTY SHOES TO BE LEFT IN LOBBY OR SCULLERY
ALL NIGHTCLOTHES TO BE LEFT ON CHAIR OR BED
NO CLOTHES TO BE LEFT ON FLOORS
ALL BATHROOMS TO BE LEFT AS FOUND

She stopped for breath. "Anything else?"

"I'll think," said Dad.

"The other one is more legal. It must be signed, it's all about not holding us responsible for death, illness, theft, injury, etcetera, etcetera. And about children coming here at their own risk. I'll get it copied if you are all agreeable."

"Let's get a solicitor to look at it first," suggested Dad.

"Someone telephoned this morning about your having two ponies to get fit before camp," continued Mummy, looking at Ben and me. "They want you to name a price," she said.

"In or out?"

120

"I didn't ask. Here's the number."

"Everything is going to be all right, isn't it?" I said, taking the number which was on a scrap of paper. "We can go on being a guest house?"

Mummy nodded. "And we can choose our guests now," she said.

Lisa, Phillipa, Georgie and Paul were coming towards the house, pushing each other and laughing. Mrs Mills waved her trowel at them and called, "Keep off the flowerbeds."

There was sunlight everywhere. I watched them coming without really seeing them, seeing instead new guests, strange ponies coming, strange riders. I hoped we would choose well.

"Isn't it lovely to sit and know everything's all right after all," said Ben. "That Mary's coming back and that Paul's staying, that we've succeeded in spite of everything."

"It's a miracle," James said. "And I vote we have the old colonel, because I'm sick of mowing the lawn."

"No. I want Commander Cooley. He sounds like MI5," said Ben.

"There isn't any hurry to decide," Mummy said. "Tomorrow will do."

"There goes the telephone again," James cried. "And that will be another one." He went to answer it.

"Perhaps we should take the delinquent boy," said Mummy. "It might make all the difference to him."

"It's people wanting to come for the weekend," said James, coming back. "Two children who are mad about riding and two parents who are mad about walking, three dogs and a tortoise."

But whom we took next, and how Mary behaved, and what pony we bought for Paul – well, that all belongs to another story.

121

Mystery at
Black Pony Inn

CONTENTS

One
We buy a horse

It was May. We were sitting on upturned buckets in the stable-yard talking about the future. My brother Ben was chewing a piece of straw. Lisa was cuddling Twinkle, our black cat. James, who is the eldest, had a school book in one hand, but he wasn't reading it. In a month's time he would be taking his GCSEs, but it wasn't a day for work, it was a day for plans, for sitting around in the sunshine, dreaming impossible dreams.

We had been running the inn for several months now. We had suffered calamity and found Paul's pony dead and Mary with a broken leg; but Mary was getting better and Paul wanted a new pony, and we had a new guest called Colonel Hunter, who was impossibly old and whom Lisa was always trying to marry off to Mrs Mills, who was a paying guest in her eighties. The ponies watched us over the rail fence. They had shiny summer coats now and their sides were round and full.

"I'm not having this Commander Cooley on Solitaire, whatever anyone says," Ben said. Commander Cooley was to be our next paying guest. He was said to be rich and handsome.

"He's got to ride something. He's coming to ride. It's on doctor's orders, he's had a nervous breakdown," retorted James, who doesn't ride.

"We'll have to buy a horse," I said. "Something large

and patient, which will carry anyone – a horse we can trust."

"Dad will only let us have three hundred pounds. We can't buy anything with that," answered Ben. "That's less than meat price."

"Not if it's thin. We'll go to the market – okay?" I asked.

"It's a devil of a risk," replied Ben.

"We'll risk it then." I hated the market. My own horse, Lorraine, had come from there. But we had known something about her. This time we would be buying in the dark. It would be an appalling gamble.

"It must have a vet's certificate and be warranted," said Ben. "We don't want another Apollo." Apollo had been Paul's pony. He had had a tumour on the brain, which had killed him.

"If we don't get something soon, Commander Cooley will be riding Solitaire *and* Lorraine; and all the horses in *Horse and Hound* are five hundred pounds and then we have to get to see them," I said. "The market is our only hope."

"Okay, Mummy and I will stock up at the CaterMart while you're there," James said.

"Remember to ask Dad for the money. They like cash at the market." He walked away with the school book still in his hand, looking taller than ever.

Lisa was talking to her piebald pony, Jigsaw. Limpet, the little black which had taught us all to ride, was nibbling her hair. Grey Lorraine was gazing into the distance while Ben's Welsh cob, Solitaire, stood eyeing the buckets hopefully. It was Sunday and the church bells had started to ring beyond the common.

"Mummy says Commander Cooley is tall and slim and incredibly handsome. I expect Mary will fall in love with him," said Ben.

128

"But he's forty," I objected. "And that's old enough to be her father."

We saw that Colonel Hunter was coming towards us. "He's going to talk about India," said Ben.

But he only called, "None of you going to church?" in a disapproving voice and walked away across the common towards the sound of bells.

Presently Mary joined us, walking with a stick. Her leg was still in plaster after her accident with Apollo, and she looked pale and bad-tempered.

"School again tomorrow," she said. "And how I hate the boys on the bus. Can't your mother take us? Do we always have to go by bus?"

"Yes," I said.

"You needn't talk to the boys. They don't like you either. The dislike is mutual," said Ben.

"Thank you very much," replied Mary.

I didn't want to go inside to help get lunch. I wanted to sit there for ever dreaming about the future, making plans, the sun warm on my back.

"There's a commander coming in two weeks' time. He's very handsome," Lisa told Mary. "Perhaps he'll take you to school."

"He's got a Mercedes," said Ben.

"And loads of money, because he wants to ride every day and he's paying fifteen pounds a week extra for the best bedroom," I added.

"Which is Mummy and Dad's. How do you like that? He's turning them out. I hate him," cried Lisa, her eyes suddenly full of tears. "Why should they give up their bedroom?"

"They don't have to. What a baby you are," retorted Mary, going back towards the house. "They just want the money. That's why they're doing it."

"I wish there were children coming," said Lisa. "I'm

sick of the old Colonel. All he talks about is India."

"You can't expect children in term time. Anyway, Paul will be here for his half-term in a couple of weeks. He'll play with you."

Lisa was nine, small, thin and determined. I was twelve, with brown hair and blue eyes. Ben was just fourteen and James was sixteen. We had turned our house into a guest house when no one would buy it and Dad's firm had gone bust.

But at the moment we hadn't many guests – just ancient Mrs Mills, the Colonel, Mary, and Paul at half-term. It wasn't enough to make a profit, so the Commander was to be a welcome addition.

We found Mummy inside making a pudding. "We've decided to go to the market next Saturday to buy a horse. There's nothing in *Horse and Hound* which will do, and Mrs Sims has only high-class horses at four hundred for an unschooled four-year-old," Ben said. Mrs Sims was our local dealer.

"Have you tried all the riding-schools?" Mummy asked.

Ben nodded. "So many horses went for meat last autumn that there's now a shortage," he said.

"Be careful then," replied Mummy, who isn't horsy. "Don't buy a dangerous animal."

Dad came in then so we told him our plan. "So you want three hundred pounds," he said. "Can't the Commander ride Lorraine or Solitaire?"

"Impossible," replied Ben. "You know he said that he hadn't ridden for years and they're as gassy as old champagne at the moment. And anyway he weighs twelve stone and they're only fourteen two."

"Three hundred pounds is cheap, absolutely rock bottom for these days," I said. "Lots of people are spending thousands."

"If he rides every day and pays by the hour, we'll soon have the money back," argued Ben.

"You know things never work out like that," Dad replied wearily. "Well, all right, you can have the money; but only because I've just sold my big car and bought a little one. It won't be there again."

"Thank you!" we screamed.

And so it was settled. We just had to live through another five and a half days until Saturday.

Saturday dawned warm and fine; even Ben was up early lunging Solitaire in the paddock before breakfast, saying, "We must be there early to see the horses arriving. We must hear the gossip about them."

Lisa was rushing round the kitchen chivvying everyone. James was making a list for the CaterMart. Mrs Mills was perched at the corner of the kitchen table eating lots of bread and marmalade and drinking an enormous cup of coffee. The Colonel had *The Times* and breakfast on a tray in the dining-room. He had the same breakfast every morning – Shredded Wheat, a soft-boiled egg, toast in a toast rack, butter and a very expensive marmalade, plus coffee in a jug with hot milk and lump sugar.

Ben and I ate vast bowls of cereal, then we found Dad and he gave us three hundred pounds in twenties in an envelope. "And don't lose it," he said. Suddenly I thought again of the risk we were taking and there was a funny feeling in my stomach.

Ben said, "We may not buy anything, Dad. Don't worry. We're not complete idiots."

But we both knew without looking at each other that because we had the money we would buy something, come what may, simply because the chance might never come again.

132

"I spent last night reading about choosing a pony. I read five different books on the subject," said Ben.

"Buy a good one then," said Dad. "Or I'll wring your necks." James had brought the Land Rover round to the front door.

"I'll take Mary up her breakfast in bed," said Mrs Mills. "Don't worry. And I'll see to the Colonel's tray and do the spuds. Have a good time."

Mummy loaded boxes into the car, thinking that the CaterMart might have run out.

I said, "Who's got the money?"

Ben said "Me" and tapped his back trouser pocket.

Lisa had put on riding-clothes and carried a crash-cap. "I may be offered a ride. You can try them sometimes," she said, looking defensive.

"Not big horses, not when you're only nine," snapped Ben.

Mummy started the Land Rover. "Remember that you don't *have* to buy a horse," she said. "There's still a week before he comes."

"But there's only Saturdays; we're at school all the rest of the week," I argued.

"There's the evenings, and Sundays," Mummy replied. "You don't have to rush. Remember, more haste, less speed."

We had considered hitching on the trailer, but it seemed to be tempting fate too far, and anyway Mummy had to go home to get the Colonel's lunch.

It was nine miles to Radcott, where the sale was held monthly in the cattle market. We had sent for the catalogue and had marked possible buys; there was a grey mare of fifteen two which I fancied and a dun gelding of sixteen hands which Ben had chosen. They were both aged. Lisa had marked lots of ponies which we had no idea of bidding for.

There were mares with foals at foot, and harness horses, and a lot of first-class hunters being sold because the hunting season was over.

"Get something steady anyway," said Mummy, when we reached the suburbs of Radcott. "Because then Mike can ride it. He's large and quite hefty and we must teach him sometime. After all, he's coming because he's mad on horses, and he will still be with us long after Commander Cooley's gone, God willing."

"Mike!" I cried.

"Not that awful delinquent boy you were talking about, the one the social worker wanted us to have because he was mad on horses and living in a bed and breakfast place? You can't mean it? Not him?" cried Ben.

I remembered now. Dad had said he needed a home. Mummy had said you had to do something for Society sometimes, and this was to be our "good deed".

"But he was a thief!" cried Ben.

"Only because his parents were awful," replied Mummy.

"We're just a home for lame ducks," Ben cried angrily. "We're not a guest house at all. Just think, there's Mary who's neurotic and has a broken leg, there's old Mrs Mills who's eighty, and the Colonel who's incredibly ancient and crazy about India, and then there's Commander Cooley coming who has had a nervous breakdown; and now, to crown it all, this terrible boy . . ."

"Why can't we have children?" shrieked Lisa. "Nice children. Children of my age. Like the others we had, like Phillipa and her sister. They were great."

"If you keep shouting I shall crash the Land Rover," replied Mummy calmly. "Children don't come in termtime. There will be plenty in the holidays."

"I bet Mike is paying a pittance," cried Ben.

"The social services are paying for him, and he's going to help. All you kids are going to eat together in the kitchen, while the Commander and Colonel Hunter and Mrs Mills eat in the dining-room with Dad and me," announced Mummy.

"Crikey!" shouted Ben.

We were near the market now and there were horses and trailers everywhere, mixed up with shoppers clutching bags.

"When's this boy coming?" shrieked Ben. "And where's he sleeping? I suppose you're giving him my room."

"He's going in my sewing-room," Mummy said. "He doesn't need a big room. He has hardly any belongings, poor boy."

There were horses being trotted up and down. Ponies

plaited, ponies without shoes. Mummy dropped us in the carpark.

"Ring up when you want to come home and say whether you want the trailer or not. Good luck," she said before driving away.

"Crikey, I'm scared. Supposing we make a mistake?" cried Ben, scratching his head.

"Look at all those little ponies," shrieked Lisa.

We went inside. The horses stood in pens. Some looked sad and lost. Others were neighing and bewildered. We walked from one to another. There were ponies from Wales which were two and already quiet to ride. There were young ponies little more than foals, shod, with their ribs sticking out, covered with lice.

Suddenly I knew I was going to cry. Lisa had stopped talking. "I wish we could buy ten or twelve of them," said Ben.

"I wish we had a farm of acres and acres," cried Lisa.

There were old ponies with wind-galls and sad, patient eyes, wondering why they were there. There were noble hunters anxiously neighing, looking for their friends, like people searching for friends at railway stations. Foals without their mothers huddled together and mares without their foals were passionately searching with their eyes. There were lame horses, and ponies with sweet itch, and horses so thin that they were goose-rumped, their hocks sickle and their necks ewe.

"It's like a slave market," said Ben, rubbing his eyes.

I had forgotten that it was so awful. I wished I had brought dark glasses because I could feel tears pricking behind my eyes. The fitter, fatter horses were plaited and some of the ponies were fat and round and had their hoofs oiled. They all had a number stuck on their quarters. People wrenched their mouths open, talked and spat, and some of the women were crying.

136

"Come on," said Ben. "Perk up. It's going to start in a minute."

"I can't choose," I replied. "They all look so sad I want to buy them all."

"It must be the same at Battersea Dogs' Home," replied Ben. "We've simply got to choose."

The dun Ben had marked in the catalogue had a wild eye and straight, contracted feet. The grey I had chosen was light of bone and very thin. "She won't carry twelve stone," said Ben. "I'm sorry, but she just won't."

Lisa wouldn't come with us, but sat staring at a pen of little ponies straight off the Welsh hills.

Outside in the bright sunshine the bidding had started. There was a big skewbald that had belonged to a riding-school which we had marked, and a bay that had been hunted seven seasons and was warranted

sound. Then there was a mare with a pot-belly and deep poverty marks in her quarters. She had been used for pony trekking and was nine, with cracked hoofs and a hopeless expression on her tired face. She was bay, too, with a streak of white stretching from forehead to nose. She was supposed to be by a horse called The Greek.

Time seemed to be running away. The horses were selling quickly. The skewbald fetched three hundred and fifty pounds, probably for meat. Ben bid for the hunter, which went up to four hundred. Now there was only the bay mare left on our list and we started to feel desperate.

"There's plenty more we haven't looked at properly," said Ben.

"If we had come last month, they would have been cheaper," I answered.

"Dad hadn't the money then," retorted Ben.

The mare was led up. "She'll never carry twelve stone," I said.

"She's fifteen two," replied Ben, "and she's got plenty of bone. Look at her hocks. And she's got good feet if they weren't cracked. And her legs aren't blemished."

We were so busy talking we didn't listen to what the auctioneer was saying. We had talked to the mare for a long time. Now she looked at us with her tired eyes and seemed to recognise us.

"I'm bid a hundred," shouted the auctioneer. "Come on, she's a fine mare, by The Greek, quiet to ride. I'm bid two hundred and ten, two hundred and fifteen – come along . . ."

Ben was bidding now. There was a knot in my stomach. Supposing she died, supposing she had an incurable disease, a tumour like Apollo?

"Two hundred and fifty. I'm bid two hundred and fifty."

"There's no meat on her," said someone. "Just look at her quarters."

"Someone should be prosecuted," replied another.

"It's a crying shame," said a woman.

"Stop," I said to Ben. "Stop. We'll never get her fat in time. She'll die. There's no vet's certificate. She'll be another Apollo." I tried to grab his arm, to pull him away.

But he simply started smiling while the auctioneer yelled, "Two hundred and fifty, your last chance, two hundred and fifty, going, going, gone."

"She's ours," said Ben. "And she only cost two hundred and fifty, so Dad can have fifty back."

"We can buy another one with it, please, Ben, please," cried Lisa, suddenly beside us. "There's the sweetest little grey, she's only two at the moment and she's shod, please, Ben, please."

"We can't, we haven't got the grazing," I replied quickly.

"We can tether her on the rough grass in the garden, or on the common – we've got common rights."

"All right, let's look at her," said Ben, and I knew we were lost.

Two
Two wrecks

Lisa dragged us by our arms to the pen full of small ponies. The grey she wanted was the smallest. She still had her winter coat and there were bare patches where she had rubbed herself because she had lice. Her tiny hoofs were shod and the shoes were worn down to almost nothing, which meant she had been worked. I looked at her teeth. She had two in the centre which were second ones, the others were milk.

"Well, can we?" asked Lisa.

"Yes, do," said a lady in dark glasses. "I wish I could, but I live in a flat, in a street. I can't keep a pony in my living-room."

The auctioneer's men started to lead away the ponies one by one.

"She'll go for meat otherwise," the lady said. "To France, cut up into little steaks."

"Dad won't be pleased," said Ben.

"He never said anything about change," retorted Lisa.

We went outside again. The ponies weren't fetching much, forty pounds was about the limit.

"I'll look after her," said Lisa. "I swear I will."

A man dragged the little grey outside. She stood huddled with her tail close to her quarters. For ages no one bid, then Ben raised a hand.

I stood waiting with mixed feelings. I wanted the

140

pony, but I kept thinking that we were buying another pony without permission, that it would be another mouth to feed and shouldn't be ridden for at least two years.

Lisa stood close to Ben, her eyes on his face.

"Thirty-five, going, going, gone," the auctioneer shouted.

"We've still got some change," shrieked Lisa. "Thank you, thank you."

"We are not buying another," said Ben, giving his name, and I was glad suddenly that he was there looking old for his age, old enough to be treated as an adult by the auctioneer.

We went to look at our mare. "We will have to give her a Greek name, if she's by The Greek," Ben said. "And the little pony should have a mountain name or something to do with flowers. Do you agree?"

I nodded. Much seemed to have happened in a very short time, too much.

"Who's going to telephone home?" I asked.

"You," replied Ben.

"No, you're the eldest."

"Lisa, then, she can twist Dad round her little finger," said Ben.

We found a phone box. Lisa couldn't stop giggling. "Hello Dad," she said. "I've got a surprise for you – we've bought two, yes, two for the price of one. *And* we've still got some change. Yes, a darling little pony for me."

We could hear Dad saying "Oh no!" and "I never gave you permission," but he wasn't really angry. He never was with Lisa. She was one more person he gave the benefit of a doubt. Lisa put down the receiver at last.

"It's okay. He isn't cross," she said.

"Let's have a cup of coffee," I suggested. "They won't

141

be here with the trailer for a good hour, at least."

"Okay. We can't take away our horses until after the sale ends anyway, and they're still selling tack," Ben replied.

Our horses! I thought. If only they turn out to be all right.

The cafe was full of large farmers. We bought steaming cups of coffee and hunks of lardy cake. "I'm so happy, so very happy," Lisa said. "Let's call my grey Periwinkle. Darling, darling Periwinkle who will never be eaten by the French now."

"Or the Belgians," I said.

"What about Misty?" suggested Ben.

"Or Moonlight?" I asked.

"No, Periwinkle. The others are so common, and we can call her Winkle for short. Or even Winkie," replied Lisa.

We went back and looked at our purchases. We ran our hands down the mare's legs. She looked thinner than ever.

"She's riddled with worms. Let's go to the shop here and buy some worm powder. There's no time to lose," said Ben.

"She's got a sweet head," I said.

The sale was over now. We bought louse and worm powders and then Ben went to the office to pay for the horses. Lisa stayed with Periwinkle. I tried to make friends with the bay, but she seemed lifeless and totally uninterested in everything.

Then James appeared, calling, "Why did you buy two, you lunatics? What good is a two-year-old?"

"She will be a champion one day and she was terribly cheap," replied Lisa.

The trailer was ready in the carpark with its ramp down. The bay mare loaded quite well, after some

hesitation, but it needed us pushing and shoving to get Periwinkle in. At last the ramp was up and we were driving home in the bright May afternoon.

"I must say you seem to have bought two wrecks," Mummy said.

"They will soon pick up. The summer grass will fatten them, they just need worming," replied Ben, speaking like an expert.

"We don't want any more vet's bills," she replied.

"Just a couple of worm counts after they've been dosed," said Ben, making everything sound easy, "and they will be as right as rain by June."

"The boy's come," said Mummy after a short silence.

"Which boy?" asked Ben.

"Mike. The social worker wanted tomorrow off to go somewhere with her boyfriend, so she brought him today," replied Mummy. "And the Commander's cases have come and lots of mysterious boxes, so I hope he isn't going to come early too."

"If he does it will mean more money," replied Ben. "And we need money."

"What's Mike like?" I asked.

"Large and strong. He said he would do the tack for you. His grandfather worked at Newmarket," replied Mummy.

Things seemed to be happening fast. It was as though everything had suddenly been speeded up. I had the feeling that the peace of the last few weeks would soon be broken. I was filled with sudden misgivings. I wished Mike hadn't come, that the Commander was only twelve and a girl, and that we had bought a fat horse instead of our poor, thin, bay mare. There seemed to be troubles ahead, enough to sink a battleship.

We were nearly home now. There were children playing on the common and sunlight everywhere. Men were working in their cottage gardens, and beyond the common everything was clean and tidy like in a picture – dipping woods, soft green fields full of growing wheat, and smooth, summer-coated cows, clean at last after the long, muddy winter. Mike was waiting for us. He flung open the yard gate. He was large, with a shock of red hair and freckles, and the first thing I noticed were his hands, which were large too.

"I've done all the harness," he called. "I found some

144

shoe polish in the house. It looks great."

Ben and I looked at each other and said nothing. Lisa said, "It will come off on Jigsaw's white bits and on our jodhpurs. He must be mad. No one uses shoe polish nowadays."

"Don't say anything. He's only trying to help," Mummy said. "We don't want to upset him on his first day here."

Mrs Mills came out of the house in her pinny. "Let's see what you've bought!" she exclaimed.

The Colonel came after her. "We're all agog," he exclaimed. "Can't wait to see 'em."

I couldn't look at Ben. "They are cheap and poor. We bought them because we were sorry for them and we couldn't afford anything better," he said.

The ramp was down now. Periwinkle was jumping about, so we backed her out first. "Put her in a box. We don't want the others to get their lice and worms," muttered Ben.

"Well, she won't carry a commander; she's not even polo-pony size," grumbled the Colonel.

The bay mare came down slowly, so that it was easy to see the poverty marks on her quarters, her ribs standing out like the sides of a toast-rack, her distended stomach, and her poor thin neck which made her head look twice as large as it should have been. Ben backed her down and suddenly I felt like crying again.

"Well, she won't carry the Commander either. She's as weak as a kitten," announced the Colonel, turning away in disgust.

"I think they are both sweet," said Mrs Mills, "especially the little grey."

Mike offered to get them water. I bedded down the boxes and they both started to eat the straw. Ben started making mashes laced with worm powder for them. Lisa filled up two haynets. James and Mummy unhitched the trailer. Then Ben and I started to delouse the bay.

Presently Mary appeared and stared at us over the loose-box doors. "Whatever have you bought now?" she asked.

"Why don't you help, instead of standing there?" retorted Ben angrily.

"No fear. I don't want to catch lice," she said.

She was dressed in smart trousers and a shirt which had cost twenty-five pounds. I remembered that she had promised once to help all the time if we would have her back, but she hadn't kept her word.

Presently Mrs Mills called "Tea!" and we shook our coats and went inside to drink steaming mugs of tea in the kitchen. The hall was full of the Commander's luggage, which had his initials on it. It was beautiful luggage.

"I expect he'll change for dinner," Mummy said. "I hope we can live up to him."

Dad was out organising the sale of his factory. He had found himself a job in someone else's, which I found immeasurably sad, though he said it was simply "life". You went up and down, he said, and if you stayed alive and had enough to eat you should be grateful.

Ben telephoned the blacksmith. "One is two and definitely needs her shoes off; the other needs a new set – she's fifteen two with biggish hoofs and very poor."

Mike drank with loud sips, putting both hands round the mug. "I'm still on probation," he said. "I have to report to the officer every Friday after school."

"Why?" asked Lisa. "What did you do?"

"I broke into a 'ouse and assaulted a teacher," he said with pride in his voice. "It was the third 'ouse me and my mates had done."

I could see now that he didn't belong to our world. He was like a stranger from another country. I wished again that he hadn't come. "You're not going to do this house, are you?" asked Ben.

"Not likely, mate. You're my friends," Mike said.

Mummy was moving furniture from her bedroom to the attic already. I rushed upstairs to help. "I shall enjoy sleeping up here," she said.

"But you won't have your own bathroom any more," I replied.

"I don't care. It's so lovely to be getting lots of money in these hard times."

"Well, watch it. Remember we've got a thief," said Ben coming in, his arms full of blankets.

"He's not one any more. He's reformed," replied Mummy. "It wasn't his fault. If you lived in a bed and breakfast place and no one cared for you, you might go wrong."

"Thank you," replied Ben. "I would get a job, or go to school or read books."

"His father is in prison," Mummy said, as though that was the final answer.

"We need a safe," said Ben, "one with a difficult combination."

"We need time," I replied. "Time for our new mare to get fat, time for Periwinkle to grow, time to prepare for exams and school our horses. There's never enough, is there?"

"Mike will help," Mummy said, dusting the windowsill. "He's a good boy really; he's just unfortunate. You must learn to be more tolerant. You always think the worst of everybody."

"We're all thinking the best of the Commander. By all accounts he's a real gentleman, rich and talented. Just a bit nervous, of course, but that's overwork, in the Navy no doubt. But what is he really like, I wonder?" asked Ben.

His arrival hung over us like a cloud. All the next week letters kept coming for him, important looking letters which Mrs Mills thought must be for her. Then a parcel came. And some new riding-breeches were delivered from a shop in Radcott.

We anxiously scanned the bay mare for an improvement in condition. We deloused her again and turned her out in the bottom paddock where there was plenty of grass and Periwinkle already installed. And we decided to call her Cassandra.

Mike came to school with us each morning. Mary said that he smelled and sat at the other end of the bus; but he soon made friends with some boys from the village who were mad on football, and every evening after school he played with them on the common.

And then on Friday a postcard finally arrived, saying

briefly: *Delayed. Coming Next Week. Cooley.*

We didn't know whether to laugh with relief or regret the loss of a weekend's money.

"I hate waiting," said Mummy.

"We moved out of our room a week too soon," grumbled Dad.

"It gives Cassandra a few more days to get fat," replied Ben. "She certainly doesn't look up to twelve stone at the moment."

"Well, he's got to ride something. I can't have six horses eating their heads off and not a penny in return," snapped Dad. We stood looking at each other, all on edge because Commander Cooley wasn't coming when expected.

"It's the letters. I hate having to keep his letters and not having an address to send them to," confessed Mummy.

"And it's eerie having his luggage and not him," James said.

"And we may hate him," added Lisa.

"Or he may hate us," I said.

"It all adds up," said Ben, "but I expect he'll be okay. He must be a very special person if he's a naval commander and quite young. Someone who can command."

"And who expects to be waited on," said Lisa.

"We're only in a fuss because we've been waiting so long," I said.

"He'll be okay, I promise," Mummy said. "I've vetted him personally and he's a sweetie."

"Touch wood," I cried, but no one paid any attention to me.

"Mum, you're in love with him!" yelled Lisa.

"Shut up," shouted Dad.

"I hope he doesn't come," I said, holding on to the windowsill which, being old, was made of wood. "He's caused enough trouble already – he's bagged the best bedroom, worried us stiff and made us buy a horse. He must be horrible to need so much. I would never think of turning anyone out of their bedroom, never . . . but he has just because he wants a view and his own bathroom."

"And peace and quiet," added Mummy.

I looked out of the window and thought: We're quarrelling about him already, what will it be like when he's here? And I was filled with awful foreboding. I had the feeling that he was going to break us up, pull us apart.

"If we don't like him, we can kick him out," Dad said, putting an arm round me. "What are you afraid of, Harriet?"

"I don't know. I just feel doomed," I replied. "As if he's going to bring us misery. Don't ask me why. I just feel it deep in my bones."

Three
The Commander comes

A letter came from the American boy, Paul, saying that he would be having half-term in three weeks and would someone fetch him?

The bay mare grew fatter. Periwinkle shed her coat. James ranted over his GCSEs, yelling at everyone to be quiet, shutting himself in his bedroom hour after hour revising. Ben and I rode in the evenings, schooling in the paddock, improving our dressage, putting up jumps. But all the time, deep down, we were waiting for Commander Cooley, wondering whether he would shatter our peace, drive Mummy into hysterics with his demands, argue with the Colonel, get on the wrong side of Dad. But then when he came at last he was charming. He was tall and slim and wore a blazer with braid on it, trousers, suede shoes and a collar and tie. He said that everything was ideal, perfect, out of this world.

"I know I shall get well here," he said. "Everything is so tranquil, so far from the 'madding crowd', so altogether marvellous."

Lisa adored him. He told her sea stories, and his room was full of choc-bars and drink.

We found him installed one evening when we returned from school and took him to the stables to see the horses. He agreed that Cassandra was still a bit thin, "But I don't mind waiting a few days longer to ride. I've waited long enough as it it," he said.

"You are a fool, Harriet," said Ben later. "I knew he would be all right, but you always get in such a fuss and all over nothing. I don't know what's the matter with you. You've got an anxiety complex or something."

I wanted to touch wood again but I didn't. I was afraid that Ben would see me and laugh. Afterwards, when everything was terrifying and the house was bursting with tension and alarm, I wished I had. It might have made a difference – one never knows.

The next day we lunged Cassandra and the day after I rode her round the paddock with Ben riding in front. She was very quiet and wandered rather, but followed Solitaire willingly enough. We were filling her up with sugar beet and oats now, making her feeds a little larger every day.

Mike didn't help much. He came home from school, grabbed a great hunk of bread and butter, then disappeared to play with his local friends.

Mummy was worried. She was afraid he would get in with bad company and rob someone. He wasn't doing very well at school either. Ben said he was "just thick". But really I think he was too old and too mature to be shut up in a classroom every day wearing a blazer. He wanted to be out in the world working, buying himself a motor-bike. He just wasn't interested in maths or Julius Caesar.

And so the days passed. Mummy, Dad, Colonel Hunter and the Commander all ate together in the dining-room. Mrs Mills wouldn't; she ate with the rest of us in the kitchen. "I can't hear what any of them say," she confessed to us, "and they won't shout."

Another week went by and now it was less than a week to half-term. Commander Cooley started to ride Cassandra, only walking her at first and promising that he would treat her like delicate china.

Mary stopped needing a stick and ran up a huge telephone bill ringing up her boyfriend every evening. Periwinkle grew fatter. Then Mary suddenly wished to be treated like an adult.

"I want to eat in the dining-room – I can't bear Mike's manners another minute. He eats like a pig and Mrs Mills shouts all the time," she said.

"But of course you can," replied Mummy, taking the wind out of her sails. "And James can too if he likes."

"No thank you, I prefer the kitchen. I can't stand any more talk about the good old days in India when we still had an empire, thank God," he replied.

Half-term was nearly here now. Paul's room was ready. Lisa picked flowers and put them on the dressing-table.

Commander Cooley started to ride Cassandra farther. Once I went with him on Lorraine. He rode easily on a loose rein. He didn't use his legs at all, but sang a lot and talked to Cassandra. As for the mare, she was putting on weight all the time and her hoofs looked better trimmed and shod, and dressed every day with Cornucresine to help them grow strong. Periwinkle was growing too. Lisa had got rid of the last of her winter coat with the rubber currycomb and her lice had gone with it, dead or alive. We could see that she had a fine tapering muzzle now, and a kind eye with a twinkle in it; and her neck was light and elegant.

Some people rang up and asked us to have their ponies until the holidays. "We want them fit for the summer holidays," they said.

Ben had answered the phone. "You mean just exercised, not schooled?" he asked. He talked for some time. "The ponies are called Sea Cadet and Mermaid," he said, putting down the phone at last. "The owners are

153

coming to see us next weekend. They are called Cummings. Their children go to boarding school. Cadet's fourteen two and Mermaid is fourteen hands. We'll have to get some more hay from somewhere if they are going to be in."

Half-term started on Thursday. Mummy disappeared at an early hour to fetch Paul. James got out a pile of books and started revising. Mike and Colonel Hunter decided to mow the lawn. Mrs Mills started weeding under the apple-trees. Mary sat about getting in everybody's way. Lisa jumped up and down saying, "I wish Paul would come. Why is it taking so long? I can't wait to see him." Commander Cooley relaxed in a deckchair, recovering from his nervous breakdown.

Ben and I wandered down to the stable. "You know the Cummings are coming tomorrow at three," he said. "I do hope they like it here and think we are okay, because it'll give us a lot of money."

"They must be terribly rich," I replied. "I expect they've got a heated swimming-pool and a Rolls-Royce."

"I expect so too," Ben said. "Lucky devils."

Paul arrived at eleven-thirty looking just as always – well scrubbed behind the ears, clean, friendly, uncomplicated. "Say, it's good to be home," he said. "Everything looks kind of different. The horses all look just fine, don't they?"

We showed him Cassandra and Periwinkle. Lisa followed him like a dog, asking him questions about school, about his parents, about anything she could think up; anything to be noticed.

When we introduced him to Commander Cooley they seemed to become friends at once. Paul called him "sir", and Commander Cooley said, "I've got some cassettes from your country, you must hear them. They are right up to date, the very latest."

And Paul said, "My, I would like that, sir." And they fixed up to listen to them together after lunch.

Then Mike came and shook Paul's hand and said, "Pleased to meet you," but without any pleasure in his voice, and Paul seemed to look at him with instant dislike.

And suddenly the scene seemed set, but for what none of us knew. Later we all rode, Paul on Jigsaw because he had grown too big for Limpet, Lisa on Limpet, Commander Cooley on Cassandra, me on Lorraine and Ben on Solitaire. We hacked through the woods, and though Lisa was longing to talk to Paul, he rode beside Commander Cooley discussing the American Navy and what his father did and a host of other things.

Then Commander Cooley took a huge bar of chocolate from his pocket and gave us all pieces and told us that he was getting better every day and how he loved being with us; and then waited for us to say something complimentary back.

Ben looked at me and I said, "It's great having you, too," but I only half meant it, because somewhere inside me I still had reservations about him.

None of us knew, of course, that this was to be our last day of peace for some time. It seemed then that the peace was endless, that the woods would go on being green, the sun shining for ever. We cantered over a hill and the Commander started to sing and suddenly we were all joining in. The horses seemed to enjoy the songs and they walked with ears pricked and long swinging strides. And because we were all in good tempers, Ben and I made good resolutions as we rode, deciding that we would start teaching Mike to ride and help Mummy more, and not quarrel. Then we started to discuss Mary and then suddenly we were back on the common and nearly home.

We untacked the ponies together in the yard and Commander Cooley rubbed down Cassandra, whistling all the time. Then we turned them all out and stood watching them roll as the sun started to go down above the treetops.

"Don't forget to come up to my room after dinner, Paul," said Commander Cooley, turning to go indoors at last. "I've got plenty of chocolates and some rare stamps you might like to see, as well as some tapes you haven't heard."

We found Mummy cooking supper and she said, "Wow! Isn't everyone getting on well? Really, Commander Cooley is quite an asset," and the Colonel, who was passing through the kitchen, gave a disapproving snort.

156

"Don't listen to him," Mummy said. "He's getting very old, poor chap, and he feels out of things, unlike the Commander, who will be back on active service in a few weeks' time. He can't help being jealous, poor old fellow."

"The Commander's sure been everywhere – Malta, the States, South America, Asia, everywhere. He's some guy," said Paul.

Mike stood listening. "I wish we had another telly," he said. "The Commander and the Colonel always want to watch the boring programmes. I never see what I want to. At the approved school there were five sets."

"Everybody wash for supper," said Mummy, looking at Mike's hands. "Go on, hurry up. It's chops."

A few minutes later Paul came downstairs shouting, "My money's gone. All of it. I've been robbed."

Mummy was dishing up the chops, decorating them with parsley for the dining-room. Mike had disappeared. "Go and look again," she said. "It must be there somewhere."

"I'll help you," offered ever willing Mrs Mills. "I'm good at finding things."

"It was in my money-box; it was locked. There was thirty pounds."

I felt sick inside suddenly. I looked at Ben. Lisa said, "It wasn't me. I never go into his room. It must be Mike. We all know he was a thief."

Dad came in at that moment, looking tired. "Who's a thief?" he asked.

"No one. Paul's just lost his money," replied Mummy, putting the chops back into the oven.

"It's not there," said Paul. "I've looked everywhere. I put it in my money-box when I came home and locked it. It's shut, but not locked any more and the money's gone."

Ben went out of the back door. "Let's keep calm," suggested Mummy. "Let's have dinner and then all look. It's probably in a pocket. You probably thought you put it there and didn't. It's easily done."

"Not me. I never do that," replied Paul, and I believed him. He just wasn't that sort of person. Dad went upstairs with big strides.

Mummy started to beat the gong. "Get Ben," she said.

I ran down to the stables with Lisa at my heels. It was a clear evening with a red sky promising a fine tomorrow. Mike was fighting Ben. He held the three-pronged fork in one hand while Ben defended himself with a broom. The horses watched over the fence like spectators at a wrestling match.

"I tell you I didn't," yelled Mike. "And you shouldn't

accuse me, you foul b—," He used a word we are definitely not allowed to use.

"How dare you rob our guests," yelled Ben.

"They'll kill each other," screamed Lisa.

"Stop it," I shouted. "There's no proof, Ben. You can't accuse him."

"I didn't take it," shouted Mike, charging Ben with the fork. They were both sweating and one of Ben's hands was bleeding and Mike's face was scratched.

"Fetch James and Dad," I shouted to Lisa.

Then Paul appeared. "Leave him alone, Ben," he shouted. "I expect it was the help. It doesn't have to be him."

And suddenly they stopped fighting. Mike put down his fork and said. "Thanks, Yank. I don't rob my mates. I'm not that sort. Strangers maybe, but not my mates."

"It was probably the woman who comes to help," repeated Paul, sounding weary.

"What, Mrs Crispin?" I asked. "Not her, surely. She's so nice."

"The gardener then, or Mrs Mills gone dotty. Just forget it, will you?" asked Paul.

Mummy was beating the gong again. "We had better wash," said Ben, looking at Mike. "Please accept my apologies." And he held out his hand.

"That's all right, mate," replied Mike, shaking it. We went indoors slowly. The day seemed ruined now. Somewhere in the house there was a thief. It was a horrible thought. And it couldn't be the gardener because we hadn't got one. It had to be one of us or a guest. My mind went over all the guests. None of them would steal. It was quite impossible; they all had money, plenty of money. And then I thought of Mary, who was always buying new clothes and had only a small allowance from her mother. It must be her, I thought, there's no one else. What are we going to do? And Ben looked at me and mouthed "Mary" so that I knew he had reached the same conclusion.

Before we had supper Dad made a speech. He said. "I don't want a lot of uproar about Paul's lost money; most likely it's blown out of the window or something equally stupid. We know we have no thieves here. It's inconceivable that anyone should steal. So I'm giving Paul thirty pounds, which appears to be the amount he has lost, and if his money turns up, he can pay me back. And I don't want any more discussion, is that clear? The loss is over and done with. Of course if more goes, we will have to call in the police, but I trust it won't. I trust this is the end of the matter."

He had changed into a suit for dinner with Commander Cooley and the Colonel. He looked dark and handsome and I suddenly felt quite proud that he was my father. At the same time I thought: This won't be the end of it because we are going to go on suspecting each other, whatever he says. I shall suspect Mary and she will suspect Mike, unless she's guilty of course, and Paul will suspect poor little Mrs Crispin who is always so tired and couldn't kill a fly.

"Come on, supper," said Mummy.

Four

It's the police!

We rose early the next day, because we wanted the stables looking tidy for the Cummings. Lisa groomed Jigsaw and Limpet while Ben and I polished the brass knobs in the old-fashioned loose boxes and swept the cobbles until there wasn't a weed to be seen or a piece of straw among them.

"It's obvious Mary took the money," Ben said.

"We are not supposed to discuss it," I answered, putting the broom away.

"She's always been a liar, and look at the clothes she buys, and the lipsticks and eyeshadow. Her room is chock-a-block with them. And they're not cheap either," retorted Ben.

"She has an allowance," I answered. "She calls it guilt money from her mother for ruining her life."

"It's time she forgave her mother," Ben said. "You can't go on hating someone for ever; it isn't Christian."

I looked round the yard; everything was shipshape, the doors shut tidily, the buckets in lines, the tack in the tack room.

"Her mother *did* send her pony to the market when she went away to school," I said. "And that was a pretty awful thing to do." We were walking towards the house now, hungry for breakfast.

"But that was years ago," Ben said.

How long was years? I wondered. How long did it take to forgive and forget? Would I forgive Mummy if she sold Lorraine without telling me?

The kitchen smelled of coffee. Paul was sitting on a stool humming. "Good news," he cried. "I'm going out with the Commander. We're going for miles and miles, no kidding."

"Going out? How? In his car?" asked Ben.

"In his automobile? Not likely. On the horses, of course. Your father has given us permission. Isn't it great?" cried Paul.

"He hasn't," I said. "Not really?"

"Sure he has. Go and ask him. I'm riding Jigsaw," cried Paul.

Lisa was behind us now. She started to shake her head in disagreement.

"But he might let you fall off," Ben said.

"He's an adult, dope," replied Paul. "And he's no kid, no sir, he's sure travelled the world. He can ride too, I'm telling you. He's going to show me a ruined church. Do you know it?"

I nodded. "It stands down a lane, beyond the woods, miles away. It's said to be haunted."

We were eating cornflakes now and the sun was shining into the kitchen. Paul's right, I thought, the Commander's an adult. What are we worrying about, for goodness sake? What can go wrong? Jigsaw's so sensible, and Paul rides quite well now; he's not really a beginner any more. And Dad's given his permission.

"It isn't fair. I never have Jigsaw now," wailed Lisa.

"You have two ponies, that's why," replied Ben. "Jigsaw's supporting Periwinkle."

"I'll have my own pony come the summer," Paul said. "A real Apache pony. You can ride it, Lisa, I shan't mind."

He was already dressed in breeches and boots and a collar and tie. Commander Cooley was eating a leisurely breakfast in the dining-room. It was nine o'clock at the end of May and a day none of us would ever forget.

"We'll get the ponies ready then," Ben said.

"I don't like it," I exclaimed, following him to the stables. "You know we don't let people go out alone."

"But the Commander's been going out alone for weeks now," answered Ben.

"But Paul's only a child," I argued.

"Dad's given permission."

"But he isn't in charge of the horses," cried Lisa, suddenly beside us. "Jigsaw's being worked to death."

We caught Cassandra. Her coat was shining now and she had a lovely fine mane which needed pulling. She was fat round the middle although there were still poverty marks on her quarters, but her sickle hocks had vanished and her neck was losing its ewe look.

Ben looked tired. "I was worrying about Paul's money all night," he said. "It must be Mary. I want to search her room. It was your room once. Couldn't you search on the pretext of looking for something you lost long, long ago?"

"She might come in."

"I could keep her occupied."

"You know what Dad said," I answered. "No more discussion. We must forget it."

"She'll strike again," Ben said.

"Let's set a trap for her then. Marked notes in the tack room. I've got some five-pound notes," I suggested.

"Okay," Ben replied. "Good idea."

We oiled Cassandra's hoofs. Her tail was like spun silk. "In a few months' time, she'll be a beauty," Ben said.

"If we can get rid of her stomach," I answered. "We

163

had better have another worm count."

"I bet it's still worms," replied Ben.

"Hi," shouted Paul. "Come on, Commander. They're ready."

We held their stirrups while they mounted and pulled up their girths. I wished I could follow them, but the Cummings were coming and we couldn't do without their money.

"Have a good ride," said Ben.

"Sure will," replied Paul.

"See you later then. Don't wait lunch. We may get something at a pub. Paul would like a Coke, wouldn't you, Paul?" asked Commander Cooley.

Paul nodded, leading the way out of the yard on cheerful Jigsaw who could outwalk any horse. The yard was full of sunshine and the smell of hay and horse. "Don't worry," Ben said, "they'll be all right."

We tidied up the yard some more; then we went indoors to try to make ourselves look old and responsible for the Cummings.

"The Commander and Paul may be out for lunch," I told Mummy. "They're going to stop at a pub."

"Which way are they going?" she asked, looking worried.

"To the ruined church," I answered.

"They are supposed to leave written instructions about where they are going, in case they fall off," she said. "You know it's in the guests' charter in the hall."

"They won't fall off," replied Ben. "Cassandra is still very slow and Jigsaw's rock safe. Do stop worrying, Mummy."

"Touch wood," I shouted.

We washed our hands and combed our hair, and Mary said, "Boyfriend coming?" She was always on about boyfriends, though she knew I hadn't any.

I found my three five-pound notes, marked each one and put them in an envelope, and wrote *Fifteen pounds for the blacksmith* on the front.

"Would you like some eyeshadow?" offered Mary. "Or what about some perfume?"

"No, thank you," I said.

It was nearly twelve o'clock now, so Ben and I wandered down to the yard and swept up a few more wisps of straw and tidied up the tack room again; then I put the envelope with the money on the tack-room table. "That'll catch her," I said. "I've only put weeny dots on each note so you can't see them unless you really look."

"Well done!" said Ben. "Here they come."

A Range Rover came into the yard and the Cummings poured out of it. They were large and rich and smelled of scent. The children shouted, "What a brilliant place!"

Father held out a slim, well-manicured hand. Mother said, "Pleased to meet you, I'm sure."

They prowled round the yard like hungry dogs. The children, a boy and a girl, exclaimed over the ponies. "I do so love a grey," the girl shouted.

"I like the cob best. He looks so kind," said the boy.

"We've got two more, but they are out at the moment," Ben explained.

"Which boxes will ours have?" asked the girl, who was called Rosemary.

"The loose boxes," I replied. "So that they can look straight out."

"Would you like to come in and meet our parents and have a sherry?" asked Ben, trying to sound grown up.

"Great," shrieked the girl. "Daddy loves a stiff whisky."

We took them into the best sitting-room, which is a relic of our days of prosperity, and very smart. Dad was out, so I dragged James from his studies to do the drinks. Mummy was making pastry and her hands were covered with flour. "I'll come later," she said.

Dad's bottle of whisky only had a few dregs left in it, so everybody else had Mummy's sherry. They settled comfortably into the armchairs and sipped their drinks. I felt time ticking away. James is good at conversation and talked non-stop; so did Ben. Then Mummy came in and everyone talked some more and needed more drinks and now the sherry was finished as well as the whisky and I wondered what Dad would say when he returned and found the empty bottles.

Mummy said, "I hope your ponies are sensible. I have a horror of accidents. They don't do anything awful, do they?"

The Cummings laughed heartily and said, "Only the odd buck."

"Mermaid's had me off sometimes, but I'm a rotten rider. You'll be able to stick on all right because you're experts," Rosemary said hopefully.

"That's right," agreed the boy. "They just need work, that's what Miss Smith says."

We could hear the Colonel moving about the dining-room now, coughing in an obvious way as the hall clock struck one. I remembered that he considered punctuality "the essence of good manners".

"I must fly," said Mummy. "I've got things in the oven."

Time was passing. I started to listen for hoofs, for the Commander and Paul coming back.

"They just need plenty of work and to be mastered," said Mr Cummings. "I'm sure you'll manage." He stood up at last. "They'll come over by box tomorrow," he continued. "We'll send their tack and rugs with them."

"Thank you very much," said Ben, opening the door.

They took a very long time going, stopping to admire every flower. Mrs Mills was watching impatiently from the kitchen window, longing to start lunch. Then some-one beat the gong. They shook our hands again. Then one by one they got back into the car and fastened their safety-belts. I listened, but there were no hoof-beats coming up the road, just the song of birds and the shouting of children.

"Let us know how they go," said Mr Cummings, starting the engine.

"We will," yelled Ben, laughing with relief because they were going.

We waved to them as they drove away, then stepped outside to see whether Paul and the Commander were coming.

"Dad will be furious when he finds they've drunk all the drink," I said.

"I can't help that," retorted Ben.

I looked in the tack room and the envelope was still there.

"I bet we can't ride their horses," said Ben. "Do we really look like experts?"

I shook my head. I could feel life getting complicated again, the pressures which were coming.

"We can ride them after school," Ben said. "It's light until nearly ten o'clock."

"What about homework?" I asked.

"We can do that afterwards."

Everybody was eating lunch when we got indoors. Mrs Mills was just starting on her second jam turnover.

"Are they back?" asked Lisa.

I shook my head.

"They were going to eat at a pub. They may not be back for hours," explained Ben. "The new horses are coming tomorrow."

"They are called Mermaid and Sea Cadet," I said to no one in particular.

"So we're going to be very busy," added Ben.

Later I helped clear the table and stack the dishwasher. It was two o'clock now and there was still no sign of the Commander and Paul. Ben went out on his bike to look for them, but was soon back, shouting, "No luck. They must be making a day of it."

We were pretending that we weren't worried, but deep down I think we were all feeling the first gnawings of anxiety.

"If only they had written down where they were going," grumbled Mummy. "I think I had better switch the oven off, don't you? There's no point in keeping their lunch hot any longer."

"They said they were eating at a pub," replied Ben. "I told you."

"How long does it take to get to the ruined church and back?" asked James.

"About two hours," I said.

"But the Commander's grown up and used to commanding men. Whatever are you worrying about?" asked Mary, suddenly appearing.

"Let's go out in the Land Rover and look for them," suggested Ben.

"We'll wait until half-past three," replied Mummy.

"Really, you are peculiar," said Mary. "Fancy worrying about a full-grown man."

"It's Paul," I said.

"It's Jigsaw I'm worried about. I want Jigsaw," shouted Lisa.

We made a pot of tea and drank it. I thought of the money in the saddle room and now it seemed a mean, petty trick to try and catch someone with it.

Mike came in saying, "I smelled the tea. Aren't they back? Crikey, they've gone a long way. When did they leave then?"

"Around ten," I answered.

"Still, the Commander's got some sense, 'asn't he? Must have to be a commander. Stands to reason, don't it."

Usually Mummy corrected his grammar. Now she let it pass. It was ten to four. Ben started to pace the room. James returned downstairs from another bout of his revising. "Aren't they back yet?" he asked.

"No," yelled Ben, loud enough to split our eardrums.

James rattled the empty teapot. "He's grown up, anyway. We aren't responsible."

"We are for Paul," replied Mummy, putting on a coat though the sun was shining and the kitchen stifling. "Someone had better stay," she said.

"Not me," shouted Lisa. "I'm always left."

Then the telephone rang. Lisa grabbed it first. "It's the police," she said in a small, frightened voice.

James took the receiver from her. My heart started to beat against my sides like a sledgehammer. Ben sat down, holding his head in his hands, muttering, "What now, for heaven's sake?"

Mummy took her coat off and put on an apron automatically, like someone sleepwalking.

"The horses have been found wandering on the B450," James said. "The police want them removed. There's no sign of any riders."

Five

Fifty thousand pounds

None of us moved for a moment, though I think we all turned a shade paler.

"Have they got their tack on?" shouted Ben.

"They didn't say," replied James

"Are they all right?" screamed Lisa.

"No, one of the horses is injured. We had better get the trailer hitched up," replied James.

"But where are Paul and the Commander?" asked Mummy in a bewildered voice. "I don't understand."

"I'll watch the phone," said Colonel Hunter, suddenly appearing. "I'm used to emergencies, dealt with plenty in my time. Of course it was donkey's years ago, but I haven't lost the touch. I wouldn't put too much trust in the Commander; he's not quite right somewhere. I've known it all along, but didn't like to mention it. I'm used to judging men. He's never been in the Services. I can vouch for that."

"I'll keep the kettle on and get the Colonel's tea," offered Mrs Mills.

"I'll get some loose boxes ready for the 'orses," Mike said. "Water and hay, the lot."

Suddenly we were all running in different directions, full of fear and panic. "Which one is injured, James? Did they say?" shouted Lisa.

"No," shouted James, "I've told you once. No."

We hitched up the trailer with shaking hands banging against each other and getting oil on our clothes from the hitch-up part. Then James said, "I'll stay. I don't mind. The Colonel needs support. He's too old to go it alone."

"Get some oats in case they won't load. In a bucket, you fool, not in your pockets," yelled Ben.

I fetched headcollars, cotton wool, bandages. I was feeling sick now.

"Ready?" asked Mummy, starting the engine and looking small and tense in the Land Rover, too small for what lay ahead.

Mike waved us out. Lisa sat in the back, the rest of us in the front. "Which is the B450?" asked Ben suddenly.

"I don't know, but it might be the road to Radcott," Mummy answered.

"There must be a map or an AA book somewhere in here," shouted Ben. "Where is it?"

I was thinking about what the Colonel had said. He had said not to put trust in the Commander. What did he mean? He was an old man but he knew the world and the ways of men. I felt cold now. I started to pray for Paul. God let us find him soon, I prayed. God make him all right.

We drove for miles. The roads were full of sightseers. They drove very slowly, admiring cottages and flowers and the sudden glimpse of woods. But they didn't get out to look. We couldn't pass them because there wasn't room with the trailer. Ben ground his teeth. Mummy's hands grew whiter and tenser on the steering-wheel, then Lisa started to moan in the back.

We stopped to ask walkers the way to the B450, but though they were full of suggestions, none of them knew. And suddenly life became a nightmare without end and I wasn't cold any more, but sweating.

Mummy was crying now, which was something I had never seen before. Ben was swearing, using words I had never heard.

"Surely they could have telephoned?" said Mummy through her tears.

"If only it wasn't Paul. Things always happen to him. Why wasn't it me?" I asked.

"Or me?" screamed Lisa.

"Or me?" said Ben. "I would have phoned hours ago."

"I wouldn't have left the horses," I said.

Lisa was leaning forward. "Look! There are the horses, and there's a police car!" she shrieked. "There they are!"

We threw ourselves out on to a grass verge.

A young policeman was holding Cassandra. "I didn't know whether to send for a vet or not," he said. "She's injured; needs stitching, I should say."

Her shoulder had a gash in it, so deep that you could see the bone. She dripped blood on to the grass. Jigsaw was happily grazing but he neighed when he saw Lisa. They both had their tack on, but their reins were broken. Mummy looked at the wound. "We can't apply a tourniquet to that," she said. "We had best get her home and send for Roy."

"What about the riders?" Ben asked, letting down the ramp.

"I don't know. I can't understand it," replied Mummy. "I wish your father was here."

Cassandra didn't want to move. I fetched the oats. She didn't want them either. I was trying not to cry. Lisa led Jigsaw up the ramp and into the trailer, calling him all sorts of pet names.

Ben pushed Cassandra. She moved slowly, at a snail's pace.

"She's shocked, that's what it is," said the policeman, who was young with fair hair.

"Is she going to die like Apollo?" called Lisa.

"No," I shouted. "And stop asking silly questions."

Mummy was asking the policeman what could have happened to the Commander and Paul, giving him a description. Slowly the mare moved, slowly and painfully, while I felt torn apart by misery and impatience, with the Colonel's words banging away in my mind.

174

"Someone must have hit her, a hit-and-run driver," the policeman said, pushing too.

We got Cassandra into the trailer, put up the ramp, and thanked the policeman, who said, "I expect you'll find the Commander and the boy home before you, but we'll keep looking until you get in touch."

"Poor Paul," said Lisa. "Poor unlucky Paul."

We started slowly, our hearts heavy, our minds filled with anxiety. "Your father will be home by now," said Mummy.

We had taken off the horses' tack. Cassandra's reins were covered with blood and hair and sweat. We didn't talk much now, just waited desperately for time to pass, for good news to come from somewhere, somehow.

We stopped at the first telephone box we came to and Ben telephoned our vet, Roy Smart. "He wasn't at home," he told us, returning. "But they're getting him on his car phone. He isn't far away."

"Will she need a lot of stitches?" asked Lisa.

"Yes, and an anti-tet injection," I answered.

"And a penicillin injection and lots of sedative," added Ben, who plans to be a vet one day.

We could see our hills now and the gentle slope of woods beyond.

"We are very unlucky people," said Ben to no one in particular.

Mike had bedded down two loose boxes. Roy was waiting in the yard. "Let's see the worst," he greeted us, smiling.

"It's bad this time," replied Ben.

We backed the mare out first. The blood was clotting, but she started bleeding again as soon as she moved. Roy took one look and dived for his case. Mrs Mills peered round the trailer, still in her pinny. "Is it bad?" she asked.

The Colonel said, "She'll never work again, I can vouch for that."

We got her into the loose box somehow, then Roy, with a grim look on his face, filled her with sedative and in few minutes she was standing with her head hanging low, her lids heavy across her eyes. And for a time we forgot that the Commander and Paul had vanished. I held her head, while Ben passed Roy what he needed in the way of needles, forceps, scissors and thread. Mike watched over the door. Lisa fed Jigsaw. Time passed slowly. Mrs Mills brought us steaming mugs of tea. Someone switched on the light. At last the job of stitching was done. But there were still two more injections to be given before Roy was able to stand back and look at the mare, and say, "I'll just have a little listen to see everything's all right inside. I'll get my stethoscope."

"He must be listening for internal injuries," said Ben.

We all fell silent as he listened and I thought how long the day had been, and how it wasn't over yet.

"It's still breathing," he said. "I won't do any internal today, she can't take any more."

"What's breathing?"

"Her foal."

"Foal!" I cried.

"Yes, didn't you know?" asked Roy.

So that was the pot-belly we had been trying to get rid of, that explained everything. Poor little mare, I thought.

"No. And we've been working her," answered Ben, his voice full of guilt.

"She's all right, anyway," said Roy gently. "She'll be foaling quite soon, in a matter of weeks, and it sounds a strong little beggar."

I imagined Cassandra with a foal. She would be very happy. She would have our best field and a long, long

rest. Roy's telephone was calling him now. He packed his equipment into his case. "I'll call tomorrow about twelve," he said, starting his engine. "Will there be someone here?"

Ben nodded. I fetched Cassandra a rug.

For a moment neither of us could think of anything but Cassandra's foal. We thanked Roy automatically, rugged up Cassandra. "Don't do up the surcingle too tight," said Ben. "It might injure the foal."

"We must get her some extra vitamins. What shall we call it?" I asked.

"Windfall," he answered. "Because it will be one if it arrives, okay?"

We went towards the house calling, "Cassandra's in foal. Cassandra's going to have a foal." Everything seemed strangely quiet. The kitchen was empty.

"Whatever's happened now?" asked Ben in an apprehensive voice. We started to run. "They're in the sitting-room," he said.

We kicked off our dirty shoes. Twinkle mewed hopefully for her supper. The kettle simmered on the top of the Aga. Everything was the same yet different. Everything seemed to be waiting for something.

I felt terribly afraid as we went towards the sitting-room. The door was closed but the hum of voices told us everyone was there. "They're holding a meeting," Ben said.

"A conference or a council of war," I replied.

We pushed the door open. No one was sitting down. Dad was pacing the room and the Colonel was talking on and on as he always did, advising everyone. Mummy looked at us out of a haggard face. Lisa rushed to me and burst into tears.

Dad shouted. "I wish we had never started this place, and where's the whisky? Just when I need some, it's gone."

"Paul has been kidnapped. The Commander has demanded £50,000 ransom money. Isn't it charming?" said James.

"Have you told the police?" asked Ben.

"We've been on to his parents. They don't want the police told. They think it's safer without the police involved," James replied.

"What about the money?" asked Ben.

"It's being cabled or something. It's got to be in dollars. The Armstrongs are coming over on the first available plane, but there's a strike on and most of their planes are grounded," continued James.

"How long have we got?" asked Ben.

"Forty-eight hours. He's phoning further instructions tomorrow."

"So he wasn't a commander?" I said.

"You all thought I stole Paul's money, but it must have been 'im all along," said Mike. "I always hated 'im. I warned Paul he was no good."

"I've checked up, he was never in the Navy at all," said the Colonel. "I always could judge a man."

So we had to wait until tomorrow. It seemed like eternity. "Can we look for them?" I asked. "They might be hiding quite near."

"No, don't say a word to anyone about it," said Dad grimly. "And remember, all future guests must supply references."

"If we look for them, he's going to shoot Paul," explained Mummy.

Somehow we cooked and ate a meal. Mrs Mills was a tower of strength. Mary was much nicer than usual and Mike insisted on doing all the washing-up of saucepans. Suddenly we seemed to have become one large family, except that nobody said a cross word to anyone, and most families bicker all the time.

Later Ben and I went down to the stables to look at Cassandra. We found her lying down and now we could see that the foal was kicking inside her. We kneeled down beside her in the straw to say we were sorry for making her work, and she nuzzled us gently and Ben said, "You're going to be here for ever and ever and we're going to feed you nothing but the best, and you'll never go back to a market or any awful trekking centre."

She smelled of antiseptic and I think she liked having us there because after a few minutes she started to eat her bed. We fetched her hay and Ben said, "I feel very old tonight, don't you?"

I nodded. "Years older. I wonder where Paul is and whether he still likes the Commander and is listening to his stories?" I said.

"I hope so. I hope he doesn't know he's kidnapped," Ben replied.

"I'm glad I haven't got a rich father," said Lisa, suddenly beside us, "or I might be kidnapped too. Poor Paul!"

"You ought to be in bed," I said, standing up.

"Do you think we'll get him back alive?" she asked.

"I expect so," I said, "with a bit of luck."

"I keep feeling sick," she said. "I've always wanted to marry Paul. I never told you, because I thought you would laugh."

"I don't think I shall ever laugh again," said Ben, leading the way towards the house.

Six

He wants to speak to you

Cassandra was very stiff the next day. Roy came at twelve, at the same moment as the Cummings' ponies arrived. We were all very irritable and counting the minutes passing in an agony of suspense.

"Yes, she is stiff, isn't she?" agreed Roy. "I think I'll give her another injection to soften the pain a bit."

Mike and Ben put the Cummings' ponies into their loose boxes while I held Cassandra. Fortunately the Cummings hadn't come in person, but the ponies were awful. First they wouldn't go into their boxes, then they raced round and round them like maniacs, churning up the straw and neighing.

"They're a pair," said Roy, packing his things away into the car. "You had better watch them. Where's the American boy, by the way? Gone back?"

"Indoors," said Ben after a moment's embarrassed pause. "He's got a cold."

"A cold, fancy staying in for a cold!" replied Roy. "Well, I'll be round tomorrow to give her a long-lasting penicillin injection which should keep her going till the stitches come out."

He drove away and we stood looking at our new lodgers without really seeing them, seeing instead Paul somewhere. I wondered if he was gagged and bound? Hungry and alone? Was he in London in a dingy room or hidden quite near in a deserted building?

I wished we had told the police, because if he died now, we would blame ourselves for ever.

Lisa was still in bed. She said she couldn't face the world any more and that she wanted to die, because life was so awful. And no one had the energy to argue with her, though Mrs Mills played Happy Families and Sevens with her, and Mummy had taken her up breakfast in bed. I think she couldn't forgive herself for having fallen for Commander Cooley, for having believed his stories and admired him, and then having discovered that he had feet of clay, or, as James said, that he was our "fallen idol".

One way and another we were all at loggerheads. Half of us wanted the police called in regardless, but Dad insisted that Mr Armstrong had wanted otherwise and since Paul was his son, he must have the last word.

Rightly or wrongly Ben and I had no energy left to ride Mermaid and Sea Cadet, so we made excuses to ourselves.

"They need a day to settle in," I said.

"And it's obvious the journey has upset them," added Ben.

So the day wore on; all of us subconsciously listening for the telephone to ring. After lunch it was agreed that we should search the Commander's room, and we all went together and pulled open the drawers, which turned out to be empty, and opened the two splendid suitcases which remained. We found these filled with newspaper and stones, which did nothing to heighten our morale.

"So the whole thing was planned from the start," said Ben.

"Yes, he meant to impress us," said James, "and we fell for it hook, line and sinker."

His car had gone too, though none of us had noticed. Mrs Mills remembered him saying it was going to be serviced, but she couldn't remember when. She was looking old today and so was the Colonel.

Mummy took the sheets off the bed, saying, "They might as well be washed. He won't be coming back."

And Ben said, "Only in handcuffs. I bet he's been in prison heaps of times."

"And was without money, which is why he took Paul's," I added.

"The minute Paul's back, we'll set the police on him," Dad said. "Pity we haven't a picture of him."

"But I have," replied Mary. "I took one of him sitting in a deckchair. He wasn't very pleased. I can see why now."

"Is it developed?" asked Dad.

She shook her head. "It's still in the camera," she said. "Shall I get it?"

Dad nodded. "The sooner we have the picture the better!" he answered.

Then the telephone rang and we all jumped. James ran downstairs, taking them two at a time. Lisa appeared in the passage in her nightie.

"It's the bank," said James, returning. "They want to speak to you, Dad. It's private."

"What now?" Mummy asked.

"The camera's gone," said Mary, returning. "There isn't a sign of it anywhere."

"There wouldn't be. Our Commander is no fool," replied Ben.

"He might have left the camera," said Mary. "He could have taken out the film."

"But he can sell it. You can always sell good cameras," replied Ben.

"His cheque has bounced," Dad told us in a flat voice, coming back upstairs. "That's a whole month's keep gone." He started to swear, calling the Commander all sorts of terrible names, while the rest of us hurriedly disappeared in different directions. Ben and I went to do the horses, with Mike and Mary close on our heels.

Cassandra was lying down again and the two new ponies had settled down a bit and were eating hay. We mucked them out again and fetched them clean water.

185

Ben said, "Someone will have to ring up Paul's school tomorrow, because he's expected back."

"What shall we say?" I wondered.

"Perhaps he'll be back by then and we won't have to," replied Ben hopefully.

Dad got out his small battered car, which had replaced the large one he once had, and drove away. Ben said, "You know where he's going?"

And I replied, "No."

"To fetch the money," he said. "£50,000 worth all in lovely crisp dollars."

"How do you know?"

"I just do."

"Well you shouldn't advertise the fact," said Mary, looking at Mike. "It just might get nicked."

"By you?" asked Mike.

"By no one," said Ben quickly. "Let's go in. It's nearly time for supper and we haven't had any tea."

That's how it had been all day. Our usual pattern of life had vanished and no one seemed to mind. The Colonel didn't even demand breakfast on a tray in the dining-room any more, but was quite happy to have it in the kitchen. Our consciousness of time had vanished; we were all waiting for only one thing – another telephone call from Commander Cooley. As for anything else, time could stand still as far as we were concerned. So food didn't taste any more, letters remained unopened, and Lisa remained in bed, her hair untouched by brush or comb, because everything became unimportant compared with the awful danger Paul might be in. I think deep down most of us wondered whether Commander Cooley might be mad.

It was certainly possible that he had a Jekyll and Hyde character, that he could be two people – one gentlemanly and charming, the other vicious beyond

186

words, capable of anything. None of us had put this into words, but I think we all felt it.

And then at last, as daylight began to fade and the song of birds became softer and sleepier, the phone rang again. Dad was waiting by it, unshaven, a glass of whisky in one hand. I looked at my hands and saw that they were shaking. Dad said hardly anything. His voice was abrupt. He sounded as though he was speaking to something loathsome and saying as little as possible. Then he asked, "Why Harriet? Why not me?" And I jerked to life. My hands stopped shaking and I found I was shivering instead.

Lisa stood beside me now, still in her nightie, with bare feet. "You're not to go near him," she said. "Please, Harriet, please."

Dad was still listening, his face creased into a frown. Mummy stood in the doorway holding a saucepan.

"Don't give him an inch. Call the police," advised the Colonel. I could hear Mrs Mills making tea in the kitchen.

"He wants to speak to you, Harriet," said Dad, holding out the receiver.

"Why me?"

"Speak," snapped Dad, his nerves at breaking point.

I said, "Hello, it's me, Harriet."

A voice said, "Listen carefully. I want you to meet me at five in the morning by the old churchyard, with the money. You can come by horse and Ben can come as far as the old arch and then hold your horse. Have you got that? And no monkey tricks. I shall have a gun and I'm a crack shot, and you both will die and Paul will too. Are you listening?"

"Yes."

"If you tell the police, Paul will die anyway. And if I die, he'll die, it's all arranged. Do you understand?"

187

"Yes."

"Count the money first and bring it in a case. I shall open it before I let you go. And if it isn't there I shall kill you too. Do you understand?"

I said I did.

"Five o'clock in the morning, then."

"What about Paul?" I whispered.

"He will return to the house within the hour." He put down his receiver.

"She can't go!" cried Mummy.

"No, you can't, I won't let you!" cried Lisa, hanging on to me.

"Why can't I take the money? I'm not scared," Ben asked. "Why does he want Harriet?"

I was trying to imagine the moment. How would he be dressed? Would Paul be there too?

"I think we should tell the police," Mummy said. "I don't want Harriet to go."

"Nor do I," shrieked Lisa.

"We must make a plan," said James. "I will be there too. I can borrow a moped. I can hide. I can be there in case I'm needed."

"But you mustn't be seen."

"Of course not."

"You can let down his tyres, that will give us more time," said Ben.

The boys were turning it into a game, making it sound as though we were going to win. I knew now that I was going; there was no way out. I put an arm round Mummy. "It's going to be all right," I said. "The boys will look after me. Besides, he wouldn't shoot a girl."

"There's less than twelve hours to go," said Mummy in a horror-stricken voice, looking at Dad. "What are we going to do?" And suddenly I knew that none of us were going to sleep a wink all night, that we were going to get up in the morning drained of all energy. But the boys were still making plans. They had a map on the table now – an old ordnance survey map which showed everything as it had been thirty years ago.

"We're looking for the hiding place," Ben said.

I leaned over their shoulders and looked too. I saw the churchyard and the lane leading to it and the open

MYSTERY AT BLACK PONY INN

hills beyond and the railway line and the road which led to where the station once had been, and then I knew where Paul was. "Look!" I cried. "There!"

"The old signal box!" cried Ben. "Does it still stand?"

The rails and the sleepers had been pulled up and taken away years ago. A young couple now lived in what had been the station. But what about the signal box?

"Nobody goes that way and it stands back from the old track a bit. But is it still there?" cried Ben.

"Yes, it's there," said Mike. "It's all locked up. But it's there all right. I've been past it with my mates. The windows are boarded up."

"The Commander could have ridden that way too," said James. "Now for a plan."

"It's quicker and shorter to gallop along the track, but would he see us from the road?" asked Ben. "And what if we've got it wrong?"

"Exactly," said Dad. "They may hold Paul many miles away. We must get him here safe and sound. That's all that matters."

"And Harriet back safe and sound," added Mummy.

"But can we trust him to return Paul?" I asked.

"If he doesn't, every policeman in the country will be after him. He wants an hour or more to get clear. Probably there's a plane waiting for him somewhere," Dad said.

Time seemed to be passing very quickly now. As Mummy had said, in less than twelve hours I would be approaching the Commander with the money. I didn't want to think about it.

"Can I dress up as Harriet?" asked Mummy.

"You can't ride. And you're not the same shape," answered Dad.

190

Mrs Mills made everyone coffee. Dad and the Colonel put brandy in theirs. The Colonel started talking about India, about Poona and the great famines. "I was there when they handed India to the Indians, you know. Greatest mistake ever made," he said.

Mrs Mills scuttled about like a little mouse. We ate a strange meal of bread and cheese, pickles, scrambled eggs and bread and jam. No one seemed to mind. It was eight o'clock now and Ben and James were still making plans. Lisa was reading like a robot, automatically, without taking any of the words in. I went upstairs to the attic and set my clock for 4 a.m. I thought of the suitcases filled with stones and newspaper and how smooth and perfect Commander Cooley had appeared, and thought I would never trust anyone again.

The last of the day was fading as I undressed and got into bed. Supposing I never come back, I thought. What will happen to Lorraine? And I saw my own funeral and everyone crying.

Then Ben knocked on the door and came in. "We're going to have a go," he said, sitting on my bed. "James and I have made a plan. It should be all right."

"Won't the Armstrongs be cross?" I asked. "You know they wanted the money paid and no fuss."

"They only said not to call the police," replied Ben. "They will be pleased to have their money back. Honestly, Harriet, we have a very, very good plan. It can't go wrong. And it doesn't involve the police. Not to begin with, anyway."

"What is it?" I asked.

"We're not telling you, because if Commander Cooley went mad and kidnapped you too, he might force you to give it away."

"How charming," I said. "Thanks for warning me. I *shall* have nice dreams now."

"If he carried you off we would save you; that's half the point of the plan – it's to safeguard you too."

Suddenly I wanted everything blotted out by sleep. I wanted to wake and know the time had come. I didn't want any more waiting.

"Would you go away?" I said. "I want to sleep, if you don't mind."

"See you at four then. Say your prayers," replied Ben, getting off my bed and wandering away smiling, in his paisley dressing-gown which was much too short.

Mummy came in next. She sat on my bed and said, "You don't have to go, Harriet. You *can* say no. You don't need to risk your life for Paul."

"I'm going and I shall be all right," I said. "Lorraine is faster than the wind. Anyway, Ben will be near. I'll be all right, I promise."

"You can say no. You don't have to go," repeated Mummy.

"I'm going," I cried, sitting up. "I've made up my mind. If I don't I shall despise myself for ever and ever. It will ruin my life. Dad is always saying that you must have a hand to burn for your country or a friend. Well, I've got one. I'm burning it tomorrow at five o'clock at the old churchyard. Okay?"

It sounded brave, but inside I was quaking, wishing that Commander Cooley had chosen Ben or James instead of me, longing for tomorrow to be over and done with for ever.

Mummy kissed me and left the room. Moonlight filtered through the curtains. A bird cried, lonely in the sky.

I tried to think of lovely things – of horse shows in the summer and the glory of winning, of Cassandra's foal arriving, of all the money we were going to make exercising the Cummings' ponies. But all the time, at the back of my mind, tomorrow waited, lurking like a shadow ready to pounce. There was no way out, no going back, no escaping. My alarm clock ticked the minutes away; soon the night was half gone already, soon the cocks would be heralding another dawn. I slept at last, dreaming of Mike coming out of a bank carrying a case – the case I had to carry – full of money.

"I've blown the safe," he said. "It's all right, no one saw me."

But at that moment the burglar alarm went off; and it went on ringing until suddenly I knew that it wasn't a burglar alarm but my own clock telling me that my hour was nigh.

I drew back the curtains and saw that dawn was breaking; the sky was growing lighter, the moonlight gone. It was another day – a day I would never forget.

Seven

In the ruined church

Mummy met me downstairs. "I've made you some tea," she said.

Dad was in the kitchen. "If you're not back within the hour, we'll send the police," he said.

I don't think either of them had slept all night. Then Ben came down fully dressed, his pockets bulging.

"Ready," he said. "It's time to go. I've got some iron rations. We can eat as we go." James was already in the yard, tinkering with a moped he had borrowed. The sun was rising. We tacked up quickly. My hands were clumsy and shaky. I cursed myself for a coward as I mounted.

Dad gave me the case of notes. "I shall be watching through these," he said, pointing to some binoculars, "and if he touches you, he won't live another day."

Now that I was mounted, I felt quite brave. "Don't worry. I shall be all right," I said. Lorraine was fresh and bouncy. I turned her round and waved goodbye.

Mike leaned from a window to call, "Be careful now," Mrs Mills's bedroom light was on, her face at the window.

I wasn't scared any more. I felt incredibly brave in a mad, light-hearted way, as though I had drunk too much. I rode with one hand holding the case, which seemed far too light for something containing so much in the way of future happiness and Paul's life. And I felt like singing.

The common was covered with morning dew, the brambles magic with cobwebs. There were rabbits everywhere and from the fields came the thick, scraping sound of cows pulling at grass.

"It's a fantastic morning," I said. "Why don't we always get up at dawn?"

"We're too lazy," replied Ben. "I hope everything goes off all right. It's a devil of a responsibility." He looked at his watch and we started to canter because suddenly time was running out again.

"How happy I shall be when it's over, when Paul is with us again," I said. "I shall sleep and sleep."

"Same here," said Ben.

Later I dropped the case and it burst open, and the

money was scattered over the ground. We were in the woods by this time and daylight had come, but we still had several miles to go.

Ben swore. "Just like Dad," he said. "Why didn't he put a strap round the case?"

"It isn't his fault," I cried, leaping off. "I let it slip."

Lorraine whirled round, stepping on the notes. Ben swore again. It would have been funny if it hadn't been so awful. We stuffed the notes back, but they looked grubby and wrinkled now, and there wasn't time to count them. "We're going to be late," cried Ben, looking at his watch.

"Let him sweat it out," I answered.

"Is it shut properly this time?"

"I hope so."

We started to gallop as the sun rose, missing trees by centimetres, our ponies racing each other, our blood racing through our veins. We came out of the wood and we had reached the lane which led to the churchyard. I remembered that the Commander and Paul had ridden this way together on Sunday, which now seemed a hundred years ago. Our ponies were sweating and on edge; they must have sensed our anxiety and knew that something was about to happen. Ben looked at his watch again. "We'll be dead on time," he said.

We could see the ruined church now – the ruined spire, the ancient tombstones. My heart was thudding in a strange way and suddenly I didn't want to go on, didn't want to face Commander Cooley. I wanted to turn round and go back and be safe at home drinking tea in the kitchen. The ponies became nervous too; they imagined things in hedges, and shied at the dawn sun shining on puddles, and smelled the air and snorted.

"They smell danger too," said Ben. "Are you all right? Do you want some chocolate?"

I shook my head. I felt too sick for chocolate.

"I wish I was going and you were staying," said Ben. "Waiting is much worse than going. I swear it is."

We had reached the broken, arched gateway, where once people had passed on their way to worship. There wasn't much left of it now. I dismounted and handed Ben my reins. My legs felt weak. "Good luck," he said.

I patted Lorraine and said, "Wait for me, I'll be back," hoping that the words would give me courage.

The old churchyard is a ghostly place at the best of times. Today everything seemed ten times worse. I stepped over the old broken tombstones, clutching the case, and as I walked I prayed, "God, make everything all right."

Behind me the ponies snorted and in front of me I could see the hills calm and beautiful in the morning light, white where the chalk showed through, untouched by time. I thought of the Romans who had marched across them centuries ago and how little really changes. If only they could speak, I thought, and then I had reached what was left of the church, and there were steps leading down into the ruin proper and ivy wrapping itself round everything which stood or grew. I knew that I had to go down the steps.

For a moment, I couldn't see anything. My eyes wouldn't focus properly and my brain wouldn't concentrate. Then I saw the Commander perched high up in the ruined spire, surveying the countryside through binoculars. He looked very tall, like someone on the look-out of a ship, I thought; and suddenly I was frightened for James, lurking somewhere in his workman's clothes on the moped.

The Commander had changed – gone was the elegance. He was still in his riding breeches, but they looked as though he had slept in them. His hair

197

was uncombed and his face unshaven. He wore an anorak over a shirt without a tie.

I shouted, "Good morning, Commander." He turned quickly, as quickly as an animal suddenly scared.

"Have you brought it?" he said, climbing down.

His voice was different too. Before it had seemed so cultured, as though its owner had taken elocution lessons, or been to a posh school. Now it was rougher, matching his appearance. I had the feeling that I was meeting the real Commander for the first time and it wasn't a nice feeling. I pointed to the case. My hands were shaking.

"Follow me then," he said.

"But it's here," I answered, holding out the case, longing to get back to Ben and safety. "Take it, please," I pleaded, and my voice came out shaky and I realised how frightened I was, more frightened than I had ever been before.

The binoculars were hanging round his neck and he had a gun; his eyes looked strange and scared, as though his whole life was at stake.

I followed him, remembering how we had welcomed him, waited on his every whim. What fools we had been! I could see his car, parked at the side of the road. He stopped where the ground sloped and there were trees. His hands were shaking too.

"Open it," he said.

He won't be pleased about the dirty notes, I thought, and my hands felt numb suddenly and my heart started to race. "Hurry!" he shouted.

He'll suspect us of taking some, I thought, and wondered whether James was watching, or, Ben, Dad, anyone, waiting to help if he went mad, somebody to shout and carry me away to safety and to home which now seemed more precious than ever before.

The case was open at last. I held it out to him and heard a dog barking in the distance for the first time. He looked through the notes quickly, scuffling them with his hands, and I saw that his nails were dirty but that his hands had stopped shaking, as though he knew now that the worst was over.

"Get back to your brother fast," he shouted, slamming the case shut. "And no monkey tricks, I know how to use this gun. I was a champion shot once and I'm not afraid of killing."

Every fibre in my body told me to run. But I stood my ground. "What about Paul?" I asked. "If he isn't released pretty soon, the whole of the world's police forces will be after you."

"He will be!" He started to run towards his car while I rushed back through the churchyard, stumbling over the broken tombstones, through the arch, back to Ben waiting with the ponies.

"My God, you were a time!" he cried. "Get on, will you?" There was sweat on his face mixed with dirt.

"He made me walk away from the churchyard. He's got a gun," I cried, struggling to mount. But the efforts I had made already seemed to have sapped my strength. My legs were not working properly and there was a hollow feeling in my stomach. "Let's go home and wait for Paul. He's got a gun. Please," I pleaded.

"It's a mile shorter along the track. Come on!" yelled Ben. "If James has let down his tyres, we'll be all right."

We raced down the lane, under an old bridge, across some rough ground and on to the track which had once been a railway. The ponies were ready to go. Their hoofs ate up the ground. The wind was in our faces and daylight had really arrived. It was nearly two miles to the signal box, but the ground was smooth and even had an embankment on each side which hid us from the road.

"Still scared?" asked Ben, smiling as he galloped.

"Yes. He's quite different. He's tough, Ben. He's not the same; he's not Commander Cooley any more."

"We're going to find out who he is quite soon and it will be very interesting," said Ben.

"If he doesn't kill us both first," I replied.

We came out of the embankment and there were placid meadows on each side of us and a smell of thyme. Sheep grazed among bushes. Rabbits scurried into holes at our approach.

"Look!" cried Ben. "Look, over there, you fool. It's his Mercedes." It was twisting along the country road like a snake ready for the kill.

"I wish we had kept away. He will kill Paul now," I cried.

"He may not have seen us, and he's still got to walk to the signal box from the road which will take him at least ten minutes," shouted Ben, his heels drumming against Solitaire's sides.

"He'll run, and he's fast," I shouted. "He's not smooth, manicured Commander Cooley any more. He's a man running for his life."

Our ponies were almost spent, but we could see the signal box and the sun had burst through and was shining.

"Come on!" shouted Ben. Lorraine, who was the fastest, streaked away from Solitaire and suddenly I was alone, racing to save Paul's life. I was travelling very fast but time seemed to pass slowly. And for ages the signal box seemed to grow no nearer. Then, suddenly, we were there. I threw myself off and rushed up the wooden steps. Everything was boarded up, the door padlocked.

"Paul!" I shrieked. "Are you there? Paul! Paul!"

201

And an answer came back. "Who's that? I'm here and no kidding. Has Dad paid up? Where is he, where's Dad?" He sounded frightened and exhausted.

"He's here, Ben," I yelled, falling down the steps.

"Okay," yelled Ben, drawing rein. "Lorraine has got her breath. Go on to the station. Tell them to send for the police. Hurry."

"What about you?"

"I'll be all right."

I was on again now, galloping, Lorraine's ears giving me courage, her speed giving me hope. Some horses rise to an occasion and will gallop until they have nothing left to give. Lorraine was of that breed. Her ears and neck were dark with sweat, her sides lathered, her breath laboured, but I knew she would go until she dropped. And I couldn't spare her, there was too much at stake – Paul's life, Ben's, perhaps even James's as well.

A dog was barking in the station but the curtains were drawn. I flung myself off and started to beat a tat-too on the door and the dog became frenzied with bark-ing. Then the young owner, who had a beard, opened the door a crack and said, "What is it? Who's there?" He was still in his pyjamas and his feet were bare. The dog peered round his legs, snarling.

"Please send for the police," I cried, suddenly breath-less. "There's a kidnapped boy in the signal box and a man with a gun."

"Okay," he said, believing me. "Odette, wake up. Go to the phone. I'll go with the girl. Call the police from the phone box. Hurry!" he yelled.

Odette had hair which hung fair and straight down her back. She was already pulling on slacks, while the man with the beard picked up a double-barrelled shot-gun, boots and a coat. "Okay," she said, "but I'll have to take Mattie."

"Fine, but hurry. Just dial 999." The man was run-ning along the track now, ahead of me. "We're not on the telephone," he shouted. "She's got to go to the phone box." Lorraine had her second wind by now and felt ready to go for ever.

Then I saw a sight that sickened me – the Comman-der's Mercedes parked less than a hundred metres from the signal box and the Commander himself running across the ground that separated him from Paul and Ben.

I started to gallop and the man with the beard called, "Wait for me. I've got a gun." But I couldn't wait. My head felt full of hammers, hammers which banged: He's going to kill them, kill them, kill, kill, kill.

But the feel of Lorraine under me gave me courage, because there is something about being on a horse which makes you feel invincible. I can't describe it but it exists, any horseman will tell you this is true. So I felt untouchable, as though no bullet could hit me as I galloped on, and the morning was like any other morning, full of the song of birds and the smell of a summer day, except for what was about to happen by the signal box.

Eight

Have they found James?

Ben was halfway up the steps. The Commander had him
covered with a gun and there was someone else there
too – a squat man with a squashed nose, wearing a dark
hat, and he had a gun too.

"Shoot them both," said the Commander. "That way
they won't talk."

"Not to kill," replied the squat man. "Let's get back
to the car. We've got the money. I don't want to be had
for murder. Shoot at his feet."

They raised their guns to shoot at Ben but at the same
moment the young man fired. He was too far away to
hit them, but they must have imagined he was the
police, for they turned and ran. And suddenly we were
all there at the signal box, struggling with the door.

"They've still got the money," cried Ben. "Are the
police coming?"

"Any minute," said the man with the beard.

"And where is James?" I asked.

"They must have got him," replied Ben.

The door was cracking, splintering under our com-
bined efforts. The young man gave one final crashing
blow with the butt of his gun and then we were inside
staring at Paul, bound to the seat where a signal man
had sat in happier times. He was very pale. "Have they
gone?" he asked. "Have they got the money?"

Ben nodded. "Listen!" he said. "Police sirens."

I went to the door and looked out. There were police cars parked along the roadside, policemen running towards the signal box, and Odette running towards them with the dog, Mattie, running beside her.

Ben had untied Paul by this time. The young man was rubbing his wrists saying, "It's just the circulation. They'll be all right in a minute."

"He was some crook," said Paul through chattering teeth. "Is Dad coming?"

"There's been a strike – all planes grounded – but he'll be here," said Ben. I stood scanning the horizon, searching for James on his moped, seeing no sign of him anywhere.

"Was James to come here?" I asked.

"Yes," replied Ben, suddenly beside me.

"Where can he be then?"

"I don't know."

Our ponies were cropping the grass below. They looked a sorry sight, soaked in sweat and mud, their flanks run up like greyhounds. Then Ben came to life. He leaped down the steps and ran towards the police shouting, "He's got away in a black Mercedes, number plate L934 MOP. He's got £50,000 in dollars and perhaps my brother. There's two of them."

Some of the police were running back now, talking into their radios. Paul was saying, "I want my parents. Why haven't they come?"

"The planes are grounded," I said.

"But there isn't any fog."

"There's a strike."

Suddenly there were more people coming. Mummy and Dad and two larger figures, and the Colonel hurrying behind. And I started to wave and shout, "Paul's all right. He's here."

206

Mummy rushed up the steps crying, "Thank heavens you're safe, Harriet. I've been so frightened," while Ben went on talking to the police.

Then I saw that the other figures were Mr and Mrs Armstrong and I turned to Paul and yelled, "Your parents are here. They've come!"

He looked at me in a dazed way and said, "My parents. Here?"

"Yes," I yelled. "Here!"

And then he stood up and began to shout, "Mom. Dad. I'm here. I'm all right. But he was some crook, no kidding."

Mrs Armstrong was running up the steps with outstretched arms, while the Colonel stood waving his stick and shouting, "Where's the other one? The dark-haired lad. The one who went out on the moped."

MYSTERY AT BLACK PONY INN

And I shouted, in a voice which was suddenly not my own any more, "I don't know."

Some of the police stayed but most of them went away. There was a policewoman who questioned Paul in a soothing voice and a young constable who wrote down everything Paul said. Other policemen disappeared with Dad while Odette brought us hot coffee in a Thermos. I was feeling very cold by this time and I kept worrying about James. The policewoman asked me a few questions about Commander Cooley and then Mummy said, "Ben has gone in one of the police cars. Can you manage to get both the ponies back, Harriet? Are you sure, absolutely sure?" And I kept nodding, though I wasn't sure at all, because suddenly everything seemed unreal and I was worrying so terribly about James.

"I think he's mad," I said, catching Lorraine.

"Who?"

"Commander Cooley. His eyes are mad, anyway." Mummy held Solitaire while I mounted.

"I must go back with Paul and his parents; they landed and came straight here," she said. "Please be careful." She looked desperately tired, more tired than she had ever looked before.

"I shall be all right," I said. "I just wish we knew where James was."

"He was supposed to let down the tyres, apparently," Mummy said.

"And the other man was there and caught him," I cried, turning towards home, not wanting to think any further.

"The police will find him," Mummy said without any conviction in her voice.

Dead or alive, I thought, riding along the track, not seeing it, not seeing anything very much any more. I was very tired. I hadn't eaten anything since the night before. But the ponies understood. They looked after me. They went like angels. I think I cried into Lorraine's mane. I can't remember much of the journey. I think Lorraine simply carried me home.

I know it seemed like midday as I passed the old familiar common, high now in grass, sweet with the scent of flowers from cottage gardens.

We didn't do the right things, I thought. We didn't really save Paul because they were going to let him go anyway, and now we've lost James and that's even worse because we haven't got £50,000 like the Armstrongs. My mind was full of mad, muddled thoughts which seemed to glide into each other without making any sense, so that I felt like a ship without a rudder, drifting hopelessly without guidance in a strong sea. The ponies didn't trot – perhaps they thought I was too weak to stay on; they walked with long swinging strides, proud and independent, taking me home.

I thought that perhaps James was home waiting for us, perhaps he was all right after all. The ponies turned through the gateway and there was the dear, familiar yard all bathed in sunlight and a little knot of people seemingly waiting for me, their faces smiling. It was like a dream, but it wasn't – it was real.

There was Roy smiling, Mrs Mills in her pinny, and Mike with his big hands all red and soapy. And Lisa laughing and proud. I seemed to be seeing them all for the first time, as though I had been away for a long time and had come back. I wanted to say, "Where's James?" But no words would come. Mike took hold of Solitaire for me.

"Come and look," shrieked Lisa. "Cassandra's had a foal. It was a bit of a job, but it's all right, a lovely little colt, isn't it, Roy?"

"It was a real cliff-hanger but they are both all right," said Roy. "But what's happened to you?"

His face seemed to be going away; they all were, growing smaller and smaller. I forced my legs to dismount. I tried to say Hurray! or Thank you, something appropriate. But now they were far away and there didn't seem any point in shouting.

I felt my feet touch the ground, then they crumpled and I thought: You're fainting, head between your knees, you fool; and everything went black and I passed out.

Roy was leaving when I came round and I was sitting in a chair in the kitchen with Mrs Mills making tea, and Mary was saying, "Cold towels on her face will bring her round."

Roy was just the same as ever, with his wellington boots turned down at the top and his rugged face smiling, all crooked and agreeable, and so strong that one knew he was capable of facing almost anything and coming through all right.

"What happened? Where are the others?" cried Lisa, her small face close to mine.

"Has anyone seen to the horses?" I asked.

"Mike has. He's a good boy, that one," said Mrs Mills. "Here, have this. There's lots of sugar in it." She handed me a cup of tea.

I wanted to say, "I hate sugar," but I knew she wouldn't hear me because she wasn't wearing her hearing-aid, and I felt too weak to shout at her.

"Look after yourself. Bye for now," said Roy, slamming the back door after him.

"He carried you. I think he kissed you. He must want to marry you," said Lisa, who is full of silly ideas culled from sloppy television programmes.

The tea had brandy in it. It burned my throat, but

gradually I felt my strength coming back.

"What about the others?" asked Lisa in a small, frightened voice. "Where are they?"

"With the police. All right, except for James; we don't know where he is."

"What about Paul?"

"He's okay. Shaken but all right," I replied. "It's James who is lost. I think they've got him."

I knew I was going to cry and I didn't want Mary to see me crying. Mrs Mills handed me a thick wedge of fruit cake. "It's full of iron," she said. "Eat it up."

"Why doesn't the silly old woman put on her hearing-aid?" asked Mary.

"Don't be beastly," shrieked Lisa.

"What's she saying?" asked Mrs Mills, putting her face near mine so that she could hear.

"Nothing," I shouted.

I wished the others would come home. Mary seemed so spiteful, and Lisa was silly and Mrs Mills deaf. I stood up. "I'm all right now. I'm going to see to the horses," I said, sniffing. "I want to look at the foal." I went outside and thought that James might be dead and no one seemed to care.

Mike was working on Solitaire and Lorraine, drying them with straw, hissing like a groom of long ago. I told him what had happened, how the Commander had changed, and that Paul was all right but James was missing. I told him the police had taken over now and he kept nodding and saying things like "Well done" and "That's all right then." Things which really didn't mean anything at all. Then, "They came straight 'ere," he said. "Straight off the plane."

"They?" I asked.

"Paul's parents. They were in a proper state, they were."

I stood looking at Cassandra's foal. He was strong
and roan, with a white streak on his face just like his
mother. Mike had made Cassandra a bran mash and her
box was bedded deep with straw. She looked very proud
and happy, and peaceful too, as though all her misery
was forgotten and only happiness lay ahead.

Mike and I turned Lorraine and Solitaire out and watched them roll. Morning seemed long ago, like a dream, like something which had never happened. I was missing Ben. When we went indoors Mrs Mills was laying the table for tea and the kettle was bubbling on the Aga.

"They must be back soon," she said.

Presently a young man came and started photographing the house and asking questions. He had long hair and a fantastic Grecian nose and Lisa fell for him at once and told him all about Paul. He took some photographs and gave Lisa a box of chocolates before he vanished, and it was only afterwards we realised he was a reporter and that now everything would be in the papers. And I remembered that the Armstrongs didn't want any fuss, and no publicity, and I felt like screaming.

Then Mike came in and said, "A man's been photographing the stables and asking questions. He gave me this," and held out a five-pound note. "Is he a cop?"

"A reporter, you fool," said Mary. "You shouldn't have told him anything."

I went upstairs to my room because I was tired of the others, and I lay on my bed thinking: What if James never comes back? And then I think I must have slept, for the next thing I knew Mummy was shaking me, saying, "Are you all right, Harriet?"

She had dark smudges of exhaustion under her eyes and she had put on an apron which smelled of onions.

"Isn't it lovely about the foal?" she asked.

"Have they found James?" I asked, sitting up.

"No. But they're still looking," she said.

Nine

Will it leave a scar?

I joined everyone downstairs. The Armstrongs had gone to a hotel for showers and a proper meal. Paul had a police guard. Ben was telling everybody what had happened.

He looked very tired, but strung up too, so that one knew he wouldn't rest until James was found.

Dad was upstairs with two policemen, going through the Commander's bedroom. The Colonel was sipping whisky in the kitchen and talking about the old days. I missed James. Often I hate him, but now I missed him. If he never comes back I shall go mad, I thought. Life will never be the same again.

Mummy was cooking. "You must keep your strength up," she said.

"What for?" I asked. "We made a right mess of things, didn't we?"

"We don't know yet. We may have done all right," replied Ben.

"Not if James is dead," I said.

"He'll be all right. Bad pennies always turn up again," replied Ben, trying to laugh.

"I don't want that word mentioned again," cried Mummy.

"What word?" asked Ben.

"Dead." Her hands were shaking.

"Sit down. I'll cook," I offered. "I'm all right now and he'll be all right, you'll see."

"It's so awful. I was such a fool. I trusted Commander Cooley; I actually liked him. That's what makes it so much worse," said Mummy.

"In future, we'll have references from every single guest – long ones," said Ben.

"If James doesn't come back, there won't be a future," replied Mummy.

Looking round I saw how dirty we all were; even the Colonel was looking less stately than usual. Mrs Mills had put on her hearing-aid at last and was asking everyone questions. Mike was sweeping the kitchen floor. I sat thinking that I had misjudged everyone. The Colonel had seemed a boring old man and yet he had great courage and endurance. We had despised Mike and thought him a thief, but he had proved a tower of strength, and honest too. As for Commander Cooley whom we had thought such a gentleman, he had turned out to be a criminal. I will never try to judge anyone again, I thought, nor will I give them the benefit of the doubt as Dad always does. I shall be on my guard.

"There's a car," said Ben, going to the window. "A police car. What now?"

Mummy's hands started to shake again.

Then a policeman knocked on the door and asked for Dad. He came rushing downstairs and they went into the sitting-room together, shutting the door after them. I think we all imagined disaster then. I know Lisa started to cry immediately without saying a word.

"It's about James, isn't it?" I asked. "If they had found him they would have brought him here."

"That's right," said Mummy, sinking into a chair.

I smelled the ill-fated onions burning and took them off the stove. No one was talking any more, just waiting.

215

"You should have gone with them," Ben told Mummy after a time.

Colonel Hunter had fallen asleep at the kitchen table, his head propped up on his hand. The clock went on ticking. Mike stopped sweeping. "Everything's going to be all right, Auntie," he said, patting Mummy's shoulder. "I promise."

He had taken to calling Mummy "Auntie". She hated it, but never complained because she was so sure he needed love and understanding, so that any small sign of affection must be welcomed, even if it meant being called Auntie. Looking at Mike now, I knew she had been right. He had changed beyond recognition. He was sane and responsible; someone you could trust. So our one and only good deed has worked out, I thought, but I couldn't rejoice, not until James was with us too, safe and whole.

Colonel Hunter sat up, muttering. "Sorry about that – been asleep. Bad manners, I know, just flaked out."

"How do you know it's going to be all right?" Lisa asked Mike. "Come on, how?"

"Because the Commander isn't that bad. He isn't a killer. He's just a con-man," replied Mike as though he knew. "I've met some criminals and they're all different; some can kill, some can't. Commander Cooley can't – he hasn't the temperament."

I remembered that Mike's father was in prison. He never visited him, nor his mother. Had he rejected them or had they rejected him?

Mary was filing her nails. She was the only one of us who had combed her hair since early morning.

We could hear Dad showing the policeman out now, saying, "Thank you very much. It was good of you to come. Everything is in the clear, then."

And Lisa started to jump up and down, crying, "What does 'in the clear' mean?"

And Ben shouted, "Shut up, I'm listening."

Then we heard the car start up, and Dad came into the kitchen and said, "Be quiet, everyone. I want to tell you exactly what has happened."

But of course we couldn't be quiet. Lisa screamed, "Is James all right? Yes or no?"

Ben said, "Have they got the money back?"

And Mummy said, "Where's James? Where?"

"In hospital," Dad said, looking weary. "But he's all right. We can fetch him presently. He's been stitched up."

"Where? Where is he stitched up?" cried Mummy.

"On the side of his face and on his left knee, and he's cracked a bone or two," said Dad, smiling. "But he's all right, so stop worrying."

"Will it leave a scar? On his face, I mean?" asked Mummy.

"I don't know. It doesn't matter much anyway," replied Dad. "Boys don't have to be pretty and they'll be honourable scars."

"That's right," said Mike approvingly to no one in particular.

"You are all so self-centred," complained Mary. "What about the Commander? Has anybody found my camera? It wasn't insured and I want it back."

"Who's self-centred now?" whispered Lisa.

"Let's begin at the beginning, shall we?" asked Dad. "Sit down and I will tell you everything the inspector said. But no interruptions, please."

Mrs Mills turned up her hearing-aid. The Colonel lit his pipe.

"The police know all about Commander Cooley. His real name isn't Cooley at all, but plain Mr Smith," began Dad. "He's been in and out of prison since his twenties. Twice for bigamy – "

"What's bigamy?" interrupted Lisa.

"Getting married when you are already married," replied Mummy.

"I thought that was called divorce," said Lisa.

"Shut up," shouted Ben.

"He was in the Navy for a short time as an ordinary seaman but was discharged for theft," continued Dad. "Since then he has been kept by various women who imagined they were his lawful wives. Two years ago he was jailed for bigamy for the second time and for cashing dud cheques, but since he is always a model prisoner he was soon released and collected some money from somewhere and came here. No one knows how he discovered that Paul would be here, but he obviously did before he came because the whole kidnap plan was set very carefully. We don't know where the Mercedes came from either, but it was probably stolen at some time or other."

"Or belonged to the other man, the one with the funny nose," cried Ben. "What about him?"

"He was in prison before the Commander, I mean plain Mr Smith," replied Dad. "And he lives five miles from here and came out six months ago, so he probably told Mr Smith about Paul. All that will come out in court."

"Will we have to give evidence in court?" asked Ben.

"I expect so, but I gather someone has already given an interview to the press," said Dad, looking at Lisa with a slight smile on his lips.

"I didn't mean to. I didn't know he was a reporter," said Lisa, blushing. "He came and asked questions, and was so nice I think I want to marry him!"

"You know Lisa," I cried. "A charming man has only to smile at her and she tells all."

"What about the money? I keep asking, but you never say," complained Ben.

"It was in the car, intact. The Armstrongs are taking it with them tomorrow when they fly out."

"Fly out?" cried Lisa. "Paul isn't leaving, is he?"

"Yes, they are taking him with them. Now that the news has broken they are afraid someone else will have a go at kidnapping him. And they haven't had much luck, have they? First they're sold a dud pony, then Paul's kidnapped. You can't say old England's treated them very well," said Dad.

"Won't he ever come back? Is he coming to say good-bye?" asked Lisa in a tearful voice.

"Yes, tomorrow. We have to pack his things up," Dad said.

It was like the end of a chapter; our relationship with Paul was over; but I couldn't blame the Armstrongs for taking him away, for he had had enough frights to last a lifetime.

"He didn't want to go. He was crying his eyes out," Dad continued. "But he'll like it when he gets there."

"What, in an apartment?" cried Lisa.

"They're buying a farm," replied Dad.

It was eight o'clock now. Mummy stared at the clock in dismay. "I haven't done anything about dinner. I haven't even taken the meat out of the freezer. It's still frozen," she cried, leaping up. "I've done nothing but cook onions. I must be mad."

"I'm quite happy with scrambled eggs," said Mrs Mills.

"I'm not. I'm dying on my feet from hunger," replied Ben.

"All I want is a nice drink," said Dad.

"I want you to be my guests," said the Colonel rather loudly. "I may be an old man but I'm not a poor one. Will you do me the honour of dining with me tonight?"

"What, all of us?" asked Ben.

"Yes, all of you."

"Me too?" asked Mrs Mills.

"Not me, sir. I've never eaten in a restaurant before," said Mike.

Colonel Hunter held out his hand. "I'm proud to

know you, Mike," he said. "If you were in my regiment I would recommend you for promotion. You are the salt of the earth, sir. Of course you are coming."

Mike took his hand, blushing to the roots of his carrot-coloured hair.

Lisa cried, "What shall I wear? My one and only dress is filthy."

"We had better see to the horses first," I said to Ben. "You know our rule, Horses before humans, and Solitaire and Lorraine were marvellous."

We remembered then that we hadn't looked at the Cummings' ponies all day. "They'll have azoturia from not being exercised," I cried. "We'll have to take them out now. We can't go out to dinner, that's all. It's still light."

"And I love a good dinner," wailed Ben.

"And I've had nothing but a sausage roll and a cup of tea for hours and hours."

"We exercised the horses," said Lisa. "So stop worrying."

"You?" cried Ben.

"She said they would get some frightful complaint, something beginning with 'a'," said Mike. "So we lunged them. We looked it up in a book and then we found the lunging rein and Ben's old hunting whip."

"They were awful. Cadet bucked and bucked, but Mike was marvellous," Lisa related.

"We gave them twenty minutes each and most of it was trotting; then we grazed them along the roadside for a bit; then Cassandra started her labour pains – at least that's what Mrs Mills called them," Mike said.

"We fetched her for advice. We didn't know what to do. Cassie kept lying down and getting up," continued Lisa.

"We looked up foaling in a book. It said a mare

mustn't be in labour more than half an hour, so we rang up Roy," Mike said.

"It was a very bad birth, according to Roy," continued Lisa, sounding grown up and knowledgeable. "The foal got stuck and we had to use a rope on it. Mrs Mills was marvellous, she held Cassandra all the time. You would never think she was eighty-something."

Suddenly I saw that Lisa was growing up; that she wasn't just a tiresome little sister any more. She was capable of responsibility too.

Ben was staring at them both. "Cassandra would have died without you. Thank heavens you were here. And thank you for lunging the Cummings' ponies," he said.

"It was a pleasure," replied Mike. "And you needn't check anybody's water buckets. I was out there at seven and I checked everything."

"Stop gossiping and get ready," called Dad. "Wash your hands. And clean your nails, Ben. We don't want the smell of stable wherever we're going. And put on a dress, Harriet. I'm going to fetch James. I'll be back in half an hour."

Colonel Hunter was on the telephone trying to book a table somewhere. But he had to telephone three places before he could find anybody who could have us all.

Mrs Mills was muttering, "I hope my suit will do," and frantically washing up cups which didn't need washing. Mary had locked herself in the bathroom so that no one else could wash. Ben started to clean his shoes. I looked through my dresses. They were all too small, but there wasn't time to do anything about it.

Outside the ponies were grazing. The sun was going down. It seemed the longest day of my life and it wasn't over yet.

Ten

The Colonel's dinner party

Dad telephoned to say he would meet us at the hotel; he
said that James was all right but still a bit sleepy, and
not to worry. So the rest of us piled into the Land Rover,
Colonel Hunter sitting in the front with Mummy, who
was driving, and the rest of us in the back – Mary, myself and Lisa on one side, Ben, Mike and Mrs Mills on
the other. Only Mary was smart. My dress felt too short
and my ankle socks kept disappearing into my shoes,
which were too small. My only other respectable clothes
were my school uniform – sensible black shoes, dark
socks or tights, a ghastly skirt and blouse, and a blazer
with a stupid crest on it. Otherwise my clothes were old
jeans or things for riding. Mrs Mills had on a suit which
smelled of mothballs, and sensible lace-up shoes which
had been handmade twenty years ago.

Ben was wearing his riding-jacket, school trousers
and jodhpur boots, and a very clean white shirt. His
hands were clean but he hadn't washed his face, which I
was sure Mummy would notice any minute, and his
neck looked decidedly grubby against his white shirt.
Mike had put on his school clothes – trousers, a shirt,
blazer, school tie and black shoes – but since the social
services had provided them secondhand, none of them
really fitted.

Mary was wearing a long skirt, an embroidered

blouse, earrings, fashionable shoes, and smelled delicious. She made me feel very young and awkward.

The Colonel kept telling Mummy which way to go, though she knew already. Mrs Mills lectured us on the versatility of Land Rovers. Mary tried to chat up Ben, but quite soon he fell asleep with his mouth open.

I wondered where the Commander was now and tried to imagine him handcuffed in a cell. I wondered why he had made such a mess of his life when he was both good-looking and clever. Then Mary started to grumble. "When are we going to arrive? This thing shakes you to pieces," she said. "And I bet the old boy's a frightful bore when we get there."

"He's jolly nice to have us. Dinner will cost him a lot of money," I said.

"Well, it hasn't been much of a day, has it?" grumbled Mary. "No proper lunch or tea, and just Mrs Mills doing all the work. Call yourself a guest house."

"You can always leave," said Ben, waking up. "We don't need you. We are perfectly happy with the Colonel and Mrs Mills and Mike until the holidays start."

We could see the hotel now, large and splendid, with a great sweep of drive and high Georgian windows. Lisa started to jump about. "Do you think Daddy'll let me drink? I love wine," she cried.

Mummy stopped the Land Rover and we all climbed out. There was no sign of James or Daddy yet.

"We'll go in and have a drink," said the Colonel. "They won't be long now."

We sat in armchairs in an elegant lounge. Lisa kept giggling. Mary sized up the waiters. I talked to Ben about what we would do the next day. Half-term was nearly over. It seemed to have come and gone like an express train, and yet encased in it were some terrible moments none of us would ever forget. The Colonel

refused help and brought us drinks himself on a tray.

He was a perfect host. He looked old and graceful, like some moustached pedigree dog. Eventually he sat down beside Mummy and talked. I had a cider to drink. I sat waiting, waiting for James. He came at last, pale and tall, one arm in a sling. He smelled like a hospital but he was smiling. And now we were complete, a collection of people who had gone through something together. Only Mary didn't belong.

"They threw me out," said James, laughing.

"Not when they were going?" cried Mummy.

"Yes, and the road felt mighty hard when I hit it!"

The Colonel was fetching James a drink, talking to Dad at the same time, and suddenly he seemed younger and merrier, perhaps because he was feeling wanted at last. "What did they say?" I asked.

"Not much, but they were hating me, and their language was something terrible, not what you would expect from the elegant Commander at all."

His face had a dressing on one cheek. Mummy made him sit down.

"You weren't concussed, were you?" she asked.

He shook his head. "I can remember everything perfectly," he said. "The only problem is the moped. No one's found it yet and I promised to return it tonight, intact."

Mrs Mills sat sipping whisky. Mike had chosen Coca-Cola. James went on talking, telling us how the man with the squashed nose had found him trying to let the air out of one of the Mercedes' tyres, how he had bundled him into the car and tied him up, issuing the most terrible threats. Then the Commander had come, crying, "I've got the money! We'll beat it!" and leaped in, revving up the engine.

The man with the squashed nose had said, "I've got kids of my own – release the American boy first, do you hear? Or I'll grass." But the Commander had driven at tremendous speed towards the signal box, still not knowing that James was in the back.

They had left him there while they had gone to the signal box and found us. James had watched it all from the window, unable to get out because his hands and legs were bound with tape and the doors locked. He had tried shouting but no one had heard. He had tried to reach the horn, but that had been impossible, and then the Commander and the other man had come back. And two minutes later they had heard the police sirens.

"We travelled very fast," James said. "Over a hundred most of the time, I should say. It was very frightening. The Commander knew I was there by then. He wanted to shoot me. He called you all names, dreadful names – I can't repeat them," continued James, "and then without warning he climbed over into the back and said, 'This will give me great pleasure,' and simply opened the door and threw me out."

"We must go in to dinner now," the Colonel said. So James stopped talking and we all trooped into a beautiful dining-room with a high ceiling and lots of gilt.

When we had finished ordering, which took a long time because no one could make up their minds, James continued:

"It seemed ages before anyone came. A dog appeared first and jumped round and round and licked my face and barked; then a snail crossed the road; and then a woman with a little boy came along. I heard the boy say, 'What's that, Mummy?' and Mummy said, 'A dummy.'

"I yelled, 'I'm not a dummy. I'm tied up and I need help.' My head was aching by this time and there was a pool of blood which I was lying in, so that my hair felt awful and my right arm felt completely numb."

"Don't tell us, it's horrible," interrupted Lisa.

"Mummy was very shocked," continued James, "and the little boy kept staring at me with eyes so wide that I was afraid they would fall out. Then Mummy started to run towards a phone box, saying, 'I'll get help,' leaving me lying at the side of the road.

"I think she didn't fancy touching me, you know what some people are like – afraid of blood. I was feeling pretty funny by this time but I remember yelling, 'Untie me, please untie me.' But she didn't stop, and the little boy kept shouting, 'Wait!'"

James pushed away his plate of smoked salmon.

Lisa said, "Go on."

"There isn't much more to tell," continued James. "She never came back, not the Mummy and the little boy, but a man with a dog came on a bike and said,

227

'What's the matter, son? Are you all right?' The understatement of the year, I should say." The waiters were listening now, the whole dining-room had fallen silent. No one seemed to be eating any more.

"So I said, 'No I'm not, mate. I'm b— awful. Can you untie me, please.' He was an old man, and first he leaned his bike against a telegraph pole and then he called his dog, which was called Patch. And all the time the pool of blood was getting bigger. It was terribly frustrating. He was very old and his hands were knotted with rheumatism and I was done up with rope and some frightfully sticky tape, and he kept saying, 'I can't do it, son, I can't do it.'

"And then at last I heard a siren and a police car arrived, and then an ambulance came full of real people who had wonderful scissors and bandages and were calm and reliable. They said, 'Okay. We'll have you on a stretcher inside three minutes. Don't worry.' And they did. It was marvellous," said James, stopping at last. And the waiters started to work again and the other diners went back to their meals.

Mummy leaned forward and kissed James.

Lisa said, "It's like a serial on television, only worse. Did they wash your hair?"

"The nurses did. Everybody in the hospital was marvellous and they got on to the police. But of course it was all spoilt by me being sick. The nurses said it was delayed shock. It was very boring anyway. And then they wanted me to stay in for the night and we had a great argument about that.

"Anyway, here I am at last, with a cracked collarbone, five stitches in my face and twelve in my knee, but otherwise not much the worse for wear. How are all the rest of you? What else happened?" finished James.

We told him as quickly as we could, but there was so

much to tell, and it took a long time. Ben told about the Armstrongs and about what he told the police and how Mrs Armstrong couldn't stop crying. "I wanted to catch up with the Mercedes. I wanted to spit in the Commander's face, just once, but we took the wrong turning and missed the fun," he said.

I told about my ride home and about my passing out. Lisa told about the reporter who was so beautiful that she wanted to marry him, and Mike told about Cassandra's foal and how beautiful it was, the most beautiful thing he had ever seen. And suddenly we all felt happy, except for Mary, who bit her nails and shouted, "I want my camera back!"

Then the grown-ups had coffee and brandy and liqueurs, and James fell asleep in a chair. A middle-aged woman came up and said, "Excuse me. I couldn't help hearing what you were saying. Was it true?"

I nodded and said, "You're not a reporter, are you?"

"No, dear, I'm not," she said "But I think you all sound very brave. Is the dark-haired boy your brother?"

I nodded again and answered, "They both are," and pointed to Ben, and suddenly I felt proud of them, which was something I had never felt before.

The Colonel was paying for the dinner and Mummy was putting on her coat, and Dad was standing behind the Colonel with his wallet in his hand, saying, "Let me help. Please."

But the Colonel simply pushed him away saying, "This is my dinner party."

The moon was shining as we travelled home and we sang in the back of the Land Rover – sad, sentimental songs.

We can't go to school tomorrow, I thought, because the Armstrongs are coming to say goodbye.

The stable-yard was full of shadows when we reached

it. The Cummings' ponies were lying down and so was Cassandra, with her foal by her side. Everything smelled marvellous, of horse and hay and summer. Bed felt marvellous too – like heaven. I undressed and pulled the bedclothes over my head and felt really safe for the first time that day. I thought: Thank goodness it's over. All I want now is peace. And then I slept and slept and slept.

Eleven
The end of it all

When I wakened my room was full of sunlight. I lay in
bed thinking that everything was all right. Paul was with
his parents, Cassandra was with her foal, James was
alive, and I felt quite stupendously happy.

I dressed slowly, looking at the sunlight outside,
thinking that at last summer had come in earnest. James
was still in bed. Ben was mucking out. Mummy was in
the kitchen stacking the dishwasher.

"Bad news," she cried when she saw me. "Look!"
She held out a letter and all my sense of happiness
started to wilt and die. What now? I thought. I took the
letter, which was written on a piece of torn, lined paper
and read:

*Dear Auntie, I have heard from my dad. He knows all
about the kidnap. He knows something else and he
wants me back. He is like the Commander and no good.
I don't think you will want me any more when you
know all. So I am going now. Thank you for everything.
But I can't escape my past.*
Mike

"What does he mean?" Mummy asked in a distracted
voice when I had finished reading. "As if things aren't
bad enough without him adding to them."

"He's been so marvellous," I said. "He's mad to go back."

"I shall have to contact the social services," Mummy said. "I can't leave them in the dark."

"I'll go after him," I answered. "I'll bring him back. We can't manage without him now. You want him back, don't you?"

Mummy looked tired beyond words. "Yes. He must have got a letter this morning. He wasn't here when I came down," she said.

"When did the postman come?"

"Seven-thirty."

And it's nine now, I thought, and cursed myself for staying in bed so long.

I found my crash-cap and ran to the stables. The yard was swept clean. Ben and Solitaire were missing. Lorraine stood waiting by the gate, her sides dirty with dried sweat from yesterday.

Mermaid whinnied hopefully. Cadet banged on his door, wanting to be noticed. I caught Lorraine and tacked her up, wondering where Mike would have gone, alone and worried at seven-thirty in the morning. He could have hitch-hiked miles away by now, or walked to Radcott and caught a bus somewhere, or met his dad in the village and gone for good. But he wouldn't have left a note then, I decided. He had left a note because he wanted to be followed.

We should have been at school. The village was quiet and empty. An old man was cutting the grass in the churchyard, his clothes the same faded colour as the older tombstones. Then I saw another elderly man sitting on the seat which had been presented to the parish at the time of the Coronation of Queen Elizabeth the Second, or so the plaque on it reads.

His name was Mr Parker, and I cantered across to

233

him and yelled, "Good morning, Mr Parker. Have you seen Mike by any chance?"

He pointed to the woods, calling, "He wouldn't speak. I asked him why he wasn't in school, but he wouldn't speak."

I shouted, "Thank you," and gave Lorraine her head. I tried to imagine how I would feel with his sort of father. And it will grow worse, I decided, as he grows more law-abiding. The woods were silent in the sunlight. Bluebells were out like a sudden blue carpet under the tall beech trees. I let Lorraine walk and thought about Paul. We were going to miss him, and if Mike never returned the house would suddenly seem empty. I remembered that none of us had wanted Mike and that we had suspected him of stealing. Ben had even accused him of it, but he had forgiven us. Then I saw him sitting on a stile, a forlorn figure staring across acres of green wheat, a rucksack on his back.

He heard Lorraine's hoofs and turned round. "Why did you come?" he asked. "I don't need you. I can manage now."

"I thought you were going back to your father," I replied. "But you don't have to – we want you back. You don't have to be responsible for your father. It's not your fault he's like he is . . ."

Mike rubbed his forehead with a hand, leaving a dirty mark. "You don't understand, Harriet. 'E wants information. 'E wants help. 'E wants to know about your mum's silver, and you know what that means . . ."

I started to laugh. "Mum hasn't any silver, she sold it all to buy sheets and the freezer when we started the inn. Come back, Mike. We need you," I said.

"You don't understand," he answered, getting off the stile. "I wrote to Dad when he was in prison, telling him about the place. I told him it was ever so posh, that kind

234

of thing. And about Paul and all 'is pocket money and
about the posh school he went to. I didn't mean no
'arm. I just wanted to let him know how happy I was."

"It doesn't matter," I answered. "It doesn't make any
difference."

"You don't understand," he said again, wiping a tear
off his cheek. "The man with the squashed nose is one
of his mates. I'm sure of that. They call him Fish Face,
on account of his nose."

"You can't be sure, you didn't see him."

"It all fits, don't it?" he asked.

I didn't know what to say. For a moment everything

did fit, it was like coming to the last bit of a jigsaw puzzle and putting it in place. We knew now why the Commander had come. And then I remembered the waiting, the suitcases which came first, the big build-up. I remembered Mummy telling us about the Commander and then about Mike.

"But the Commander wrote about coming long before you came," I cried. "He was delayed, that's why you came first. But the whole plan must have been hatched before you ever set eyes on the place. And the social services lady sent you. Your father didn't have anything to do with it, Mike, so you're in the clear. You're okay!" I shouted.

"Are you sure?"

"Yes. Ask Mummy when you get back. The Commander's letter came long before you did."

"I've been a fool, haven't I?" he asked, walking homewards through the woods with me. "But it all seemed to fit."

I nodded. "It doesn't matter," I said.

"He used to beat me and he gave Mum a black eye regular, every Saturday," he said.

I didn't know what to say. He stopped and picked me a bunch of bluebells, though I would rather he had left them growing in the wood.

It was going to be a hot day, and above the trees the sky was an endless blue. "I think we need some fierce dogs," I said as we came to the common at last. "I must ask Dad." The bluebells were already wilting in my hand.

Then I started to run, leading Lorraine, remembering that the Armstrongs were coming to say goodbye. It must be eleven by now I realised with growing panic. They've probably been and gone.

There was a big car parked at the front of the house,

with a chauffeur pacing the drive. Lisa came running to meet us. "They're here!" she shrieked. "They brought Mummy an enormous bottle of perfume and masses of flowers, and Dad the biggest bottle of whisky you've ever seen, and the Colonel a box of cigars, and Mrs Mills a book, and James a watch and me a fantastic book about horses . . . Honestly, they've gone mad, Harriet, they really have."

I left Lorraine in an empty box with her tack on and yelled to Mike to hurry. James shouted, "Here she is," as I rushed into the hall, which was full of suitcases.

Paul said, "I wanted to tell you everything, but there isn't time now."

And I said, "I'm sorry. I wanted to hear what happened to you, but I had to go after Mike."

"We wanted to buy you something special, dear," said Mrs Armstrong. "Give it to her, Bill."

They looked very wealthy standing in the hall dressed for a journey. I looked at my old jodhpurs and dirty boots and felt ashamed.

"I don't deserve anything," I said. "Please."

"We owe you a lot, Harriet," announced Mr Armstrong, stepping forward. "And we want you to accept this gift as a token of our esteem." And he took a gold necklace out of a case and put it round my neck.

"Thank you, thank you very much," I said.

And Paul cried, "You saved my life, Harriet, no kidding."

"Ben was there too, and James," I answered. "But thank you very much. It's lovely."

Paul sat on a case, staring into my face and smiling. Mr Armstrong looked at his watch and shuddered. "We must get going, or we'll never make it," he said.

Lisa sat on the biggest case, yelling at Paul, "You're not going, Paul. I'm not letting you."

237

Then the chauffeur came in and started picking up the cases and Ben pulled her off. Mrs Crispin had arrived and was dusting the banisters and listening to everything. Mike stood clutching a ten-pound note, Mary had some chocolates. It was like Christmas, but sad too, because now we were saying goodbye.

Mummy kissed Paul, Paul kissed Lisa, Lisa started to cry.

"You're all to come and stay – okay?" asked Paul in a shaky voice, beginning to cry too.

"We'll miss the plane," shouted Mr Armstrong from outside.

· "Thanks, honey," said Mrs Armstrong, kissing me on the cheek, then kissing Ben and James and Lisa, saying, "I think you're the greatest family. I do really, the very greatest."

"We're not, we're hopeless," I answered, thinking that life must go on regardless of how miserable we were feeling now.

The chauffeur stacked the last of the cases in the biggest boot I had ever seen.

"You must come on a visit. We'll be living in the mountains right near the old Apache trails," called Paul.

"Be seeing you," I yelled.

They were waving now, going out of our lives, perhaps for ever.

"I am going to stay with them," Lisa announced. "I'm going to marry Paul."

"Not that again. I thought it was going to be the reporter," moaned Ben.

Everything seemed suddenly quiet. Lisa wiped her eyes.

"Nice to have you back, Mike," said Mummy, turning towards the house.

"Nice to be back," replied Mike.

"They must have spent a fortune, an absolute fortune," mused Ben.

Dad was in the hall, looking at the newspaper. "Have you seen yourselves? Look, you're in it," he said.

I took it from him and saw a photo of me sitting in the kitchen, looking half dead, and suddenly I didn't want to remember that moment, it was too awful to remember.

"'Mystery kidnap of American boy'," read Lisa. "And look at me." She stared at herself. There was another photograph of the house. "I look awful," she said. "My tummy is sticking out."

"It always does," replied Ben.

"What did Paul say?" I asked. "What really happened to him?"

"It's a long story, and we haven't much time," replied Ben. "Let's exercise the ponies and talk as we ride. The Cummings rang up to ask after their ponies and was I embarrassed!"

239

"I bet. What did you say?" I asked, searching for my cap.

"All sorts of tripe about them settling in very well."

I felt happy suddenly, happy that it was all over, happy in a way I had never felt before. I wanted to sing, to turn somersaults, to shout, "Everything's all right. We're safe, alive, safe. And the Armstrongs are safe too." I wanted to thank someone for my happiness.

We were both running now, laughing, free of tension at last. We tacked up the ponies. I rode Mermaid because she was the smallest. She had a short, quick stride and didn't want to leave the stable-yard. Her neck was thick, and dappled like a rocking-horse. Cadet went sideways all the time, which made conversation difficult.

"He needs to learn the turn on the forehand," Ben said. "He hasn't the faintest idea what my legs mean."

"What about Paul?" I asked.

"What about him?"

"What did he say?"

"That he ached all over."

"No, the story! What actually happened?" I shrieked.

"Well, the Commander was all right at first," said Ben, pulling Cadet into a walk. "He bought Paul lots of beer at the Crooked Billet and a pork pie and a bag of crisps, and Paul felt rather funny. Then they rode on and Paul felt funnier still, and then suddenly the Commander said, 'This is where we leave the horses,' and there was the Mercedes with Squashed Nose in it. And Paul says he said, 'You can't just leave them here, they'll be killed, and what about the tack?' But our dear Commander just bundled him into the car and off they went, driving here and there for what seemed hours, and then ending up in a house which seemed to belong to Squashed Nose. It smelled terrible and the curtains were kept drawn all the time, and they ate nothing but sausages and mash, and

Paul kept worrying about the horses but he couldn't do anything because one of them watched him all the time."

"Poor Paul!" I said.

"He was really scared by this time," continued Ben, "but the Commander was very nice really. He talked politics all the time, mostly about a chap called Karl Marx, and they played cards, and then Paul had a drink of something which must have been drugged, because the next thing he knew he was in the signal box tied to a stool. He shouted and shouted, but no one heard. Then he started to pray and he was scared, and then he spent ages singing and thinking how great the United States is and how he might never see the land of his fathers again. And then suddenly he heard us and was he pleased!"

"No kidding . . . So he didn't suffer too much?" I asked.

Ben nodded, shortening his reins. "He was terribly upset about the horses and Mr Armstrong wanted to pay for Cassandra's treatment – quite mad when we shouldn't have let Paul go out with the Commander in the first place. They could have sued us for negligence," replied Ben.

"Instead they gave us wonderful presents . . ."

"That's Americans for you – they're so jolly nice," replied Ben.

"Touch wood; they may sue us yet," I cried, reaching for a tree-trunk.

"They can't change their minds now," said Ben, laughing.

"I shall miss Paul," I said.

"Not as much as Lisa," replied Ben. "Did you read the paper?"

I shook my head. "It's peculiar, but I don't want to read it," I said. "I don't think they should make money out of other people's misery, do you? And it was misery, wasn't it?"

We were trotting now and there was sunlight everywhere.

"It's all wrong in the paper anyway," Ben said. "They call Paul an ambassador's son. The police say that the Commander is only an amateur at crime, and he

242

certainly botched the kidnapping, didn't he?"

"Yes, but we shouldn't call him the Commander any more."

"He'll always be the Commander to me," replied Ben.

"He's just a wolf in sheep's clothing," I said. "We must get some fierce dogs who know the difference . . ." And I saw us crossing the common with a couple of dogs running ahead of us, the house full of children and the exhaustion gone from Mummy's face, and suddenly life was full of hope again.

Secrets at
Black Pony Inn

CONTENTS

One

Are they boys or girls?

It was July. Outside everything was parched brown and yellow by drought. The sky was a cloudless, endless blue, when all we wanted was rain. Two of the oak-trees were dying in the straight-railed paddocks, and autumn flowers were blooming already in the flower-beds.

Mummy was pacing up and down the kitchen with her hands plunged deep in her apron pockets. My eldest brother, dark-haired James, was reading the newspaper while Lisa, who was nearly ten, was plaiting the mane on a toy horse. Ben, who has fair hair and brown eyes, was reading about splints and spavins. I was thirteen, with straight hair which never stayed in place and a straight nose which I hated.

"We are not doing very well," said Mummy, and we all knew at once that she was talking about our guest house, Black Pony Inn. "We have the Colonel and old Mrs Mills, and Mike who will be leaving soon to get a job. That's all, and their money is hardly enough to pay the council tax and keep the roof over our heads. Even the ponies aren't paying for themselves any more."

"I was thinking we might run a horse show in aid of ourselves. Is that allowed?" asked Lisa, who is given to mad ideas. "Or what about a sponsored ride?"

"Definitely not," snapped Ben.

"However, there is hope," continued Mummy as

though no one had spoken. "A fantastic man called yesterday in a huge car. He asked if we would have his three children and their ponies for three weeks. I've said yes. He's ringing today to let us know definitely."

"What do you mean by 'fantastic'?" asked James, looking shrewd.

"Film star-ish!"

"Oh, Mummy!" cried Lisa. "How romantic!"

"Will he pay up when the moment comes?" asked Ben.

"All in notes, in advance, he's that sort of chap," said Mummy, laughing.

"Can we have some money for the ponies?" asked Ben. "Enough to buy their hay, but vet's bills and shoes will have to be extra; also individual lessons. I'll explain that when he comes. What's he called?"

"Mick Travers, that's what he said. He simply held out his hand and, nearly crushing mine, said, 'Mrs Pemberton? I'm Mick Travers,'" related Mummy. It was obvious that he had made a great impression.

"Make sure you count the money when it comes," said James. "He sounds too good to be true – and we've been fooled before."

"Exactly," agreed Ben. "You know we agreed everyone had to bring references. I hope he's got some really good ones. Did the Colonel see him?"

"I'm not sure. There's the telephone. That will be him. He promised to telephone at ten. It's all right, then?" asked Mummy.

"With references," called Ben.

"And with money in advance," shouted James.

"I hope the children don't need looking after all the time. I hope they're tough and independent. Do you think I shall be able to school their ponies?" asked Lisa.

I was listening to Mummy talking, saying, "Yes, that

will be lovely – teatime then. Yes, they'll be in next door rooms."

"References," shouted Ben.

"Yes, and some references, the bank insists, yes, and our accountants. You know how accountants are. We've been taken in once or twice. I'm so sorry," said Mummy. "Yes, lovely, thanks a million . . . Yes . . . Bye.

"Everything's all right. They'll be here at teatime – references and all," she said, replacing the receiver.

"We can't check the references if they bring them. We should have had them days ago. Oh, Mummy, you've got no business sense at all, you're hopeless," wailed Ben.

Dad was in London. Colonel Hunter had gone for a walk, swinging a walking-stick belonging to an age when India was ours. Mrs Mills was wrestling with weeds among the strawberries, looking like a strange bird scratching for worms. Our horses stood by the yard gate head to tail. "What are their ponies like?" I asked.

"Small, I believe," Mummy answered.

Ben raised his eyes upwards as though saying, "Heaven help us, she hasn't even asked."

"What about the children? I hope they're my age. Are they boys or girls?" cried Lisa, suddenly sounding excited.

"Two girls and a boy – Marion, Sally and Kenny. Kenny's the youngest," answered Mummy.

"They're not babies, are they?"

"No, seven to eleven."

"What about their mother?" asked Lisa.

"She didn't come," Mummy answered.

"Poor kids, with no mother around," I said. "And they don't sound big enough for a pony each."

"Perhaps their mum's dead – you know, in a car accident," suggested Lisa.

251

"Could be," replied Mummy. "But are you happy about having the ponies? They're probably tiny and terribly fat. And the money will pay the butcher, the baker and the candlestickmaker, not to mention the council tax," cried Mummy, dancing round the kitchen.

I went outside. My grey mare Lorraine was waiting to come in. I put her in one of the old-fashioned loose boxes which have Staffordshire brick floors and ancient, expensive brass fittings. Flies were everywhere. On the common outside, the gorse and bracken were already dry and the village pond was nothing but a puddle.

I thought of our paying guests who had come and gone – Mary who had caused us so much trouble, but was now abroad studying French; Commander Cooley; and Paul Armstrong, an American. They had all been nice in some way or other, but they had caused havoc in our lives. I hoped the three new children wouldn't be the same; they would miss their parents, of course, and cry themselves to sleep. Their ponies would be fat and ill-mannered. But three weeks isn't long, I thought. Even if we hate them, time will pass and their money will buy us oats and pony nuts. And they are too young to cause havoc.

Ben came to stand beside me. "She's hopeless, isn't she?" he asked.

"Who?"

"Mummy. She's got no business sense at all. Mick Travers sounds a phoney to me, and where is Mrs Travers?"

"I expect they're getting a divorce," I answered. "Anyway it's nothing to do with us."

Ben led his Welsh cob, Solitaire, into a stable, Cassie and her foal were waiting to come in, and so were Limpet and Lisa's piebald, Jigsaw. I suddenly felt old and filled with trepidation. I knew that my brothers were right; Mummy is too kind and trusting – gullible, Dad calls it – and anyone can fool her. I imagined Mick Travers looking like Paul Newman, Mummy's favourite film star. I imagined him tricking us as Commander Cooley had done.

The notes will be stolen notes, I thought. The bank will send them back, and we will be poorer than ever.

We climbed the railed fence and walked to the lower paddock. "There isn't any grass," said Ben, kicking dry earth with one foot. "And it isn't growing, so the Travers's ponies had better be fat."

"I'd better help Mummy get the attic ready. I hope I don't have to sleep with them. I like having my own room, even if it does still smell of Mary," I said.

"Dad will be surprised when he comes back. I wonder if he's got the job," replied Ben.

Once Dad had owned a factory but taxes and high wages had killed it. He's been looking for a job ever since without any success. He's self-educated and he made his money the hard way. He speaks his mind and is blunt and down-to-earth. Mummy is the opposite. She was educated in a convent and, like Lisa, is full of dreams and romance. They both make stories out of nothing and believe what they are told, automatically, without question. James and Ben are more wary and I'm somewhere in between. Dad gives everyone the benefit of the doubt, but he can be ruthless if it's needed. We all worry about money – it's almost an obsession with us, probably because we never have enough. We all go to the same school, except for Lisa who's still at primary, but in the autumn James will be transferring to our local Sixth Form College. Ben plans to be a vet. I shall work with horses; perhaps I shall go to America or Italy. I haven't decided yet. I want to explore the world of horses from one continent to another. Lisa plans to marry a millionaire and breed palominos.

I found Mummy shaking mats. "It will be lovely to have the house full again," she said.

The attic rooms had been redecorated by James and Ben, and the walls were covered with blue horses prancing across primrose wallpaper. The paint on the windows had run a little. There were rush mats on the floor and a white chest of drawers for each bed. It was all a little like a school dormitory. We made up two beds in the first room and a bed for Kenny in the one beyond. Then we left the windows open and hurried downstairs

to prepare lunch, while I tried to imagine Mick Travers sipping tea, his children chasing each other, shrieking with laughter. But I knew it wouldn't be that simple, because parents don't leave their children with strangers if they love them. Deep down within myself, I knew there must be a problem – something terrible must have happened, terrible for the children at any rate; and that we would have to deal with the misery which was left!

Horses are easier to manage, I thought, they learn to trust you and then they love you. I thought of Lorraine who had come to us so thin and wild, and of Cassie who had come from the market too, unexpectedly in foal, and how easily they had settled down and become happy.

I prayed, God, please make the Travers children normal and happy too, I can't bear any more complications. I remembered Mary and her secrets and Paul with his sick horse, and then I thought: It's too much to hope, Harriet, you oaf, they'll probably be scarred for life. I thought of Mike who was working spare time on the farm and how he had come to us through Social Services, because his father was in prison. And suddenly I saw how lucky we were with a house and parents and ponies, even if we were constantly short of money.

Colonel Hunter had come back from his walk and was in the garden, shouting at Mrs Mills because she wasn't wearing her hearing-aid and so couldn't hear him. "Who was that fellow who came yesterday evening?" he shouted. "Shifty sort, I thought, with more money than sense. I hope he's not going to be a guest."

"No. His children are coming, I think," shouted Mrs Mills. "I don't know where their mother is, poor little things."

"He's no good, I should say," replied Colonel Hunter.

Ben had his radio on and a newsreader was talking about the drought. Lisa was chasing Twinkle, our cat, round and round the kitchen table, and every moment the day was growing hotter.

"Four hours to go," said Mummy.

"Until what?" I asked.

"Until the arrival of the Traverses and their ponies," cried Mummy, looking about thirty years old and not at all like the mother of four children.

Two

Sick ponies

They came in a matching Range Rover and trailer. The children were pale and neat. They stepped into the yard without speaking.

"They look as though they're sleepwalking," gasped Lisa.

"Travers is the name," said Mick Travers, holding out his hand. His hair was greying at the sides. His eyes were brown. He was dressed in expensive trainers, in casual clothes which you knew had cost a fortune.

Ben was throwing down the ramp. Lisa was riding, and she said, "This is Jigsaw. Which of you is which?" to the children, who were standing quite still, one girl sucking her finger, another looking at the ground, and the boy twisting a handkerchief round and round in his hands.

The tallest one spoke. "I'm Sally, she's Marion, he's Kenny," she whispered.

The ponies were small and thin, so thin that my heart sank when I saw them. There was a roan, a grey and a chestnut with two white socks. Mick Travers threw up the ramp. "No time to waste. We're catching a plane," he said, throwing me a plastic bag stuffed with notes. "No need to count, it's all there," he added.

Mummy appeared, her hair on end. "References," she gasped. "You promised us references."

"They're all here," he said, handing her an envelope through the Range Rover's window.

"What about next of kin? Your address?" cried Mummy.

"It's there too. Got to catch a plane," he said, starting the engine. The children didn't say goodbye, nobody did.

Kenny simply went on twisting the handkerchief in his hands and Sally held on to Marion, while Ben and I turned their ponies out into the bottom paddock. "They look pretty lifeless," he said.

"Children or ponies?" I asked.

"Both."

"I didn't have time to count the money," I said, handing it to Mummy.

"He sure wanted to get rid of them, didn't he?" said Ben.

I nodded. I was feeling upset now. All my worst fears were coming true. Obviously we had three problem children on our hands and three starving ponies. And life has taught me that money doesn't always compensate for problems – however much there is.

The children were following Mummy towards the house. She was talking in a new, bright voice which I had never heard before.

"I expect you could do with some tea. Do you like the country?" she asked.

"I can't bear it," said Lisa, dismounting. "They're absolutely pathetic. They don't even speak. They're going to ruin the holidays. But wasn't their father smashing? Wow!"

"Probably a sheep in wolf's clothing," replied Ben, laughing. "We had better worm the ponies tomorrow and inspect their teeth. They're going to need extra food."

258

"And that means money," I added before he had time to say it.

Indoors there was a special tea laid on in the dining-room, which smelled of furniture polish. There was bread and honey, and one of Mummy's fruit cakes and a whole pile of shop cakes. The Travers children sipped milk and ate almost nothing. Sally said that she was ten, Marion nine, and Kenny nearly eight. Kenny went on twisting his handkerchief in his small white hands, and Marion sucked her thumb.

"What are your ponies called?" asked Lisa.

"Jack and Jill and Little Bo-Peep," answered Sally in a whisper.

After tea Lisa asked them to play Happy Families and reluctantly they disappeared in the direction of her bedroom.

"They don't look right to me," said Mrs Mills. "They look battered – you know what I mean."

"Or shattered," suggested James.

"I knew it would be like this," I cried, suddenly over-come with rage. "We never have anyone ordinary, sane, down-to-earth. Everybody who comes here has some ghastly problem. It isn't fair. I wish they had never come."

"Perhaps they are shy," said Mrs Mills. "Little chil-dren often are, you know."

"Their ponies are rotten too," I continued. "If they are skin and bone in July, what were they like in Janu-ary? And why didn't their beastly father stay? He didn't even kiss his kids goodbye or slap them on the back. He didn't do anything. He wasn't like a father at all."

"Steady on," said Colonel Hunter. "Don't be too harsh. You shouldn't judge people on one meeting."

"He's given a banker's reference and one from a Roman Catholic priest," said Mummy. "Do you think they are Roman Catholics? If so, they ought to go to church."

"Whatever they are, they're hopeless and their ponies have only got felt saddles and horrible little snaffles without nosebands," complained Ben. "Let's go and look at them properly. Coming, Harriet?"

The sky was still cloudless. We had come to accept the endless fine days, the parched lawn and the dusty fields.

"I knew it would be like this," I said again.

"The money's real. I looked. And they are only here for three weeks," replied Ben.

"Money isn't everything."

The ponies were coughing when we reached the lower paddock.

"It's the dust," said Ben.

"But their noses are running too," I replied.

"It could still be dust," argued Ben.

"Or something else," I answered, climbing through the fence. "I knew there was something wrong with them as soon as they got out of the trailer."

"They're sweating," muttered Ben, feeling their shoulders.

"And they've drunk from the water bath and probably touched noses with our horses by now," I said.

"We'll have to take their temperatures," replied Ben, thinking out loud.

They were friendly ponies, but their heads drooped and their eyes had little life in them, and every few moments they trembled.

"Poor, poor little ponies," I said, my arms round their necks. "Poor sick ponies, you are going to be all right now." And I thought at the same time: Supposing our horses catch whatever they've got? What then? And I saw the vet coming every day and the bills mounting

261

and Ben talking endlessly about money.

And everyone would grumble at Mummy because she had not stuck to the rules of the establishment, because nobody had signed anything; so if the ponies died Mick Travers could even sue us for negligence.

The ponies all had temperatures, the little chestnut was the worst.

"I'll make them bran mashes with black treacle in them," I said.

"We'll have to have Roy," said Ben. "At once, and he will charge extra because it's after hours." Roy is our vet. He's handsome in a rugged way and we all love him, but his bills can be devastating, and he likes to be called at the beginning of an illness, not halfway through.

"We'll have to explain everything," I said.

"Of course," answered Ben, going towards the house with bent shoulders as though he carried all the worries of the world on them.

I looked at the ponies a moment longer. Their ribs protruded and their necks were pathetically thin. Their shoes were only partly attached to their small, mis-shapen hoofs. They looked as though they had been worked too young, too much, and fed too little. Looking at them made me want to cry. In a strange way they resembled their owners; they had the same battered, hopeless look about them, as though nothing in the future could ever be as bad as what had happened in the past. Our horses were staring at them over the fence, wondering why they wouldn't come forward to sniff noses. They looked rich by comparison, I thought sadly, turning towards the house.

The children were still upstairs with Lisa. Mummy was preparing supper. "I'll feed them and Lisa first. Do you think they will eat ice cream?" she asked.

"I don't know. Their ponies are ill and I think they are sickening for something too – smallpox or typhoid, I expect," I answered gloomily.

"More like anaemia. They need feeding up," replied Mummy, breaking eggs into a basin.

"Roy's coming. He's doing the evening surgery first, but he expects to be through by six," said Ben, appearing. "How about the mashes?"

I ran to the forage room and filled a bucket with bran. Our horses neighed hopefully and dug in the dust with their hoofs. There were flies everywhere and no break in the sky. I boiled a kettle, poured a tin of black treacle on to the bran and then some hot water and stirred it all with a wooden spoon.

Then Lisa came into the kitchen. "I've showed them their rooms," she said guiltily. "I didn't know what else to do. Marion can't do anything. I think she's goofy. She won't speak. Sally says she's withdrawn. What does 'withdrawn' mean, Mummy?"

"Keeping out of things, not speaking," replied Mummy in a distracted voice.

"Kenny doesn't speak much either and Sally's awfully quiet. They're not like normal children," Lisa said.

Mummy looked at me. "Go and see them, Harriet darling, please. You're so good with small children," she said.

"But I'm making a mash," I answered. "And supposing Roy comes?" I added.

"Ben can deal with him."

"But I want to know what he says. I do really care about poor Jack and Jill and Little Bo-Peep," I argued.

"Please," pleaded Mummy.

"Why is it always me?" I asked.

"It isn't. I've been struggling with them for nearly an hour!" said Lisa.

"Why can't Ben go?" I asked, putting a towel over the mash.

"Because I might lose my temper and bash them up," he answered, smiling.

"Well, call me when Roy comes," I answered, going out of the kitchen.

The rooms in the attic face west and were full of the evening sun. Sally was sitting on a bed reading to the others who were sitting close to her, Marion sucking her thumb, Kenny still twisting his handkerchief in his hands. She was reading *Alice in Wonderland*. She looked up as I entered the room. "I'm being Mummy," she said. "She used to read this to us every evening. She read much better than me. I get stuck on some of the words."

"Would you like me to read it to you?" I asked. "I would like to because actually I've never read *Alice in Wonderland*."

"Yes, please," said Sally, making room for me on the bed.

I sat down, longing to be outside with Ben in the yard, half of me subconsciously listening for Roy's car.

"I've reached the bottom of the page," said Sally.

Soon I will ask them where Mummy is, I thought, but not yet, not until tomorrow.

I read until my eyes ached and my throat was dry. When I put down the book Marion was crying.

"What's the matter? What is it?" I asked.

"She often cries like that," said Sally, suddenly sounding old and responsible.

"Doesn't she talk?" I asked.

"Not often."

It was as though we were talking about a doll, a dog,

something which didn't understand. I wanted to scream, "Speak. Why don't you? Please speak."

"She used to talk, once upon a time," said Sally in a matter-of-fact way. "Then one day she stopped."

Kenny nodded in agreement.

Mummy called, "Supper."

"We don't have supper," said Sally. "Just milk and biscuits on a tray, please, and an apple each to clean our teeth. That's what Daddy gives us in the evening."

"But it's ready," I answered.

"No thank you, just the same. Marion isn't up to it, just milk and biscuits, please."

"There's ice cream," I insisted.

"No thank you."

I ran downstairs, glad to escape from the weird atmosphere in the attic.

"They want milk and biscuits and apples in their rooms," I told Mummy. "So forget the ice cream."

"They can't."

"They do; and they're all yours now," I cried, running outside to where I could see Roy's car parked, and then everything seemed brighter and clearer because I had escaped, because I wasn't bound by some unspeakable misery like the Travers children.

Three

No horse shows

Roy removed his stethoscope.

"They are pretty ill," he said. "And have been for some time. The chestnut's the worst. I hope he will pull through. They should have been treated months ago; their lungs are permanently damaged by now. The chestnut may still be infectious. The other two are past that stage; but for all of them it's touch and go."

"Isn't there anything you can do?" I asked.

"I can try an antibiotic, but remember it should have been administered weeks ago, now is a little late. And I can inject them with vitamin B," continued Roy, walking towards his car. "Where did they come from?"

"I don't know," replied Ben. "They came with three small children."

"Without parents?" asked Roy, staring at us in complete disbelief.

"They've brought references," I answered after a short silence, while Roy filled his syringe.

"And an address where their parents can be reached?" asked Roy.

I shook my head.

"Well, they can talk presumably; so you can ask them!" exclaimed Roy, sticking a needle into the chestnut's neck.

"The children or the ponies?" I asked.

"The children, of course."

"They are not very communicative, and they only arrived at teatime, and they're very tired," I answered.

"It is important," said Roy, as though I was being
tiresome. "I want to know where these ponies came
from and how long they've been ill. If I don't know, I
can't treat them effectively."

I ran to the house, up the stairs, and then up the second flight to the attic. The sun was still shining but the
Travers children were already in bed, looking neat and
washed. Kenny looked tiny, and Marion was sucking
her finger again. I sat down on Sally's bed.

"The vet wants to know where your ponies came
from. They're not very well; he wants to make them better," I said.

268

"From a farm with big gables, and a pond with trees round it, and ducks," replied Sally.

"The name? Do you know the name?" I asked impatiently, imagining Roy stamping up and down outside, waiting to leave.

"It had sheep too and lots and lots of ponies," she continued, sitting up, smelling of scented soap.

"Which county? Herts, Berks, Bucks, London? You must remember," I asked.

"Well, I don't. I was very upset at the time." Sally was beginning to cry.

"It doesn't matter then," I said. "But it would be nice if you could think back. Do try, it's important."

She shut her eyes and then, opening them again, said, "I'm sorry, it's no good, it's a blank. I can only remember the house and the pond and the trees."

"Well," called Ben, coming into the house, "what do they say?"

"Nothing. The ponies came from a farm with gables, a pond and trees, that's all," I answered.

"Did you ask them all?"

"No. Kenny looked too small and Marion doesn't talk," I replied.

"They must know," cried Ben, standing in the kitchen, smelling of horse and antiseptic, clutching a bottle of cough syrup.

"They seem to be in a state of shock," I answered. "Try and understand."

"I shall go mad in a minute," said Mummy, chopping parsley. "Must you always argue in the kitchen?"

I ran back to the yard with Ben. "No luck," I told Roy.

"Well, I need their address anyway. They are going to get a pretty hefty bill and I don't suppose you want to pay it, do you?" he asked with a faint smile.

I ran back to the kitchen. Mummy was frying potatoes. "Not you again?" she cried, exasperated.

"Roy wants Mick Travers' address before he goes," I said. "It's urgent."

"I haven't got it," replied Mummy. "I'm sorry, but there it is."

"But you must have, it's for the bill," I cried. My heart was fluttering in a funny way now. I thought of the bill coming to us – dozens and dozens of expensive injections, tens of visits – it could be for hundreds of pounds! "You must have it," I cried. "Supposing one of the children dies, is killed under a bus, what then?"

"We will have to contact the priest. I'm writing to the bank address tomorrow for references for Mick Travers and for his home address, so don't worry, darling, everything will be all right," replied Mummy, shaking the potato pan. "You must learn to trust people more. It's awful to be so suspicious. And the bank is sure to have his address."

"But what am I to tell Roy?"

"Tell him to send the bill care of here. Stop worrying," replied Mummy.

"The bill is to come to Mr Travers, care of here," I told Roy, who said simply, "Will do."

We watched him drive away in silence.

Then Ben said, "Which means Mummy hasn't any home address for those weak-kneed kids."

"She thinks we should trust Mick Travers," I answered.

"I don't trust anyone," replied Ben.

The ill ponies looked a little better already. We gave them more mashes, laced with the cough medicine, which they hated. Meanwhile, our horses, madly jealous, pawed the ground and neighed hopefully, their eyes following us, imploring us for feeds.

270

"We have to take our animals' temperatures every day. The moment they start to rise, we must phone Roy; if we can catch the infection at the beginning, it won't be so bad," explained Ben in a deadpan voice, with a slight choke behind it, so that I knew he was trying not to break down. "We needn't start yet, because the incubation period is several days," he added.

"Mick Travers should be called Lucifer, because he's like the devil, isn't he?" I said bitterly. "Just imagine the misery he must have caused in his life."

"We're to move our ponies into the paddock by the yard, so that they can't sniff noses any more, just in case they haven't caught the disease already," said Ben. "There isn't any grass but that can't be helped. We'll have to feed hay, it's cheaper than the vet's bills."

I felt numb. What was happening was too awful for tears. I knew that we were too poor to pay immense vet's bills, the money just wasn't there. Not in the bank, nor in the house, nor anywhere else. We were almost down to our last penny, that's why Mummy had accepted the Travers' so recklessly. It was enough money to save us from having the telephone cut off; and it would pay for the Land Rover's MOT and our twice-weekly help to clean the house. I couldn't blame Mummy. What she had done wasn't criminal. The money looked all right, and how could she know that the ponies would be sick when they came?

"No horse shows, no hunter trials, no Pony Club," said Ben. "Because even if they haven't got it, they can still carry it." He started to swear, to pick up stones and hurl them at nothing, using words I had never heard him use before. "Why can't we be rich?" he shouted. "Why haven't we got sane, sensible parents like other people?"

"There's no such thing. Look at what we have got – a lovely place in which to live, horses galore. Count your

271

blessings," I lectured. "We've got enough to eat, two legs, eyes, ears . . ."

"Oh shut up," he shouted. "You're just pathetic."

We're falling apart, I thought, imagining catastrophe that hasn't even happened. Our horses may not catch the infection. Mummy may find the Travers home address tomorrow. The children must know it. Any child over seven knows its home address.

"You're making a mountain out of a molehill," I shouted. That's the way it goes, I thought, when I'm miserable and frightened, he's the opposite, and now he's in a state, I feel quite calm. Why?

Dad was home when we went indoors, standing in the kitchen, saying, "I don't think I got it. They wanted someone they could boss around and I'm no good at taking orders. Anyway, I don't think the firm is quite straight."

He looked uncomfortable in his suit, and a mixture

of my two brothers except that his dark hair, which is just like James's, is peppered with grey, and Ben's brown eyes are lighter than his.

"We've got some strange guests," said Mummy. "And look at this! Count it! Sit down, darling, and I'll tell you everything." But Dad was already counting the money.

Next door James was playing his radio full blast, because Colonel Hunter was out to dinner with an elderly lady he had met in church, and Mrs Mills is too deaf to mind. She was already eating supper. She's always hungry and hates waiting, so often she eats at a corner of the kitchen table, nibbling quickly like a small animal, still in her pinny, with bedroom slippers on her feet, not at all like a paying guest. Lisa had not waited either. She had made herself two vast doorstep sandwiches and she was wolfing them down at a disgusting rate.

James appeared and made himself a mug of coffee, then he left, spilling it as he walked.

"I see we have our problems. But they can wait until tomorrow," said Dad, handing back the money. "Just now I think we could do with a drink. After all, we are in funds again, so if you don't mind I'll just slip down to the pub and get something to brighten up supper."

He kissed Mummy and, finding a shopping bag, disappeared in the direction of our local pub.

"Be an angel, Harriet, and just dash upstairs and look at our new guests," said Mummy.

I found them neat and tidy in their beds. Sally had her hands crossed in front of her on her counterpane. Kenny still had his handkerchief in one hand. Marion's face was gleaming wet with tears.

We've sorted out the ponies today, and it will be their turn tomorrow, I thought. The day seemed to have lasted for a week already and it seemed days since teatime. I imagined Mick Travers dining somewhere exotic,

273

while his children wept and his ponies grew worse. None of us could do it, I thought. We would be worrying about what we had left behind. Mummy can't leave us for a day without telephoning to say, "Are you all right?"

I could hear Dad coming back, whistling merrily. Mummy was scolding James for the spilt coffee. It was the end of another day. I stood hoping that tomorrow would be better, staring at the horses outside through the passage window, at the three ponies grazing painfully as though their throats hurt, at our own horses gazing into the distance, refusing to eat the few blades of grass pushing dry, withered heads through the cracked earth.

"Please God, make things better tomorrow," I prayed, going downstairs.

Mike, who has red hair and freckles, had returned from the farm, bearing dead rabbits. "Here, Auntie, I thought we could have these tomorrow," he said to Mummy.

But Lisa screamed, "You beast, you beast, killing rabbits! I won't eat them. How can you do it?"

"I didn't. Pete Symons did it, I just drove the Land Rover," replied Mike, swinging the rabbits by their legs and laughing.

"Dinner," cried Mummy. "Thank you very much, Mike. Go and wash now, there's a good boy." And I thought: Mike isn't a boy any more; he's an adolescent and that's quite different. Then I thought: We'll all be grown up soon, and I wanted time to stand still. I didn't want to grow up.

Four

Get them out, Harriet

It was raining in the morning. We had been wanting rain for weeks, but not now, with three sick ponies standing outside with almost no shelter. I leaped out of bed and rushed to Ben's room. His fair hair was all that was visible above the sheets. "It's raining," I cried. "What are we to do with the ponies? They'll die."

"We can't put them in, they'll infect the stables; we can't risk it," cried Ben, sitting up.

"What about waterproof rugs?"

"They'll infect them too."

"I'm going to look at them anyway," I answered, running back to my room to dress.

James had his radio on already. Mrs Mills was eating toast and marmalade at the kitchen table. Colonel Hunter was looking for letters in the hall, wearing an ancient tartan dressing-gown and a thick scarf wrapped round his ancient neck.

I unbolted the back door and ran through the rain to the bottom paddock; the ponies were standing huddled together, like people waiting miserably for a bus on a wet day. I fetched them feeds of oats and they cheered up a little and arched their thin necks, but the oats dribbled out of their mouths when they ate, so I knew that their throats were still sore. There was nothing wrong with our own horses.

275

Cassie's foal was trotting in circles as though she was a ballet dancer on tiptoe. My grey mare, Lorraine, was grazing. Dun Solitaire stood with his back to the rain, Jigsaw and Limpet grazed shoulder to shoulder. They all looked healthy enough.

But how long will it take them to become infected, I wondered, walking back towards the house – a week, ten days, a month? When can we look at one another and say it's all right, we're in the clear, they're not going to get it after all?

Mummy was making tea in the kitchen, while Twinkle, our cat, purred round her legs. "Your father's going to take up Mick Travers' references today," she said. "We can't go on as we are. Will you wake the children up and find out if they're Catholics. It is important because Catholics have to go to church."

"I know all that. I just wish they had never come; just looking at their poor ponies makes me feel ill," I answered.

Mrs Mills was washing up her breakfast things. "Isn't it nice to see some rain," she said. "Everything will start growing again."

"Do you think there's something wrong with Marion, Harriet, really, truthfully?" asked Mummy, looking worried.

"Yes," I said. "Definitely. I think she's very strange, crazy-mad." I only half meant what I said but Mummy took me seriously.

"Don't say that again, not ever," she cried. "I won't believe it. She's had a shock, something awful has happened. We've got to find out what; once they've told us, they will be all right. But they mustn't go round carrying it inside them any longer, poor little things. You must help, Harriet, please. You're older than Lisa and kinder than Ben. You're our only hope."

"Their pale faces frighten me, they look so fragile," I answered. "I'm scared of them. Marion cries in her sleep. I don't know anything about children; I prefer horses, they're easier to understand and much more friendly."

"But *you* are a child," argued Mummy.

"Not like them. Not knotted up inside and scared, and so clean. I tear about banging doors. Can you imagine them doing that? They creep about like ghosts. It's horrible. They aren't like children. They're like zombies."

"Don't shout," said Mummy. "I hear footsteps. It could be them."

But it wasn't. It was Lisa. She charged into the kitchen crying, "Are they dead?"

"Who?"

"The ponies, *their* ponies. They don't care, do they? They know they are ill but they don't ask after them. They're horrible."

"Don't," cried Mummy.

"But it's true," cried Lisa.

"Take them riding on Limpet and Jigsaw when it stops raining. Please," pleaded Mummy. "They've got the loveliest riding-clothes."

"They're ruining the holidays," cried Lisa. "Why do we have to run a beastly guest house? Why can't we be like other people?"

"Oh, go and do your hair and wash your face," said Mummy wearily. "You took terrible – your hair is in a mess and your teeth are turning yellow for want of cleaning. Why can't you be nice?"

"Like them, I suppose," cried Lisa, running out of the kitchen. It was still raining so hard that you could hear it running down the gutters.

"What are we going to do with them this morning?"

277

asked Mummy. "Will you play hide and seek with them?"

"If Marion will play," I answered, filling a bowl with cereal. "And if Kenny will put down his handkerchief long enough to hide."

Then the telephone rang and Mummy hurried into the hall to answer it. She returned saying, "More prospective guests, but I said no. We really can't cope with anyone else at the moment, can we?"

"Definitely not," I agreed, "though it's a pity to turn people away."

"Two keen walkers rang up yesterday. I said no to them too," continued Mummy. "It's no good having people if we haven't the time to look after them."

Later on the Traverses came down and ate breakfast. Marion didn't speak. Sally made grown-up conversation about the weather.

"Your ponies are out in it," cried Lisa at last, hating them because Mummy was spending so much time with them. "They are ill. You know that, don't you? But you don't care. You don't even ask about them."

"We haven't had them very long, and we're not horsy," said Sally in a firm grown-up voice. "Daddy bought them for us, because he thought it might help, but it didn't."

"Didn't what?" asked Mummy.

"Help."

Kenny looked out of the window. "I like boats," he said in a small voice. "I like sailing them on ponds, nice, safe ponds in parks, not on dirty village ponds."

"Our dirty village pond has dried up," replied Lisa. "So the poor ducks have nowhere to swim; but I don't suppose you like ducks either."

"Roy is here," announced Ben, coming into the kitchen in gumboots, his hair soaking wet. "And he needs help."

"Okay," I said, finding my boots.

"I'll come too," said Lisa. "But they don't care; they don't care if their ponies die."

"Must you?" I asked Lisa as we ran down the path. "We've got to live with them and they are paying an awful lot to be here, and you know we need money."

"Money, that's all you and Ben care about," shouted Lisa. "Money, money, money all day long."

"Aren't we all the same?" called Roy, laughing, his gumboots turned down at the top, his face rain-washed.

"We were taking temperatures," explained Ben. "I was just starting when Roy came."

"And how are they?" I asked.

"Better on the whole, but we're not out of the wood yet. The three small ponies need everything done, feet, worming, delousing. Start with their feet as soon as you can get your blacksmith," Roy told us. "Delouse them the moment they stop coughing. I'll leave you some powder," he continued, shaking down a thermometer. "I'll do their teeth next time I come, if they are still improving. There's no point when they're so groggy; they might collapse altogether. How are their young owners?"

"Awful," I answered.

"Like small white mice," replied Ben.

"Poor little devils," said Roy, filling a syringe. "Now one long-lasting injection for each of them and ring me if any of your ponies starts to run a temperature, particularly the foal; otherwise I won't be calling for a couple of days. Okay?"

"Okay," I replied, holding Jack's head while he coughed and trembled.

"They *are* better," said Roy, when he had finished sticking needles into their poor thin necks. "It's a pity they can't be in, but there it is. Keep up the good work –

279

plenty of dampened feeds, damp hay, black treacle in mashes, as much as they will eat, but little and often, that's the golden rule."

"Yes," agreed Ben looking glum.

"They're not going to die then?" asked Lisa.

"Not if we're lucky, but it will be a pretty close shave," answered Roy. "They look as though they've been short of food for a very long time, so when illness struck they had nothing to fall back on. It's a shame really, because they are quite a nice-looking bunch of ponies."

"They were bought for some peculiar reason," said Lisa with a sniff. "Not for love at all. Their owners don't even like riding."

Roy winked at me. "All the better for you, Lisa," he said. "You'll have three more to ride when they've recovered."

"Thank you very much. I haven't time to ride Jigsaw,

thanks to them," Lisa replied, screwing up her small face.

"What's got into her?" asked Roy. "She used to be a nice little girl."

"Jealousy," said Ben. "Mummy complex."

"Shut up," shouted Lisa, running away towards the house.

"You've got a handful there," said Roy, getting into his car.

"Bran mashes next," said Ben, when he had gone. "Have we got any black treacle left?" I shook my head. "Any money then?"

I shook my head again. "Then we must ask Mum for our share," Ben replied.

The rain had stopped. Everything was sparkling wet. Clouds moved fast across the rain-swept sky. Behind them was light, growing larger and brighter all the time.

"Let's skip the black treacle this time. I'll go to the village shop later and see if they've got any. Their throats must be getting better," I said.

"But they're not getting fatter, they're growing thinner if anything," complained Ben.

We washed our hands in a bucket of rainwater before we talked to our own horses. Cassie's foal, Windfall, who is roan with a white streak down her muzzle and a wicked eye, sucked our fingers. Cassie looked warm and maternal with sleepy, happy eyes. Lorraine was restless, Solitaire trotted round us in circles, his big hoofs slipping on the wet grass. Lisa's Jigsaw stared over the gate, longing for excitement, and little black Limpet, who had taught us all to ride, nuzzled our pockets.

"Mummy's calling," said Ben after a time. "Come on, we had better go in."

I didn't want to go indoors. In spite of the sick ponies, everything seemed calm and peaceful outside and the sun was coming out again. I didn't want to face the arguing, or Mrs Mills shouting because she couldn't hear, or Colonel Hunter, a lonely, forgotten old man with no reason for living any more, talking about India, or Lisa on edge, hating the Traverses because they kept Mummy busy and she wanted more of Mummy to herself. Or James, pale with worry over the result of his GCSEs, which were yet to come, neither man nor child, moody, bad-tempered, liable to flare up at the slightest provocation. Nor Dad who would be facing the reality that he had failed once again to get a job, facing it in the clear light of morning.

"What are you waiting for?" asked Ben. "Mummy's calling you."

And I thought of the Traverses and the mess they were in, without a mother, with Kenny a twisted mass of nerves and Marion in a world of her own and Sally trying to be a mother at ten years old.

Suddenly I wanted to run away to a land where there were no complications, no school, no money, no arguments – just horses and things growing and sun and rain and flowers.

Dad was in the dining-room when I went in at last. "Why did you take so long?" he asked. "Didn't you hear Mummy calling?"

"Yes, I was thinking," I said. "I can't be running all the time."

James had made coffee. Mummy looked as though she had been crying. Lisa was staring out of the window.

"I've been following up the references," Dad said. "They're phoney. The bank has never heard of Mick Travers, and the priest doesn't exist."

"How do you know?" I asked.

"Because the appropriate people have never heard of such a priest," replied Dad.

"But what if something happens to them?" I asked. "Who do we tell?"

"Exactly," replied Dad. "Thank heavens someone has some sense around here."

"We are going to let them stay here for three weeks and then we'll contact the police," said Mummy. "I won't have the police informed otherwise, it isn't fair. And I won't have them questioned by the police – they are too young."

"Where are they now?" I asked.

"Upstairs in their rooms looking at books," replied Mummy.

"The sun is shining now, get them out, Harriet," said Dad. "Find out something. Marion may need a doctor. She's scared stiff of me. If I look at her she puts her hands over her face to blot me out, and the others aren't much better."

"Looking at them breaks my heart," exclaimed Mummy.

"Get them riding. It's our only hope," said Dad. "Lisa's useless and they're scared of Ben."

"It's always me. I've tried once and failed. Why can't James try?" I asked.

"They're scared of me; they run away from me like small white rabbits running to their holes," said James, spilling coffee.

It's a day to be happy, I thought, going upstairs; they should be chasing each other round the garden, or cuddling Twinkle, or kicking balls about.

I put on a dry tee-shirt and went up to the attic, where I found them doing absolutely nothing.

"Come on, we're going outside," I said. "The sun's shining now. Come on, move."

"What about Marion?" asked Sally.

"She's coming too."

"She won't," said Sally, "She won't move off the bed."

"We're going to the village shop to buy sweets," I said. "You like sweets, don't you? I'm going to get some money for sweets. Please come or I will cry."

Kenny got off his bed and combed his hair with a small pink comb. Sally looked frightened. "Marion doesn't behave in shops, sometimes she snatches things," she said.

"It doesn't matter. Old Mrs Fieldhouse doesn't mind. It's not a big 'help yourself' sort of shop. It's in the front room of a cottage. And we've known Mrs Fieldhouse for years. You can't stay in here for ever. The sun's shining," I said.

I took hold of Marion's hand and pulled her to her

feet. "Come on, walk," I said. "Walk to the shop and I will buy you sweets, lots and lots." She opened her eyes and looked at me in a strange way, as though she was seeing me for the first time.

"Later we will ride," I continued, going downstairs, still holding Marion's hand. "We'll ride Limpet and Jig-saw. We'll walk and trot, and put the tack on and take it off again. You're here to enjoy yourselves, not to sit in your rooms all day."

I went through the hall because I wanted to avoid Lisa and I kept Marion's hand in a vice-like grip. She looked straight ahead of her and none of them spoke a word, but I felt a sudden fleeting triumph. It's like lunging a horse, I thought, when he suddenly gives in and starts going round. It's the same sort of triumph.

Five

What have you done?

I held Marion's hand all the way across the common to our village shop, which stands close to the church and is built of brick and flint. Then Sally produced a pound coin from her pocket.

"You don't need to treat us," she said. "After all, you're paid to look after us, so we should do the treating. You're really our servants, aren't you?"

I stared into her small face and hated her. "No, actually we're not. You are our guests, our paying guests if you like, but guests just the same," I replied, knowing that my voice had suddenly gone hard so that Marion flinched as though I had threatened her and snatched her hand away. And now I felt alone and despised. "Go in on your own then," I said, and knew my good deed had gone sour.

Sally dragged Marion in with her, whispering, "Behave yourself, will you, or a wicked man will catch you." Kenny followed at their heels like a dog.

I stood looking at the trees, loving them, thinking: They never change, they've stood there for centuries. How much they must have seen!

I could hear Mrs Fieldhouse saying, "Naughty girl. Put that down at once." And then Sally came out shouting:

"She smacked Marion, I'll tell the police, that's assault, isn't it?" And I suddenly realised that they really were horrible children, just as Lisa had insisted all along.

"No you won't. Mrs Fieldhouse has been here for years and everyone knows she doesn't assault people," I said.

The grass on the common was still wet and they kept looking at their white socks and scowling because now they were wet too.

They didn't offer me their sweets. They just stuffed them in their mouths as they walked and whispered among themselves like conspirators. This is the last time I shall be kind to them whatever Mummy says, I thought. I won't help them again, not even if they're drowning or being kicked to death by one of their ponies.

"Daddy paid you enough anyway," said Sally. "I watched him count the money. It was a great deal."

"It won't pay for the vet, or the blacksmith," I answered. "That will be extra."

Marion was holding Sally's hand now and muttering something as she walked, and suddenly I was angry and hurt enough to ask, "And what's the matter with her? She doesn't talk properly; she's crazy, isn't she?"

For one awful moment time seemed to stand still, and I knew I shouldn't have said it, that it was inexcusable and unforgivable.

Marion stopped and started hitting her forehead with her hands.

Sally screamed, "Now look what you've done!" and Kenny turned whiter, if that was possible.

But now I had gone so far I wasn't turning back. They had called me a servant and scorned my offer to treat them to sweets and I was hurt, and hurt people like to hurt back, or that's my experience anyway. So I stood quite still and said, "Where's your mother? Come on,

say. Where is she? Is she dead? Murdered? Did she run away? I'm only asking. I won't tell anyone. We'll know in the end anyway. Lots of mothers run away. It's quite normal, nothing to be ashamed of." I still wanted to hurt them and I went on and on in the same way. "Did she fight with your father? Are they divorced? Does she love anyone else?" And all the time deep inside I was hating myself for asking.

Then quite suddenly Sally faced me and said, "You're a nasty, rude, inquisitive person. If you had been brought up properly by a nanny like we were, you would know better, but obviously you've been dragged up. You look like it too, so does your father. Anyone can see he's not a gentleman. We can find our own way back. We don't need you. You smell."

Kenny ran ahead while Sally dragged Marion with her. All the beauty seemed to have vanished from the day. I felt sick suddenly. I walked homewards in a daze, thinking, what have I done now? They'll leave, I decided, and Mummy will be furious. But I won't say I'm sorry. It's more than I can stomach.

I watched them go indoors and then I tacked up Lorraine and rode across the common to the beechwoods where the sun danced through the branches of trees, making strange patterns on the damp, sweet-smelling earth. It seemed days and days since I had ridden alone just to please myself. And the sun and the whispering trees soothed me and I tried desperately to forget their insults, to forget and forgive, but I couldn't. Lorraine walked with a long swinging stride and I wished I could ride on and on until I reached another land, where horses were never ill, and money didn't matter, and the sun always shone and I was alone, just me and Lorraine and some other animals who ate only grass, so that there would be no killing and no sadness. But I came to the end of the woods eventually and there was nothing but fields of ripening corn and the cry of a bird.

When I thought of Mummy struggling alone with lunch in the kitchen, I knew it was time to go back.

Ben met me at the yard gate. "What have you done?" he cried. "The Travers children are screaming and yelling. They want to leave but there's nowhere to send them. And James has gone mad and thrown his radio out of a window. It's bedlam. What have you done?"

"Nothing. They did it. They called me a servant," I answered, dismounting.

"Is that all?"

"All?"

"You must have annoyed them first," said Ben.

"I didn't."

"Well, you've certainly upset the applecart. Dad says you've got to go straight in and apologise," said Ben.

"Oh yeah," I answered. "He'll have to think again then. I'm not apologising, and that's final."

I turned Lorraine out again. I was near to tears but I wasn't going to cry. I had to be strong. I wasn't going to crawl before three small kids. I've sunk low in my life, but nothing was going to make me sink that low.

"Dad wanted me to ask them questions, and I did," I answered.

"Marion's gone bonkers. They've all gone crazy," said Ben.

"They were crazy already," I answered, "and so is their father. Fancy dumping them here and leaving no address. He doesn't want them, can't you see? No one wants them. And now they are here for good with their miserable ponies. Time is passing. Supposing their precious dad never comes back? We'll be the mugs then, won't we?"

"There's always homes for orphans," said Ben with a faint smile.

I stood looking at our horses. Windfall was standing with her legs tucked under her, she looked small and ill, and she wasn't taking any interest in anything. My heart started to beat in a funny way and I said, "We haven't taken their temperatures today, have we? And just look at Windfall." Suddenly we were both climbing through the fence, feeling her neck, half-carrying her towards the stables, while Cassie watched us with sad, worried eyes, nickering softly.

"See what they've done," I cried. "Them and their miserable father. She's going to die, and it's their fault. Oh, how I hate them!"

"I'll telephone Roy. He should be home for lunch," cried Ben, looking at his watch.

I bedded the box down and led Cassie in. She stood with her head hanging over Windfall, not taking much

interest in anything. Supposing she's ill too and her milk stops, I thought. What then?

Now Lisa was leaning over the door, saying, "What's happening? Are they ill?"

"They may be dying," I said.

"Oh no! What a terrible day," cried Lisa. "And Marion's had a sort of fit, and Mummy's sent for a doctor and Sally won't stop crying and Kenny has shut himself in his room and locked the door and James says he's sure he's committing suicide! And Dad's in an awful rage and Mrs Mills is wandering round with cups of tea,

291

which no one wants. And Colonel Hunter says we should send for the police. Why did they come, Harriet? Why are we so unlucky?"

"Not unlucky, just plain stupid," I said, kneeling in the straw beside Windfall.

"Roy's coming. I've told Mummy not to keep lunch but she says there isn't any anyway, so that's all right. Mrs Mills is looking after Colonel Hunter and Mike's at the farm again, and I don't feel like lunch anyway, so it doesn't matter as far as I'm concerned," said Ben, returning.

"Okay," I answered, near to tears.

"You stay here, Lisa, and Harriet and I will check the others. Come on," said Ben, waving the horse thermometer.

"Lorraine's all right. I would have known if she was ill. She went like a dream," I answered, and suddenly the ride did seem like a dream, or at least something too good to be true.

Presently James turned up with mugs of coffee, which we didn't want. "A doctor has come. He's talking to Mummy and Dad now," he said. "Sally won't stop crying and Kenny spent ten minutes screaming. Mrs Mills is sitting with them now, without her hearing-aid."

I didn't want coffee but James drinks it like some people smoke cigarettes and he expects everyone else to do the same. My mugful was lukewarm and had too much sugar in it.

"Perhaps the doctor will sort them out," said Ben.

"He runs a special clinic but we can't do much until their dad turns up in eighteen days' time," said James.

"We'll all be mad by then," replied Ben, throwing his coffee away when James wasn't looking. Roy arrived at last, looking cross, and gave Windfall three injections.

"I shan't be free again until nine tonight, ring me

then," he said. He looked tired and his car was splashed with mud and his eyes were heavy with lack of sleep. "All right? Bye for now, then," he said.

"Will she live?" shouted Lisa.

"I can't say yet," he replied, leaving at great speed without waving; and we all felt deflated because we had wanted hope and he hadn't given us any.

"That's that then," said Ben. "We had better go in."

"And face the music," I added.

"It's no good putting it off," said Ben.

"If only Windfall lives," I said. "She's so sweet with her dear little roan face, and Cassie will never get over it if she dies."

"You're making me cry," said Lisa.

"I've been crying inside all day," I answered.

"It could have been marvellous. The grass is growing again, the ground is soft enough to jump on. It should have been a nice day," said Ben.

The doctor was leaving. He was a stranger to us, in a lightweight suit, with fair hair and a jaunty step which made you think he might have springs in his shoes. His hands looked clean and manicured. He appeared the perfect doctor for the Travers children.

He smiled at us and said, "They are all right now. You can go in. There's no need to lurk any more." And I thought: He's nicer than he looks.

We found Mummy and Dad sipping sherry in the kitchen.

"It's all right, they are sedated," said Dad. "They won't speak to you again, Harriet, not ever; but later on I'll try to find their nearest relatives and then they can go. They must have family somewhere."

"What did the doctor say?" asked Ben.

"That they are highly disturbed and should be with a relative," answered Mummy.

293

"We will have to give back some of the money, of course," said Dad.

"What about the ponies?" I asked.

"We'll sort that out when we've found a relative," said Dad.

"There's some lunch in the oven now," said Mummy. "Help yourselves."

"Windfall is very ill," I answered. "And we aren't very hungry." And I thought: No one will ever understand how awful it was on the common.

"Of course, if we don't find any family we're sunk," said Dad, pouring himself another glass of sherry.

Six

Wait!

The next days were terrible, dark days at Black Pony Inn. The Travers children remained mostly in their rooms. No relatives were found. They told Dad that their mother had been called Smith and that she had a relative called Smith in Australia, but what hope is there of finding a Smith in England or Australia? (If only they had had a strange name like Pumkin something might have emerged.) They said their father had no relations anywhere; that they had no grannies and no aunts. Were they shielding their father from something? Or someone? It was impossible to know. The doctor had said that they mustn't be upset, so Dad didn't dare press them for answers.

As for the ponies, our yard was now a hospital. Ben and I seemed to spend all our time toiling backwards and forwards with hot mashes. Roy came every day and all the horses except for Limpet and Jigsaw coughed night and day. Ben and I had reached the limits of despair and had now ceased to mourn. We were resigned to the bills, to our almost sleepless nights when we even heard coughing in our dreams, to the Travers children's complete silence in our presence, to our horses being unrideable for months ahead; to broken winds in the future and permanently congested lungs. They were all out of danger now. The Travers' ponies were even filling out a little and their ribs protruded less, their necks grew thicker and the poverty marks in their quarters were less defined.

Then August came with no more rain. The ground grew dry again; the grass stopped growing. The sky was the same endless blue.

More than a week passed like this. Lisa rode Limpet and Jigsaw, who stayed fat and well in spite of everything, while Ben and I thought of Pony Club Camp starting without us. In our imaginations we saw the tents strung out across a field, the horse lines, the bustle and noise, the laughter and fights.

"I don't think we'll ever go again," said Ben.

James watched the postman for his GCSE results. He was up before any of us, lurking in the hall, his face grey with worry. It was no use Mummy saying, "They don't matter. You won't die if they are bad." Or Dad saying, "I never went to university," because James merely replied, "Yes, I will," and, "Well, look at you!"

And then one day the three Travers children appeared dressed for riding. Ben and I were mucking out, arguing over the wheelbarrow, shouting at one another. They appeared pale but refined as they looked at us.

"Excuse me, but can we ride today?" asked Sally. "Daddy will be collecting us in less than a week now and he'll be so disappointed if we haven't ridden."

Ben brushed sweat from his eyes.

"Your ponies aren't fit enough," I answered, "they're still ill, still coughing, but you can ride Limpet and Jigsaw if you like."

I caught the ponies while they watched. I couldn't believe that they would soon be going, that three weeks had almost gone. I saw my return to school in the same old clothes, with nothing new to show to anyone. I saw endless corridors, the flights of concrete stairs each painted a different colour to help you to find your way. Soon the summer would be gone. While I saw all this, I tacked up the two ponies automatically, pulling up the girths, letting down the stirrups, not really knowing that I was doing it. Ben emptied the wheelbarrow.

"How much can you ride?" I asked, looking for leading reins.

"I have cantered," said Sally. "But Kenny isn't very safe. And Marion really needs two people, one to lead and one to hold on to her. They can start first, then I can hold on to Marion."

Kenny mounted Limpet. Ben adjusted the stirrups. Marion refused to get up for a time but finally I half-lifted her, and half-pushed her into the saddle. Lisa had gone to play with a friend across the common. Mrs

Mills appeared and said, "You do look nice. Have a nice ride. I'll sweep up the yard for you, Harriet."

I often wished that I was as nice and kind as Mrs Mills, for she seemed to live wholly to help other people.

"Thanks a million," I said; and then to Marion, "All right, we're moving." We walked across the common and Marion put her fingers in Jigsaw's tangled mane and laughed.

"She's enjoying it," cried Sally. "Won't Daddy be pleased. He wants us to be riders."

"Well, riders you are," said Ben, pushing down Kenny's heels as he spoke.

The common was dry, so dry that a thrown-down cigarette end could set it alight. I was beginning to forget what mud looked like. Our jerseys and thick shirts lay forgotten in drawers, it seemed impossible that we would ever need them again.

"Gosh, it's hot. It must be ninety," said Ben. "If you ride tomorrow, make it early."

When we reached the stable-yard again, Kenny and Marion dismounted and Sally told Marion to hold Kenny's hand and mounted Jigsaw herself. She rode round the paddock, toes down, arms flapping.

I was glad that Lisa was out of the way for I could imagine her comments had she been there.

Ben untacked Limpet. "We'll charge them for this," he said.

"Can we?"

"Of course, they had a lesson, didn't they?"

"Heels down," I shouted to Sally, "toes up. You're calf-cuddling; he'll run away."

Luckily the paddock is small and presently she stopped. "That was lovely. Thank you very much," she said, sliding to the ground and handing me Jigsaw's reins. "We'll do it again tomorrow, please," she added.

"Make it early then," replied Ben. "Let's say nine o'clock, before the heat and the flies start."

She took Marion's hand. "A mother before her time," muttered Ben.

"Poor thing," I answered.

"She likes it, she likes power. She's what our black-smith calls a little madam. But one day I shall be rich. I shall make my fortune being a vet in the United States and I shall come back here and buy a mansion with a swimming-pool. I shall be richer than her or her beastly father," said Ben, kicking the ground. "I shall be so rich, I shall have everything."

I didn't answer. I thought: I don't really want money, not money to keep, just enough so that I don't have to worry all the time and can keep a horse and a dog, and take a holiday occasionally.

"I bet their dad won't pay the vet's bills," said Ben.

"He's rich. They won't mean a thing to him," I answered.

We went indoors to eat a cold lunch in the kitchen. Mummy was pleased that the Travers children had rid-den. "Try and get them out every day," she told us. "I want them to have some colour in their cheeks before their father fetches them. I want him to know he's had his money's worth."

"He's had that all right," replied Ben.

The next day they came to the stables again punctu-ally at nine. I had tacked up the ponies ready for them but Ben had vanished on his bike without telling any-one, so there was only Lisa, buzzing like a discontented wasp, to help.

"I can't go with you today," said Sally, "because Daddy may telephone. He said he would today if he could and it's written in my diary, so I know I've got it right. It says: *Daddy nine-thirty a.m.* But Marion likes you now, Harriet, so you can manage, can't you? And can Lisa take Kenny? And I'll be here waiting for my ride by ten."

They were wearing clean white shirts and I wondered how many white shirts Mummy had washed for them during the last eighteen days. "All right," I answered. "Jump up, Marion, we'll go for a proper ride today."

Lisa was muttering "Bossy boots", her whole small face contorted with fury because she likes to be in charge herself. Mummy says it's because she was born in April and that Aries people are all like that.

Marion mounted without any fuss. She even picked up her reins and smiled.

"Right, I'll go in then. See you at ten," said Sally in a small, bossy voice. "Have a good ride, Marion. Keep your heels down, Kenny."

"Okay, ready?" I asked. "Off we go then."

There were children playing on the common. Jigsaw shied at their football. Limpet hung back, making Lisa's arm ache. It was hot already, without a breath of air anywhere.

"We'll go to the woods because it will be cool under the trees. Do you like this hot weather?" I asked Marion. But she only smiled back and I said, "Do talk, please. I'm sure you can," and she smiled again.

Lisa was teaching Kenny the points of the horse as she walked. I could hear him repeating, "Withers, loins, croup," after her in a small, timid voice.

I tried the same thing on Marion, only nothing happened, but I thought that at least she was coming with me, at least she was beginning to trust us. "Tomorrow you may be able to ride your own ponies," I said. "Won't that be lovely? They've almost stopped coughing." The horizon seemed full of hope again – just another week and they'll all be better, and there may be more guests coming and Dad may get a job, and James may get super exam results, I thought. It's silly to despair. By now we had reached the woods and they were dark and welcoming and I wasn't holding on to Marion any more; she was sitting calmly and happily on Jigsaw, looking normal, and I saw for the first time how pretty she was when she was happy, with a beautiful broad forehead and large brown eyes.

"Trotting," called Lisa.

"Hold on," I said. "We're trotting." She bumped up and down, giggling and I went on making bright conversation. "Your daddy will be back soon," I said. "Isn't that marvellous? Where will you go then?" She didn't answer, which reminded me of when I was small and talked to dolls who never answered either, only then I had invented the answers myself. I tried to do the same now. "I bet you're pleased. Say yes," I pleaded, and she smiled and went on smiling, and because of that the woods seemed to smile too.

Presently I could hear Kenny laughing behind me and I thought: We're getting somewhere at last. Perhaps they're better without their elder sister. Perhaps they hate being bossed. Perhaps she's the evil force which had caused everything. It was a terrible thought and perhaps it helped in some mystic way to cause what happened next. Or maybe I was just too pleased with myself and it was the old story of "Pride goes before a fall".

The track wound on and on to where at last the woods met the open fields, which were now golden stubble, and beyond the fields, over the crest of a hill, was the road. I knew the way by heart, but now I stopped to call to Lisa: "Everything all right? Shall we go home across the fields?" Kenny was sucking sweets. Lisa's hair was all over the place and there was a hole in one toe of her plimsolls. She was wearing on old shirt of Ben's which had come out of her jeans. She looked a mess, but at least a happy mess.

"Anything you like," she called, her mouth full of sweets.

I nearly called back, "You're ruining your teeth as usual," but I didn't because I didn't want to spoil the day; instead I said to Marion, "Now we go across the fields. The corn has just been carried, a month earlier than usual because of the hot weather."

She smiled again and said, "How lovely!" and it was the first time she had ever spoken to me.

Jigsaw was pleased to be going home and danced a little. It was ten o'clock and I wondered whether Sally was waiting for us in the yard, walking up and down like a nervous mother. Perhaps Ben was back now, guilty because he had forgotten we were taking the Travers children riding at nine.

Rabbits ran out of the stubble at our approach, pheasants flew heavenwards. There wasn't a cloud in the sky, not a breath of wind. The ponies were sweating and my boots were sticking to my feet.

"Let's trot," I said. "Hold on." And it was then, quite suddenly out of the blue, that a gun went off. I jumped myself but Jigsaw hardly moved and I heard Kenny still laughing behind; but it had an extraordinary effect on Marion. She gave a piercing shriek, a louder and more terrified shriek than I have ever heard before and then she threw herself off Jigsaw and started to run across the stubble, doubled up like a terrified animal.

I shouted, "Wait. Come back." And then I leaped on Jigsaw and galloped after her. I rode past her and threw myself off, crying, "It's all right, Marion. Everything's all right. No one's going to hurt us, I promise." Jigsaw blew hot air down my neck and went round in circles.

I squatted on the ground, saying, "Come on, please." I could hear lorries going along the road just over the hill. And then suddenly she was running again and, leaving Jigsaw, I ran after her. I'm not a fast runner and I hardly gained on her and ahead lay the road!

I heard Lisa calling "Harriet, wait!" and Kenny's small thin voice crying "Marion, come back!" I stumbled in a rabbit-hole and fell, and when I picked myself up Marion had already reached the wire fence which was all that separated us from the road.

In the distance Kenny was screaming, and I had no breath left; fear made me weak and my knees buckled under me as I reached the fence. Marion was through, hurtling down the bank to the road. My shirt caught on the wire and ripped. A car hooted, someone screamed; then I was rolling down a bank, dry grass in my mouth, shouting, "Stop, Marion! Wait!" And I knew I was too late.

Seven

An accident

She wasn't dead. She lay in the road screaming, while a woman got up from under a moped saying, "I hadn't a hope. I did my best. Why wasn't she under control?"

Someone yelled out of a car window, "Get off the road, you fools." And I saw that a long line of cars was waiting, with angry faces staring out of windows.

I knew that Marion wasn't hurt because injured people lie very still and she was screaming and kicking like a small child deprived of its favourite toy. The woman on the moped had torn her slacks and was desperately trying to hold them together. Someone called, "Do you want an ambulance?"

And we both shook our heads. It was all a little like a dream. It seemed impossible, and yet it was actually happening. I pulled Marion off the road, still screaming. "She isn't hurt," I said. "Just naughty. I told her to wait and she wouldn't." I was surprised to see that my hands were shaking, because I felt very calm now and in complete control of the situation.

"My moped's smashed," said the woman, "and it wasn't my fault. Someone will have to pay. And just look at my slacks; they cost me thirty pounds. New last week. It's all wrong, isn't it?" She had a tanned face and light brown hair stuffed inside a helmet, and a cotton shirt. She looked about forty.

"She's withdrawn, you know, difficult," I answered.

Lisa and Kenny were sliding down the bank now. Kenny was weeping. "You should have caught her," said Lisa in a small accusing voice. "I could have."

I didn't say anything because I knew it was true. Lisa is a very fast runner and I'm a very slow one; I don't know how it happened; sometimes life isn't fair, though I must say I wouldn't want to be Lisa even if she can run. Marion was starting to struggle again. She wasn't crying any more. She just wanted her own way which meant running away from us.

"I've tied the ponies to trees," said Lisa.

"Well, something's got to be done," said the woman with the moped. "I can't go on like this. You had better give me your address, hadn't you?"

None of us had paper or a pencil, of course. By now the sun was merciless. The tar on the road started to melt and stick to our feet, our hands were sticky with sweat, our heads started to ache.

"Let's find a phone-box and phone home," I suggested. "Mummy will sort everything out. She can even take your moped to be mended in the Land Rover."

"I'm supposed to be at work and just look at my slacks," said the woman.

We started to walk along the edge of the road. Marion hung back, but she didn't scream. Kenny held Lisa's hand. The woman pushed her moped. She had managed to fix her slacks together somehow. The walk seemed to last for ever. Cars hooted at us, men laughed, and all the time the day grew hotter.

"The ponies will be eaten alive by flies," said Lisa after a time. "Poor Jigsaw."

My arm was aching from pulling Marion. There was a bruise coming up on her forehead and one of her hands was scratched. Kenny didn't speak, but I could

see that his small face was twisted with anxiety.

It was still half a mile to the phone-box which stood in a layby just three-quarters of a mile from home. Cars rushed by like express trains, leaving a smell of exhaust fumes behind them. We didn't talk, because we were in single file and the noise of cars drowned conversation. I hoped that the ponies were still tied up. I imagined Mummy running to answer the telephone. We could see the kiosk now. A lorry thundered by, splashing our shoes with wet tar. Sweat ran down our faces like tears. Marion lagged and dragged. Kenny hung on to Lisa as though she was his last connection with life.

When we reached the phone-box, Marion wouldn't go inside.

"She hates small places," said Kenny.

I didn't dare let go of her hand. "You phone, Lisa. Don't alarm Mummy. Just tell her to pick us up," I said.

"Give me 10p, then," she said. But none of us had 10p. I had no money at all, Lisa only had two 2p pieces, Kenny, surprisingly, had a five-pound note, and the woman had a crisp new tenner.

Marion, sensing fresh trouble, started to cry.

"Dial 100 and reverse the charges," I told Lisa. "Don't waste time."

A car stopped and a man in jeans and a blue shirt said, "Do you need help?"

"We're all right now, thank you," I answered.

"I don't know what they're saying at work. I'm half an hour late already," said the woman.

"Would you like a lift?" asked the man.

"No, I'll stick with my moped, thanks all the same," she said.

Lisa came out of the phone-box. "She's coming," she said. "Can I go back for the ponies now? Kenny's all right with you."

"Can you manage them? You know what Jigsaw's like leading Limpet," I answered.

"I'll ride Limpet then. Anyway, I'm nearly ten now. I'm not a baby any more. I'll go back through the woods. Anyway, I'm going," she said. "I don't care what you say."

Kenny held on to my shirt. The woman with the moped started to grumble again. Lisa ran back along the road. I can't control anyone, I thought, not even my little sister. A mass of rubbish was scattered in the layby – old bottles, cigarette packets, paper bags and a host of indescribable things. Someone had scratched *Pete loves Caroline* on the phone-box.

Then the woman said, "Here's a Land Rover," and there was Mummy coming towards us, looking small and worried in our blue Land Rover. Kenny started to smile and jump up and down.

"Are you all right?" called Mummy, stopping in the layby with a whine of brakes. "Where are the ponies? Where's Lisa?"

"It's a long story – can we get in? We have to take this lady's moped to be repaired and she's late for work as it is," I said.

"I certainly am!" exclaimed the woman. "Are you their mother? If you are, I'm surprised at you! Fancy letting these mites out alone on horses. You ought to be ashamed of yourself."

"I'm not a mite," I answered.

"Let's get the moped in," answered Mummy. "We'll discuss other things later."

I wished that Ben had come. He can lift mopeds in one hand. It kept slipping back and the woman became angry and accused us of bending the mudguard and breaking a brake cable, while Marion whimpered like a sick puppy. But at last it was inside the Land Rover and we were climbing into the seats, which felt like hot plates to sit on.

"Have you got a safety pin?" asked the woman. "My slacks are torn."

Mummy shook her head. Her arms looked thin against the steering wheel and her hands were clenched so tight that her knuckles showed white through the skin; otherwise she seemed completely calm. "Where do you want to go?" she asked.

"To Headleys, the moped shop, and then to work," the woman replied. "I hope you are insured against accidents like this."

"I hope so too," replied Mummy.

Marion was very quiet; she seemed changed, as though somehow the whole accident had changed her outlook. She wasn't even sucking her finger; she looked almost normal staring out of the window.

"Is Sally all right?" I asked.

"Yes and no. She believes her father is coming tomorrow and she's started packing," answered Mummy.

We had reached the outskirts of the town now.

I envied Lisa taking the ponies home. The streets were buzzing with people. Mummy stopped outside a motor-cycle shop. "It's a double yellow line," she said, "so leave the back down. If I get a parking ticket, I'll go mad. What's your name, by the way?"

"Smithers, Mrs Smithers," the woman answered.

A man came out from the shop and took the moped inside. Mummy and Mrs Smithers exchanged addresses and then we dropped her in the middle of the town and drove homewards.

"Why did you do it?" Mummy asked when we reached the traffic-lights.

"Do what?" I cried.

"Go out alone with Marion. Surely you know she

310

needs two people. All disabled riders have at least two people with them, it's a rule."

"But she's not disabled," I answered.

"You know what I mean," replied Mummy. "Mentally disabled."

Kenny sat crouched in the back like a small white mouse, hardly breathing.

"You always blame me," I said. "Always, always, always." And all the misery and the fear of the morning seemed to overwhelm me. I could feel tears streaming down my face, mixing with the sweat already there. I remembered that Ben should have come and yet I was getting the blame. It was unjust, unfair, more than I could bear. "You always blame me," I cried again. "I do my best. Do you think I wanted to go out with Marion? Do you?"

"It's the expense," said Mummy, "I don't know if we're insured against that sort of accident. I can't bear any more expense."

"But she could have been killed, what then? With no next of kin to be informed. Why don't you count your blessings? Or Mrs Smithers could have been terribly injured," I cried. "We're lucky, can't you see?"

"Lucky?" cried Mummy. "Since when?"

"Now."

We were both at breaking point. The Land Rover kept swerving and the heat was unbearable. I had never endured such heat before.

"You're going to crash in a minute," I shouted at Mummy. "Please watch the road."

"You should think before you act," shouted Mummy. "Mrs Mills could have come with you. I could have got Mike back from the farm. You shouldn't have gone alone . . ."

"You always blame me," I screamed.

"You know that isn't true," shouted Mummy, narrowly missing a parked bus. "But this time it *was* your fault."

"It wasn't," I screamed. "Ben was meant to come. Why don't you blame him . . .?"

But now a new voice screamed, "Don't. Please don't." It was a voice we had never heard before, louder than Sally's, braver than Kenny's. I looked at Marion in amazement. "Don't," she said. "Don't. I can't bear it."

And her voice did something to us both. We both fell silent automatically, with surprise.

Then Mummy said, "We won't, darling. We'll stop now, at once." She put her arm round Marion while the Land Rover swerved dangerously again.

"Mummy and Daddy fought. It didn't do any good," said Marion. "They fought and fought," she said as tears ran down her face.

"It's all over now," answered Mummy. "You're here with us, and Daddy will fetch you tomorrow."

"I don't like Daddy," she said.

"She never did," said Kenny. "She was always on Mummy's side. Then Mummy ran away and she never got over it. Not speaking was her way of paying Daddy back."

His small face looked twisted with hate.

"It's all over now. Look, we're home," said Mummy.

Lisa was in the yard untacking Jigsaw and Limpet. She looked hot and cross. Ben was mending the stable broom which had come apart.

"Let's bathe your poor eye, and put sticking-plaster on your hand," said Mummy.

"She's talking," I said to Ben.

"Who?"

"Marion."

"Is that going to make things better or worse?" he asked.

"I don't know. It was a terrible morning," I said. "But perhaps good will come out of it. Perhaps we will know the truth at last – the whole truth and nothing but the truth."

"About time too!" said Ben.

Eight

Packed and ready to go

I walked indoors. There were suitcases in the hall.

"What on earth?" I asked.

"They are Sally's. Didn't you know her daddy's due tomorrow," said James with a laugh.

"I hope he brings a horse box for his ponies," I replied. "There's hardly a blade of grass left anywhere."

Mummy was bathing Marion's face. "Is it really three weeks?" I asked.

"It must be," said James.

Colonel Hunter was sitting in the dining-room waiting for lunch. He had a habit of sitting there from twelve-thirty until one o'clock every day, his grey moustache drooping, looking like a reproachful dog waiting for his dinner. Mrs Mills was outside, gardening in spite of the heat. Mike was on the farm, bringing in the last of the harvest. Kenny stood looking out of the kitchen window. Dad was nowhere to be seen. Lisa came in, banging the back door after her. "I'm too hot to eat anything," she wailed. "Is there a Coke anywhere?"

"Will you have the ponies ready tomorrow for loading, Harriet?" asked Sally. "Daddy will be here during the morning. You won't mix up their tack, will you?"

"Certainly not, but don't ride them too fast when you get home, they're still coughing now and again," I answered.

"Daddy will know what to do," replied Sally. "He doesn't need telling."

Mummy dabbed Marion's bruise with witch hazel and put a plaster on her hand. Sally sat in the dining-room with Colonel Hunter, waiting to be served lunch. Kenny and Lisa talked and I heard him laughing; then he started to chase her round the kitchen table like a normal child of seven, and suddenly I wished they weren't leaving tomorrow because I wanted to see the tangles in their minds unravelled, to see them happy again. I wanted to know what they were really like.

Marion was talking to Mummy in a quiet undertone.

"Okay, lunch," said Mummy when she had finished. "Will you put out the knives and forks for me?" And I knew we had won; at the last moment, just in time, we had broken down the barriers.

"I want to ride again tomorrow. I don't mind if I do fall off," Kenny told Lisa.

"We'll have to ride early if your daddy's coming," she answered.

"Oh, who cares about him," he said.

It was a wonderful lunch because Kenny started to make jokes and Marion insisted on helping Mummy clear away. It was as though a cloud had suddenly been lifted from the horizon, and the whole house felt different. Ben came in late and didn't say much. I think he was disappointed at missing the accident. He likes any form of excitement.

Marion upset the water jug but we made a joke of it. Only Sally remained silent and somehow disapproving.

After lunch Kenny, Lisa and I rushed down to the stables to get Jack, Jill and Little Bo-Peep ready for their approaching journey.

"They must look their best," said Lisa. "Come on, I'll show you how to groom, Kenny."

315

Marion had decided to help Mummy make cakes. There were flies everywhere and dust, and we felt dizzy with the heat, but it didn't seem to matter. Lisa fetched a hoof pick and together they picked out hoofs.

"Daddy doesn't know a thing about horses," confessed Kenny. "Mummy used to say he didn't know one end from another. When she was with us, he wouldn't let us have ponies, and, when she went, he bought them. Funny, wasn't it?"

"Mean, I think," replied Lisa. "Come on, let's do Bo-Peep's hoofs now."

"Daddy tried to shoot Mummy once. That's why Marion doesn't like guns going off. It was terrible. I watched through the banisters," Kenny said.

"Parents always quarrel. You should see ours sometimes," replied Lisa with a sniff.

"Not like ours, though," said Kenny. "Not as badly, anyway. And yours are still together. We don't know where Mummy is. Daddy says she's gone off with someone and deserted us because she doesn't care for us, but I don't think so. He thinks she's gone off with a boyfriend, but she never had one. I think she's hurt or dead. Otherwise she would have written. She loved us. I know she did . . ."

"Don't cry," said Lisa. "Here, have my hanky. We'll find her."

"How?" said Kenny, sobbing.

"Somehow, somewhere. We'll get the police to look. When did it all happen, anyway?" asked Lisa.

"I can't remember. Weeks and weeks ago. It was terrible, really terrible. That's why Marion is how she is. She loved Mummy. She was always a bit peculiar and she couldn't take it," said Kenny.

"So now there's just you three and Daddy?" asked Lisa.

316

"Yes, but I think he's sold the house. There was a for sale notice up outside. People at school kept asking questions – where are you going next? that sort of thing, – and even Sally didn't know the answers. It was embarrassing," he said, stumbling over the word. "We didn't know what to say. Then the head teacher went to see Daddy."

"How ghastly," said Lisa.

"Then Daddy bought the ponies. He thought it might cheer us up. He didn't like Marion not talking. He said she was losing touch with everything. But the ponies didn't help, because we can't even saddle them, if you want to know, not even Sally . . ." Kenny was crying harder now.

"It's too hot here, let's go into the tack room for a bit," said Lisa, taking his hand.

I left them together. Lisa can be infuriating but she can be nice too and I knew she would help Kenny more than I could.

I turned the ponies loose again and watered the others in the stables, thinking that they were nicer than humans; they didn't fight over their children. I looked at Cassie and Windfall and there was nothing complicated about them; they were simply happy together. Poor Kenny, I thought, poor Marion and poor, bossy, muddled Sally. And I felt guilty because I had hated and despised them for something which wasn't their fault.

The rest of the day passed very quickly. Later in the afternoon Marion fell into an exhausted sleep sitting at the kitchen table. Kenny refused to have milk and biscuits in his bedroom for supper. Sally read a book, only stopping to look at the clock from time to time, as though counting the hours until morning.

In the evening they all watched television with Lisa,

while Ben and I dosed our sick horses and watched the sun going down in a great fiery glow.

"If only it would rain," complained Ben.

I wakened early next morning but Sally was already up, carrying wellington boots down the attic stairs.

"We are all packed now," she said. "Are the ponies ready?"

"But it's only twenty past seven," I complained.

"His plane may land at six," answered Sally. "I don't suppose you know about the time zones, do you?"

"I do go to school," I answered.

There were no clouds in the sky today, but the faintest of breezes.

"I shall leave our beds as they are," continued Sally.

"I'm not taking them to bits." She had dark circles under her eyes, but she had done her hair and was dressed in a skirt and blouse and white socks.

"I hope he comes soon for your sake," I said.

"I want you to have everything ready because Daddy never has much time. You see, he's an important person," she replied. She returned to the attic, a small, determined figure, calling, "Get up now, everything is packed."

I found Mrs Mills already up, eating her toast and marmalade in the kitchen. "Have you seen the postman? I'm expecting a letter," she said.

I shook my head. She is always expecting a letter and it never comes.

"It's the post. It gets worse and worse. It was much better when it was a penny post. Even the old mail coaches must have been quicker than the post today," she grumbled.

"Down with silly old motor-cars," I answered, stepping outside into a strange, threatening heat, which made one think of thunder.

The Travers's ponies were looking much better. I marvelled at their improved appearance before I watered Cassie and Windfall, who were still stabled. Nothing moved but flies and the horses' tails; it was as though everything was waiting for the storm to break. I started to muck out and presently Ben appeared, waving a piece of paper, calling, "I've written out their bill. It's huge, I'm afraid, though I've only charged a couple of quid each for the riding lessons."

"What are they doing?" I asked, moving the wheelbarrow.

"Waiting, everybody is waiting. Mrs Mills for a letter which will never come, Mike for a call from a girl friend, James for his GCSE results, Colonel Hunter for *The Times* . . ." said Ben.

319

"And the Traverses?"

"For Daddy, of course," cried Ben.

"What about Mike's girl?"

"She's called Karen and she's older than he is."

I could not imagine anyone becoming romantic over Mike. His face is very pink and his hands very large and his hair really is the colour of carrots. He can kill a rabbit with a flick of his wrist, as though it was nothing more important than a sprig of heather. Or he can be the gentlest person in the world with a sick horse. Mummy insists that we saved him from a life of crime, but I think Social Services would have saved him anyway.

"He's supposed to help us with the horses," I said.

"He's in love," replied Ben, as though that explained everything.

"Excuses, excuses, always excuses," I answered, which is what my favourite teacher at school is forever saying.

We finished mucking out and wandered indoors. The Travers children were standing in the hall looking out of the windows which face the road.

"Still waiting?" I asked.

Sally nodded.

"What about breakfast?"

"We feel sick with excitement," she said.

"Speak for yourself," replied Ben. "Come on, Marion and Kenny – breakfast."

Ten minutes later the storm broke. Ben and I rushed outside to put the ponies in. "They can't travel wet," yelled Ben.

"I only wish we knew when he was coming," I answered. "He's so inconsiderate."

"They haven't had a single card from him," said Ben.

"He's a monster," I answered. "A hideous, unkind devil."

"He makes you sick, doesn't he?" asked Ben.

"I didn't think you cared," I shouted against the noise of falling rain.

"I can't bear their poor little faces," yelled Ben. "They look starved somehow."

"Like their ponies," I yelled, slamming loose-box doors.

"Emotionally, not physically," yelled Ben.

We ran back to the house with water streaming down our necks. Lisa was playing noughts and crosses with Kenny. Marion was helping Mummy stack the dishwasher. Sally was watching the clock. How long will they wait? I wondered. Surely soon they'll start playing games or complaining, or fighting. But they didn't.

When the thunderstorm ended, I went outside again. Everything looked wet and new. The stable-yard was washed clean, the dust had changed colour and become earth. The awful tension had gone; the sun was coming out to dry the leaves.

I groomed Little Bo-Peep and then Jack and Jill. I fetched some scissors and trimmed their fetlocks. They were becoming quite handsome in spite of their narrow chests. They nudged my pockets and their eyes stared at empty buckets as though willing them to contain oats.

In a strange way they resembled their owners, and as with them, we were becoming friends too late. I found their headcollars and wiped them over with a damp cloth, while Lorraine watched me with resentful, jealous eyes, grudging them my attention. By now everything was dry again and the rain might never have been.

Lisa came to the stables. "They're still waiting," she said. "It's unbearable. I wish he would come." Her eyes were brimming with tears.

"But it's only eleven o'clock," I answered. "There's a whole afternoon ahead of us."

"If only he had sent them just one postcard," she said. "Or telephoned. I can't bear their faces. They just sit and sit with their little suitcases."

"It will soon be over," I answered. "He will come in a big car, loaded with presents, and they will jump for joy, and disappear with their dear little ponies in a cloud of dust, and we will be able to laugh about the whole episode in a few months, and say, 'Do you remember those three weird children who hardly spoke?'"

"I shan't. I shall keep wondering what's happened to them," replied Lisa, sniffing. "And what about their mother?"

"It's not our business," I answered.

"Well, I think it is. I think we should advertise for her . . . something like 'Lost, one mother. Dark hair. Dimples'."

"They will be gone in a minute, so do shut up," I replied, beginning to laugh.

"Kenny needs a mother," Lisa said obstinately.

"It's not our business," I answered.

"And we'll never see Jack and Jill and Little Bo-Peep again. I wish they had never come," said Lisa.

"Don't be maudlin and sentimental," I answered. "People come and go – that's business."

"I hate you. You've got a heart of stone," cried Lisa, disappearing full tilt towards the house.

It was like that all day. The Traverses waited and gradually the whole house waited. It was though we were waiting for a miracle to happen, something which would change our whole lives. We took it in turns to wait for the telephone to ring. We hardly ate any lunch. The afternoon was the hottest of the year and we lay about listening for the sound of a car which never came, and watching the hands of the clock which hardly seemed to move.

Mummy made special cakes for tea. Sally combed her hair again and retied her bow. Then Marion sat on Mummy's knee, sucking her finger, while Kenny went back to twisting a handkerchief in his hands. Later the telephone rang and all our hearts leaped with hope but it was only a wrong number. Sally started to cry then

and wouldn't be consoled and Marion stopped speaking and Kenny fell into an exhausted sleep.

And so the day wore on and suppertime came. Ben carried their cases upstairs again and Sally started to cry louder than ever and none of us knew what to say. Ben cooked the supper and James rose to the occasion and started to tell funny stories, while outside twilight came slow and unrelenting.

"We must have mixed up the days," said Mummy at last.

"No," answered Sally. "Look, here it is in my diary. He wrote it himself. It says: *Daddy returns*. Which means the plane must have crashed," and suddenly she was shaken by tremendous sobs.

"No, it hasn't. I've listened to the news every hour," replied James quickly. "There hasn't been a single crash of any kind all day, not even a road blocked by a petrol tanker – nothing."

Finally we carried Marion and Kenny to bed and Sally followed, tear-stained and utterly defeated, like a doll with its stuffing taken out. We put them to bed and we read to them and Mummy stayed with Sally for a long time until she fell asleep.

We were all very disheartened by this time and Dad had appeared and was very angry.

"God, what a man!" he cried. "How can he do it? He should be sent to prison."

"I knew he wasn't any good," said Colonel Hunter. "He was too dressy for a start."

"He's not fit to be a father," Mrs Mills said in a disheartened voice. "Poor little children."

"Supposing he never turns up?" asked James.

"Don't be ridiculous," answered Dad. "He'll be here tomorrow. He must have missed the plane."

I went upstairs to bed, tired to the marrow of my

bones by the emotion of the day. My bed was a haven. I climbed into it thinking: They need a mother, a relation, someone who cares, and I wondered what we could do if their father never came for them, if they stayed on and on with their ponies and no one ever claimed them.

Nine

Where are you?

By the morning Kenny had come to terms with the situation. He came downstairs quite early looking for Lisa. "I want to ride," he said. "I want to be a jockey. I don't care about Daddy, I hate him. When can I ride?"

"In half an hour. Have some breakfast first," I said.

"And I want to stay here," he continued in a small, determined voice. "I don't want to leave, ever."

"Super," I answered, searching for cornflakes. Marion appeared next, looking for Mummy.

Then Mrs Mills came looking for letters and I heard Colonel Hunter calling, "Has the newspaper come?"

"Kenny's going to be a jockey when he's grown up," I said to no one in particular.

The post came next. I looked for postcards but there was nothing but a pile of bills for Dad and James's GCSE results, which made me tear upstairs shouting, "James, they've come!"

"Push them under the door and go away," he said in a muffled voice. "I don't want to talk about them – just go away."

I knew the bills would upset Dad, because most of them were final demands in red. I rushed downstairs again, praying that James's results would be good.

"Any important letters?" asked Mummy. "Anything from Mick Travers?"

I shook my head as Sally appeared looking pale and quiet. She refused to eat any breakfast. Finally she asked, "Did anything come by post?" and we all shook our heads, feeling awful.

"I expect he'll be here soon," she said. "He would have written otherwise." And none of us had to ask who "he" was.

Then James came rushing downstairs crying, "I've got three top grades and three second grades. I've done all right. I can go to the Sixth Form College. Hurray!"

Mummy started to laugh with relief and Mrs Mills shouted, "Well done, young man."

Then Lisa arrived waving a piece of paper and crying, "I've got a super idea. You know Mrs Holman's gymkhana in aid of Save the Children, for twelve and unders, well, Sally, Marion and Kenny can go, they're all young enough. It's Saturday week."

"We shall be gone by then," replied Sally.

"I shan't. I'm not going. I'm staying," replied Kenny.

"So am I," said Marion.

"You can't. Daddy won't pay for you," Sally answered.

"I don't care."

"Just look at the classes – Leading Rein under Ten, Jumping classes, Handy Pony, Musical Ponies – there's everything. Let's start practising straight away. Jack and Jill will do very well in the leading rein. We can plait them up. Bags lead Kenny," cried Lisa, dancing round the kitchen.

"We will be gone. He'll come today," said Sally.

But Lisa wouldn't listen. She cried, "Get your hats on. Where are the bending poles? Are you coming, Harriet?"

Suddenly she was a live wire and the others caught her enthusiasm, except for Sally who said, "I shall be eleven by then. My birthday's soon."

"But it's under twelves. When is your birthday, anyway?" asked Lisa, pulling a face.

"I'm not saying."

"All right, don't," retorted Lisa, sticking out her tongue.

"Lisa!" cried Mummy. "What terrible behaviour."

"I don't care," shouted Lisa, rushing outside with Kenny and Marion at her heels.

"Look at these bills!" cried Dad, coming into the kitchen. "Who keeps using the telephone? It's double what it was last time."

"It's because it keeps going up," replied Mummy.

Sally was sitting by the telephone in the hall, like a dog waiting by his lead and hoping for a walk.

I said, "It's no good waiting and waiting, come outside for a bit, please." But she shook her head.

"Do cheer up," I said. "Probably a train broke down or he had a puncture; or the nearest airport to where he is has gone on strike. Or the storm stopped his ship sailing, or fog grounded all planes."

"You'll never understand – he's the only person I've got left," she said.

I went outside. Ben was knocking in bending poles. Lisa was tacking up Jack and Jill. "Don't trot if they cough," I said.

"I'm not an imbecile," answered Lisa.

Sometimes I love Lisa, sometimes I hate her; today I hated her. She had taken over, and from now on she would see Kenny and Marion as her responsibility. She would boss them day and night. She would tell me to shut up whenever I made a suggestion. She would behave as though she was my age when she was years younger. I felt furious.

"Don't pay any attention to her," said Ben, smiling. "They will be gone soon. Their daddy will come with lots of lovely lolly."

But their daddy didn't come. The whole day passed and there was still no sign of Mick Travers. And another day passed and another.

We waited for telephone calls, searched the hall regularly for letters. Mrs Mills walked about muttering "Poor children", while Colonel Hunter said, "I knew he was a cad." And Dad worried because we were feeding three children for nothing, plus three ponies.

Roy's bill came and we had to buy more hay because there was no grass left. James walked about in a happy trance because of his exam results, imagining a glorious future. Ben wandered about moaning over the hay situation. Lisa continued practising for the approaching gymkhana and the sun continued shining from the same relentless blue sky, until the fields had cracks in them

329

and the grass was the colour of straw. Marion and Kenny were happy. Their faces were no longer pale and clean, they became tanned and very beautiful with their pale, pale hair. Only Sally continued to mourn. Mummy was as happy as James but for a different reason.

"What does money matter compared to what we have achieved?" she cried. "Look at Marion; she's a normal, happy child now. It's a miracle."

"They must go eventually," Dad said. "We can't afford three extra children."

"You can't drive them away," retorted Mummy. "They need us."

"We're not a charity," argued Dad. "I wish we were."

Two days later Dad and Mummy travelled to London, leaving us in charge of the Travers children.

"Don't leave them alone, not for a minute. Promise?" said Mummy.

"Okay," I answered.

"Don't take them riding until we get back. I've left a cold lunch for you all in the larder. Look after the Colonel, Harriet," she said.

"Okay, but why me?" I asked.

"We'll ring up at lunch-time to see that everything is all right," she continued as though I had never spoken.

"Oh, really," cried Ben, "What do you think is going to happen?"

"One never knows."

"What are you doing? Buying clothes?" asked Lisa.

"No. Searching for clues," said Mummy. "Sally has given me a description of her mother, it's very vague, but better than nothing."

I imagined them walking up and down Oxford Street looking at the passers-by. Neither of them ever looks right in London. Mummy's clothes are always several years out of date and Dad strides through the streets as though on a country walk, his head turning all ways, as though there was a lovely view of fields just over the hill.

"I should go to Somerset House," said Mrs Mills.

"Try Scotland Yard," advised the Colonel.

"Don't worry, we'll be all right," said James.

We watched them go. Mummy was wearing a cotton dress and sandals, while Dad had tucked a cravat into an open-necked shirt, which he wore with an ancient pair of cavalry twill trousers. He had borrowed Ben's dark glasses.

"I suppose we can groom the ponies," said Lisa. "Where are Kenny and Marion?"

"Lying on the lawn, poor little things," answered Mrs Mills.

Sally was sitting in the hall doing nothing. I think she was doing what the Victorians called "sinking into a decline". Her poor face was etched with lines which shouldn't have been there. I felt very sorry for her. "Mummy and Dad have gone to London to sort things out," I said.

"What about the fares?" she answered. "It must be very expensive."

"Well, they won't go for nothing," I answered.

"Daddy has never been like this before," she said.

"Why don't you come outside? James will answer the telephone," I suggested.

"No, thank you."

I felt inadequate. I couldn't think of anything else to say.

"I like sitting here. I watch the clock and the telephone and the letterbox all at once. I like it," she told me.

I wandered outside. Lisa, Kenny and Marion were practising musical poles on their feet. "Now for the sack race," shouted Lisa. Later I put lunch on the table and chatted to Colonel Hunter. The day seemed to be passing very slowly and my brothers kept making silly remarks.

After lunch we all went outside to build jumps in the paddock and Mrs Mills promised to look after Sally, who was reading in the hall.

Mummy and Dad hadn't telephoned but Ben said, "Don't worry. No news is good news."

Lisa, Kenny and Marion started to play schools in the saddle room. I painted a jump pole red and white. I worked very slowly and the paint dried almost at once, such was the heat of the day.

As I worked, I wondered what it felt like to lose first your mother and then your father, and what would happen to the three Traverses if neither ever turned up. The heat and the smell of paint made my head ache.

Presently I called, "Are you all right, Lisa? I'm just going indoors for an aspirin."

"Yes," she called back, "what do you think, I'm not two years old."

I found Mrs Mills asleep in the kitchen. Colonel Hunter was dozing in a deckchair on the lawn. James was playing his stereo full blast upstairs. I blocked my ears and looked in the hall for Sally; she wasn't there.

I ran upstairs, stopping to thump on James's door and yelled, "Turn it down."

Sally wasn't in any of the attic rooms. I searched the dining-room and the best sitting-room, and the other sitting-room and all the time my spirits were going further

and further down, and my heart was thumping faster and faster.

Then I started to shout, "Sally, Sally, where are you?"

Mrs Mills woke up and said, "Oh dear, I must have dropped off. Where's that girl?"

"I don't know," I answered.

"She can't be far, she was here a minute ago," said Mrs Mills, scrambling to her feet.

I picked up a piece of paper from the kitchen table. On it were written the simple words: *Goodbye. Sally.*

I held on to the table to stop myself fainting.

"She's gone," I cried. "It says 'Goodbye'."

James was suddenly beside me, crying, "But why?"

I was consumed with a terrible sense of failure. Then the telephone rang and it was Mummy.

"Where have you been? I've been ringing for ages; there wasn't any answer. Are you all out?" she asked.

"Not really," I answered, hating James for not having heard because he had thoughtlessly played his stereo full blast, inwardly cursing poor Mrs Mills for falling asleep. "We've lost Sally," I said. "She's disappeared."

"I thought something must have happened," replied Mummy in a small, frightened voice. "Because she would have answered, wouldn't she? I mean, she's been sitting beside the telephone for days; that's why I was so worried. Oh dear . . . I haven't any more change," she cried and was cut off.

I put down the receiver with a shaking hand. I imagined her standing in a phone-box, white-faced, and Dad in a fury. I imagined Sally run over, dead, her small pinched face still for ever; then I was running towards the stables calling, "Lisa, Ben, Sally's gone. We need a search party. Stop playing. It's an emergency."

Colonel Hunter leaped from his chair, calling, "I'm at your disposal."

334

Mrs Mills followed me, her grey hair on end, her pinny flapping, her slippered feet making no sound on the path. And Marion said, "Our family is always running away. She'll come back."

"Mummy didn't," replied Kenny. "And she never will, as long as Daddy lives."

Ten
I'll shoot

I leaped on Lorraine while Lisa mounted Jigsaw off the fence and Ben fetched his bike. We are used to searching, though this time we didn't need headcollars and oats. Mrs Mills started running down the drive on foot. Colonel Hunter said, "I'll look after Kenny and Marion. Come on," and he took their hands and they looked small and trusting beside him. "Do you know *If* by Rudyard Kipling?" he continued, starting to recite. I thought how helpful he was, before I turned Lorraine's grey head towards the common.

"I'll go right, you go left. Meet you in the woods," cried Lisa.

"I'll search the village," shouted Ben, pedalling through the gate. We were all in deadly earnest. We had searched before and found tragedy and it was something we would never forget, so my hair was standing up along my spine as I crossed the common and more and more dreadful thoughts rushed through my mind – Sally dying in a ditch, the police searching with dogs, darkness coming and an endless, awful night. And then the morning and the awful awakening to a new day of fear and desperation. It was almost more than I could bear.

There was no one in the woods and I started to call, "Sally, come back, please come back." And the woods echoed my voice and were suddenly hateful and I thought I should never love them again.

Next I imagined Mummy and Dad returning, their exhausted faces creased with worry. I imagined them saying, "We trusted you and you failed us." And hot tears ran down my face and I tasted salt on my lips. Lorraine kept coughing but I rode her on relentlessly, because if her wind broke it would be just one more awful thing among so many that it would hardly count.

Soon I met two people walking arm in arm. They were middle-aged with sturdy legs and walking-boots. "We heard you calling. Are you looking for a dog?" they asked.

"No, a small girl with very fair hair, called Sally," I answered.

"Oh dear," cried the man.

"She'll turn up, dear, not to worry," said the lady. "I expect you've had a tiff, haven't you, dear?"

I nodded and rode on while they continued on their way, unperturbed and unflappable, stopping to prod the ground at intervals.

Presently I met Lisa, galloping madly, Jigsaw dripping with sweat, his eyes shining with excitement.

"Any luck? I said, any luck?" she shouted before I had time to reply.

"Nothing," I answered.

"We need a pack of hounds – bloodhounds," she said.

"Why did she do it?" I cried. But I thought I knew – she had reached breaking point, she couldn't wait and hope any longer. She had had to do something.

"We are doomed," cried Lisa. "We never have any luck; first the horses are ill, and the children are strange, and then this. It isn't fair. Supposing we never find her?"

"Shut up," I shouted.

"What will happen?"

"I don't know."

We parted again. Lisa jumped a stile and fell off. I galloped through the woods missing trees by centimetres, calling, "Sally, Sally, come back." Lorraine must have thought me mad, but she didn't argue or hesitate. Finally I reached a road and everything was suddenly normal, with cars travelling up and down full of sweating passengers and coaches hurtling by with holiday-makers peering through the windows, afraid of missing something. Lorraine dripped sweat and coughed incessantly and my heart felt as heavy as lead.

"We had better go home," I said at last. I dismounted and walked and the sun beat on my head like fire and the tar stuck to my feet. I couldn't even cry.

And then at last I heard Ben calling, "Found! It's all

right, she's found." He came down the road pedalling his bike, his face wreathed in a smile which almost reached his ears. "Mrs Mills found her hiding in some bushes on the common. We all went too far, too fast; she's given her a drink and put her to bed. The old Colonel is being grandad and reading Kipling to the other two, and they're loving it. Kenny's sitting on his knee. It's fantastic."

"Have Mummy and Dad turned up yet?" I asked.

"No, not yet. But not to worry," said Ben.

It was like sunshine after a long storm. My heart stopped pounding. I felt weak at the knees and dizzy with relief. "I hope she's sorry," I said.

"I doubt it. Where's Lisa?" asked Ben.

"Not far away," I answered.

"I'll go and fetch her," he said.

I walked on slowly, thanking God for what had happened and everything started to look beautiful again.

I looked at Lorraine and cursed myself for panicking. Children were kicking balls on the common. The pond was completely dry.

It's all right, Harriet, I said to myself. Calm down. Sally's in bed, no one can blame you for anything. You're home, high and dry. But the day wasn't done yet. Awful moments still lay ahead, but I didn't know that then; at that moment I felt only a great sense of relief and that incredible feeling of happiness which comes after you've been tested in some way and survived.

When I went indoors Mrs Mills was getting tea. She looked smaller than usual and guilty, like an animal which knows it's done something wrong.

"It wasn't your fault. We all go to sleep sometimes. James should have been around helping," I told her, for I know how it feels to be consumed with guilt, to think you've let everyone down, and when those awful words, "if only" and "too late" keep coming to mind.

"You do too much, anyway," I continued. "You are a paying guest, you shouldn't be getting tea for the rest of us. You should be behaving like a rich old lady."

"I don't like rich old ladies," she replied, clattering knives. "I like families, things happening, that's why I'm so lucky to be here."

"Things certainly happen here," I muttered, pouring hot water on to tea leaves.

"I'm fond of your mother and I don't like letting her down," continued Mrs Mills. She had put her hearing-aid on for once so there was no need to shout.

Ben put his head round the door to say, "I'm just popping down the village to see Simon – all right?" Simon is his best friend.

"No," I answered. "We need you."

But he was gone before I finished speaking.

Lisa came in next saying, "I fell off. What's for tea? Where's Mummy?"

"The train takes two hours. She won't be home for some time yet," I answered.

"Lorraine's coughing. I think you've broken her wind," said Lisa, who has not one atom of tact.

"Thank you for telling me."

We all ate tea in different places; then Lisa, Marion and Kenny settled down in front of the television and James went out for a walk and I waited for our parents' return.

I was half asleep when the front doorbell rang. I got out of the kitchen chair and lumbered across the hall with pins and needles in my feet. I wondered who it could be at that time. We weren't expecting anybody and it was too early for Mummy and Dad, and they wouldn't ring the bell anyway.

There were two men outside. "Good evening," they said. "We've come for the Travers children."

"For the Travers children?" I repeated to gain time. "Who are you? We weren't expecting you."

"Their father sent us, Mr Mick Travers," the largest replied. I looked them up and down. They were both large and they wore gloves in spite of the heat and one was bearded. They looked like retired boxers or the sort of men you see at fairs manning the bumper cars. Somehow they didn't look right for Sally, Marion and Kenny. And suddenly I was very frightened. But now they were standing in the hall, appraising everything with their eyes, as though one day they might come back and take

it. I wished that Ben and James were at home. I needed a man to stand up to them. "You had better wait," I said. And they sat on the two chairs in the hall with their caps on their knees.

I went back to Mrs Mills in the kitchen. "Some men have come for the Travers children. What are we going to do?" I asked. My voice was shaky.

"What do they look like?"

"All wrong," I answered.

"Let me deal with them," she said.

She looked small and indomitable staring at them.

"Well, and who are you?" she asked. "Where are your references and your letter from Mr Travers authorising you to collect his children? Come on, young men, speak up," she said.

"Look, he's our mate. He asked us to do him a favour. Get the kiddies, will you, Gran; they'll recognise us," said the one with a beard.

"We haven't a lot of time," said the other.

They stood up and pushed past Mrs Mills. I barred the way and at that moment the three children appeared, followed by the Colonel.

"I've come from your daddy. I'm taking you home. Come along now. You want to go home to Daddy, don't you?" asked the one with a beard.

"We haven't got a home to go to," replied Kenny in a small, frightened voice.

"I don't know you," said Sally.

"Yes you do. I'm your Uncle Sammy."

"Get the police," said Mrs Mills. "Quick."

"Oh no you don't," cried the bearded one, ripping out the telephone wires.

I knew then that they were criminals. I knew too that they were determined to take the children. I prayed for Mummy and Dad to come back, for Ben to come in

342

laughing with Simon, for someone to rescue us. Please God, help us, I prayed. The Colonel and the three children were backing away up the stairs with the two men following them. For an awful moment time seemed to stand still.

I felt numb with fear. It was like one of those dreams when you want to scream and can't. I couldn't think. My mind was just a terrifying blank.

"We're taking you anyway. Are you coming easy? Or are we going to have a fight?" asked the bearded one. "We won't hurt you, we promise."

Lisa appeared and started throwing shoes at them. "Go away," she yelled. "Leave them alone."

Their feet were halfway up the stairs now, big feet in boots. The children started to run. Marion screamed.

And then suddenly Colonel Hunter appeared holding a revolver. "I'm an old soldier. It's loaded and if you take another step I'll shoot," he said.

Now the men were retreating, backing down the stairs, saying, "It's all right, Guv, no harm meant," and I

was running outside, looking at their car, taking down the number, scribbling it on the calendar which I had snatched from the kitchen wall.

Colonel Hunter followed them until they were outside, his hand steady on the revolver. "Now clear off," he yelled. "Coming here and frightening women and children!" He slammed the front door after them and did up the chain.

"I'll put the kettle on," said Mrs Mills. "We need a cup of tea." And I saw that she was very pale and shaking all over.

"I should have a licence for this thing; I kept it after the war. It hasn't any ammunition anyway, but they weren't to know," said Colonel Hunter. "You had better lock the doors and put the shutters up, Harriet, they may come back."

Our house is old enough to have shutters inside to make it like a fortress. The doors have chains and enormous bolts too. I went round shutting everything and bolting and barring, then I put the lights on. After that I found Lisa, Sally, Marion and Kenny crouched together in one of the attic bedrooms. "It's all right, they've gone. Come and have some hot tea with sugar in it. You need something," I said.

"I feel all funny inside and my heart keeps fluttering," said Lisa. "Do you think they'll come back?"

"If they do, we're ready this time," said Mrs Mills. "I'll pour boiling water on them from the upstairs windows. They won't like that."

"Colonel Hunter is such a brave old man. I wish he was our grandad," said Sally.

"So do I," agreed Kenny.

It was strange sitting in the house with the shutters closed tight across the windows, but we felt safe now and gradually we began to laugh a little, even Sally.

Colonel Hunter didn't talk much. I think he was exhausted by his efforts.

He sat with his revolver across his knee, waiting. Then at last we heard the familiar noise of our own car and a few minutes later Dad started banging on the back door, crying, "What's happened? Is there a siege or something?"

I let them in, bolting the door after them. "This is our fortress," I began. "It's a long story."

"Oh Mummy!" cried Lisa. "I'm so glad you're home. It's been such a dreadful day."

"To begin at the end, Mr Pemberton," said Colonel Hunter, coming back to reality with a start, "I think you should go to the phone-box and telephone the police without delay, our attackers having wrecked your telephone beyond immediate repair. Your daughter, Harriet, with great presence of mind, has written down their car number. I think you should hurry."

I handed Dad the calendar I had written on. "They came to take away Sally, Marion and Kenny," I explained.

"And we didn't know them," shouted Kenny.

"They tried to take the children by force," explained Colonel Hunter. "I protected them with my trusty revolver."

"I threw shoes at them," said Lisa.

"Description?" asked Dad.

"Swarthy, both six foot or more, well built, one bearded," replied Colonel Hunter.

"Crooks," I said, "boxers. Like men who work bumper cars at fairs."

"Plain clothes," continued Colonel Hunter. "Gloves for fear of fingerprints, so they must have been convicted at some time or other."

"Right," cried Dad, making for the door.

We started to tell Mummy what had happened. Then my brothers came back and we unshuttered the windows and started to tell our story again, then Dad returned and said, "The police will be here any moment." Mrs Mills put the kettle on again, Mummy took off her uncomfortable sandals, and Marion climbed on to her knee. And now there was only Mike to come home.

"Did you have any luck?" I asked Mummy.

"Yes, we've started the ball rolling," she said. "There's a mass of complications. For one thing they weren't Travers in the beginning, their name was Ansell. Do you remember being Sally Ansell?" Mummy asked, looking at Sally. "Because you only changed your name three years ago by deed poll."

"Yes," whispered Sally, looking shamefaced.

"And your daddy has been married twice," continued Mummy. "You should have told us things like that; it would have made life easier. Like where you were born – you're American, Sally, you never told us that you were born in New York. We only want to help you, darling. We want to find your parents so you can go home and live a normal life."

"We haven't got a home," said Kenny.

"And I don't like my parents," added Marion.

We could hear heavy boots on the path. "It's the police," said Mummy. "Now don't be scared. Tell them everything – the truth. They want to help you; they want to find your mummy."

"I can't tell them everything, some things are too bad to tell," said Sally.

A policewoman talked to Lisa and the Traverses. She was very kind and called them "love" and "dear" and had brought a packet of sweets with her. They disappeared into the dining-room, while the rest of us talked to two officers in the kitchen.

My brothers were furious at missing everything. Mrs
Mills was rather excited and Colonel Hunter was calm
and efficient and called the policemen "officer". I told
them just what had happened and one of them wrote
down everything I said. I told them about the ponies and
what the children had said about their mother, and explained how nervous they were. Then one of the officers
said "Thank you", and I wandered outside and said
goodnight to the ponies. It was almost dark by now, and
I saw that there was a policeman standing by the gate
keeping guard. I felt very safe. Presently the police left
and the sky was full of stars.

"They know the men," Dad said later over supper.
"They belong to a high-powered gang in London.
Things are moving pretty fast now. They could be trying

347

to blackmail Mick Travers, which might explain a lot."

"I wish we could find Mrs Travers," said Mummy. "I don't mind keeping the children but it's so expensive and we're not being paid a thing."

"And their ponies are having hay, which is no joke," chipped in Ben.

Lisa and the Traverses had suppers on trays. They were all exhausted and Lisa could do nothing but cry, while Sally's eyes seemed to be sinking into the back of her head with exhaustion. And Marion hung on to Mummy like a two-year-old and Kenny wouldn't be separated from a dilapidated teddy bear.

Mrs Mills fell asleep at supper. Dad and Colonel Hunter sipped brandy, while James made the rest of us coffee, and so the day ended, a day none of us would ever forget.

Eleven
The gymkhana

We overslept the next day and were wakened by the
telephone engineer coming to repair the telephone. We
expected letters and none came; we expected policemen
to call and none came. The Colonel was very tired by his
brave exploits of yesterday and spent most of his time
dozing. There was no work for Mike on the farm so he
stood about the kitchen getting in everyone's way. Mrs
Mills related the events of the day before over and over
again, driving us to distraction. Sally was very quiet.
Kenny was excited and talked non-stop. "I can't remember being Ansell, or only dimly," he said. "It's all very
exciting, isn't it?"

Marion followed Mummy everywhere until Lisa took
the three of them riding, saying, "Only two days to the
show now. We must practise. You don't want to be last,
do you?"

Ben and James were sulking, hating themselves, I suppose, for missing what we now called The Siege. The
sun continued shining. It was impossible to imagine it
would ever stop.

Dad sat going through his accounts pulling a face,
fuming over the price of everything, muttering, "We
can't go on like this, something will have to go up in
price."

Then Ben came into the kitchen dragging a large dog

behind him, saying, "He's just been delivered. It's Sally's birthday and we didn't know. Isn't he lovely?"

"What's he doing here?" cried Mummy.

"He's Sally's birthday present. He's an Alsatian," said Ben. "Don't be beastly, please."

"I don't know what your father will say!" cried Mummy. "Where did he come from? He's enormous. He isn't an Alsatian. He's a Great Dane."

"A man came in a van. There's a note attached to his collar," said Ben. "He's called Zed."

I opened the back door and yelled, "Sally! Happy birthday! Come in quickly, there's a present."

Dad appeared in the kitchen and said, "What's this? He's not going to live here, is he?"

"It looks like it," replied Ben, still smiling. "He's a beauty, isn't he?"

"What about his food?" wailed Dad. "He'll cost twenty pounds a week to feed. Oh my God! You're driving me to drink!"

Lisa and the others came into the kitchen at that moment and I cried, "Happy birthday, Sally. He's yours." And her face suddenly lit up.

"There's a message on his collar," explained Ben.

She took it off and read it. "He's from Dad," she cried. "He's a birthday present. It says: *To love and protect you always*. Oh, I'm so happy."

Lisa disappeared and returned with a book of hers wrapped in tissue paper. "Happy birthday," she said, giving it to Sally.

"Where will he sleep?" asked Kenny. "He's too big to sleep on Sally's bed."

"I wish he was mine," said Marion.

"There's an old mattress in the loft. He can sleep on that with a blanket," said Mummy.

He had dark-coloured legs and a dark muzzle, and

the rest of him was dun-coloured.

"I knew Daddy wouldn't forget," said Sally, stroking him. "He must have known those awful men would turn up and try to drag us away. They won't dare with Zed guarding us."

"It shows those men were fakes, because if they came from your daddy, he wouldn't have sent you a present here today, now would he? It stands to reason, don't it?" exclaimed Mike.

"Doesn't it," corrected Mummy.

Zed looked at the food on the table and drooled. He was the biggest dog I had ever seen.

"Take him outside with you," said Mummy.

"Back to practising," said Lisa. "Because tomorrow we'll have to start grooming the ponies and washing their white bits, and there's the tack. We must take it to bits, all of it."

"I'll tie him to the fence," said Sally.

"I will have to tell the police," Dad said after they had gone. "Did you look at the van or the man, Ben?"

"Not properly. I was so excited by Zed," replied Ben.

I ran down to the fields and held potatoes for the potato race. Lisa won, of course, but the Traverses were not far behind.

"I shan't be able to go into the consolation race, so you can win that," said Lisa with a smile.

I nearly said, "Shut up, nasty conceited little brat," but it was too hot for arguments.

"Now for the egg and spoon," said Lisa.

All the horses were looking better, but the hay was getting low again and still there wasn't a cloud in the sky.

"I don't want anyone to fetch us. I want to stay here for ever," said Kenny, taking my hand.

"Same here," agreed Marion. "I want to learn to ride as well as Lisa."

"But we must know what has happened to your parents. You must care a bit," I answered.

"Well, they've both walked out on us," replied Kenny. "And I shan't get a dog for my birthday."

The day of the gymkhana dawned fine. I could hear Lisa and the Travers children going along the passage at dawn, trying to be quiet but failing completely. A door slammed, then another; there was muffled laughter and the sound of a huge dog scampering – Zed, of course, who had stolen food the night before from the kitchen table and half killed Twinkle. The noises suddenly made me feel old. I wished that I was still twelve and could be riding in the gymkhana too.

Later I heard Mrs Mills shuffling downstairs in search of a letter and Colonel Hunter opening his window to lean out and smell the air, as he did every morning. Then I heard Mike whistling along the path, out of tune as usual, and the clock in the hall chimed seven times. And now sunshine flooded my room, showing the dust which hung suspended in the air, and suddenly it was unnatural to be in bed. I got up slowly. I could see Lisa in the yard plaiting manes. Sally was threading needles for her while Kenny sat on the fence and watched and Marion stroked rather than groomed grey Little Bo- Peep, who was too narrow for a Welsh mountain pony and the wrong colour for a Dartmoor.

They had all been washed the night before and Jigsaw had spent the night in the stable, rugged and bandaged, so that his white bits looked as white as the whitest snow.

Zed looked pathetic tied to the fence. His lead was too short for him to sit down. I could hear Dad talking to Mummy, saying, "It can't go on. We can't afford it . . ." and Mummy wearily answering, "Give us a bit more time."

"Three children, one dog the size of a pony – if he was a miniature poodle it wouldn't be so bad – and then three ponies. It just isn't fair," wailed Dad.

"Something will happen. It must," replied Mummy.

I was dressed now. I went outside and complimented Lisa on her plaits, but she only said, "Go away, please. I'm going mad. I've lost three needles already."

I fed our own horses and Ben appeared and hitched up the trailer. "We're taking two loads, it's the only way," he said.

"Can't they hack?" I asked.

"They might run away. Little Bo-Peep isn't a hundred per cent in traffic," he said.

Windfall was still coughing and when she coughed her whole small, fluffy body shook. Zed started to howl. I returned to the house and found a young woman in glasses talking to Mummy in the kitchen. She had a pale face and straight red hair.

"Please leave it until tomorrow," Mummy said. "They're just off to a show. Just look out of the window and see how happy they look. Don't spoil it today, please."

"What about the dog?" asked the young woman.

"He belongs to Sally."

"We can't take him into care. He will have to stay with you," she said.

"I think they should all stay," replied Mummy.

"What about schools? Doesn't one need a special school?"

"Certainly not," replied Mummy sharply.

"Social Services want to take them into care, poor little kids," Mummy said when the woman had gone. "But I won't let them. We'll foster them here."

I knew she was talking about the Traverses. "That woman seems awfully young to decide the fate of the children's lives," I said.

"Exactly," agreed Mummy.

An hour later we were loading Jack and Jill, who were in Class One at the gymkhana. I was to lead Marion on Jill, while Ben and Mummy returned and fetched Little Bo-Peep and Jigsaw. Lisa was leading Kenny. The three children were all wearing gloves and were far better dressed than poor Lisa, who wore one of my old riding-coats, Ben's old boots, a shirt which was

missing a top button and a Pony Club tie frayed at the
bottom. Her jodhpurs were her own, but too short in
the leg, so that a piece of white sock showed between
them and her boots. And her hat was faded, having been
Ben's before mine. But she didn't seem to mind. There
was a streak of dirt across her face and her hair needed
combing but that was Lisa – too busy getting on with
life to bother with small details like cleanliness.

The ponies loaded without trouble. Mrs Mills called
"Good luck" and Colonel Hunter shouted "Bring home
some ribbons."

Mummy drove cautiously out of the drive, while
Marion laughed and Sally announced, "Our first show

355

ever. I wish Daddy was here to see us." Zed drooled in the back of the Land Rover and we could hear the ponies moving in the trailer behind, but we were on our way with the sun in our eyes and hope in our hearts. This is the way to live, I thought, day by day, not worrying about the future, every day as though it was your last.

The show was only a few miles away. Mummy unloaded and drove away again. Lisa fussed with tail bandages and last-minute grooming efforts. Then one of Jill's plaits came undone and had to be replaited. Then Class One was being called to the collecting ring and there was the usual panic. But at last Kenny and Marion were mounted and ready to enter the ring for the Leading Rein Class. Lisa was laughing and happy while Sally looked anxious, holding Zed, and I was thinking about the young woman who had called, and wondering whether she could remove the children by force if necessary, and thinking how awful that would be.

Then we were in the ring walking round, keeping our distance, each one of us trying to show our pony to his best advantage. In the distance I could hear Ben shouting, "Get out, I'll back it, Mummy. You're going to hit something in a minute," and I knew that Mummy had returned and couldn't turn the trailer.

Presently we were called in and Jill was standing fifth and Jack was second and our hopes started to rise. We trotted each in turn and the judge looked at legs and teeth and asked kind questions like "How old are you?" or "Have you had your pony long?"

There were twenty-two entries in the class and some of the mothers were better dressed than their children, with carnations in their buttonholes and chalk-white leading reins and beautifully done hair. There were fathers too, anxiously making their ponies stand with

legs in the right place, and small, anxious children in black coats looking as though their lives depended on winning. Lisa's plaits looked fat and amateurish compared to some of the others and our ponies still looked on the thin side. But, though we were soon moved down, we were not at the bottom of the row. Marion was very silent and Kenny talked to Lisa in a whisper, as though he was at the theatre and didn't want to upset the actors. The judge wore a silk dress and a big hat and she said that Jill was sweet and just the sort of pony she would like for her grandchildren, but she awarded first prize to a showy bay who wouldn't stand still, and second to a chestnut who threw his head up and down, and third to a black with an Araby head and a beautifully pulled tail.

Lisa made a face at me when she saw the others being led out to stand in front and Kenny whispered, "Aren't we getting a prize?"

A dappled grey was awarded the fourth rosette and the rest of us were given pink specials.

Afterwards parents surged forward to take photographs and Dad appeared and muttered, "I should have brought my camera, sorry."

Sally answered, "If Daddy was here he would be hard at work; he's got a lovely camera, it cost three hundred pounds."

"I can't compete with that," muttered Dad.

Lisa left me in charge while she mounted Jigsaw for the Twelve and Under Jumping, which was about to begin, and Kenny said, "It was fun, anyway, and I've got my first rosette."

Marion joined Mummy and I saw that Mrs Mills had come too and was stroking Zed. Everything seemed perfectly normal and well organised and yet, after just a moment, all would be changed. For while we were concentrating on the gymkhana someone else was observing us, staring at the Travers children, calculating, deciding, looking at Mummy, comparing us to one another, summing us up and coming to a conclusion which would have far-reaching effects.

Twelve

Great news

Ten minutes later a tall, slim woman approached Mummy. She wore a denim skirt and a checked shirt, and fashionable shoes. She caught Mummy's eye and said, "I know I sound impertinent but are those children yours?"

I was holding Jack and Jill while Lisa waited in the collecting ring for her jumping class, watched by Sally, Marion and Kenny. Sally still held Zed. Ben was leading Little Bo-Peep up and down.

"Which children?" asked Mummy.

"The blonde ones."

"I don't know whether I want to answer that question," replied Mummy evasively, no doubt remembering the men who had tried to take the Traverses away by force. "Who are you, anyway?"

"It's a long story," said the woman. "My name is Christine, Christine Lightfoot. I'm a nurse."

"Well, thank you for introducing yourself," replied Mummy. "But whether those children are mine or not is none of your business."

"But you are not their mother, are you?" continued Christine Lightfoot. "Because they are not like you at all, not their hair, the shape of their faces or anything else. You may be their foster mother but I think I have their real mother in my hospital."

"You must be mad," replied Mummy. "Unless you have her in the mortuary."

"No, in my ward actually. I'm a Sister," explained Christine Lightfoot. "And I have a woman of roughly thirty in my ward who has lost her memory. She cracked her skull and, until yesterday, had no recollection of anything. Now she is talking about children, she is sure she has some. She has blonde hair and the same eyes as the middle girl over there. She can only remember walking out of a house and catching a train; she is still trying to recall her name. Could she be their mother? Please tell me . . ."

Lisa was jumping and she came galloping out of the ring shouting, "I've done a clear round," as though it was a miracle.

She threw herself on to the ground. "There's only six clear rounds," she yelled, "so I may get a rosette."

"Yes," said Mummy. "It's a long story. Their father brought them to our guest house and then disappeared. Their mother has been lost for some time."

"And was never reported missing?" asked Christine Lightfoot.

"I suspect not," replied Mummy.

I was feeling funny inside now, half surprise, half relief.

"What do you want me to do?" asked Mummy.

"Bring them to see her."

"Where is the hospital?"

"In West London."

"Won't it upset them?"

"It must be done; every child needs its real mother," said Christine Lightfoot.

"Couldn't you have found out who she was? It would have saved so much agony all round," asked Mummy.

"She was only wearing underwear, a dress and sandals. There wasn't anything to identify her by. Whoever knocked her down had taken her bag and money. There was just her; of course we told the police but there are so many lost people it's just incredible," explained Christine Lightfoot.

"I'm jumping third. Aren't you going to watch? It's against the clock," shouted Lisa, completely oblivious of our conversation.

"I'm on duty tomorrow," said Christine Lightfoot. "I'm just home for the day. But I am so very, very glad I came."

Ben was telling Lisa which corners to cut. I said, "It's

362

nearly over. It looks as if their mother has been found," and he looked at me as though I was mad.

Everything seemed unreal and impossible and yet there was Lisa, real enough, jumping against the clock like an old hand. She was clear again with the fastest time so far and a great cheer went up among her supporters. Dad was with Mummy now and they were writing notes on the back of a cheque book.

Mrs Mills was sitting on the grass eating a bun and, in another ring, working ponies were being judged.

Supposing she isn't their mother after all? Will they survive the disappointment? Or don't they really care? I asked myself. Or are they just pretending not to care, because they care too much? How can one tell? Nothing seemed to make sense. We had tried to solve their problem and now it seemed to be solved just by an encounter at a horse show. It was almost too incredible to be true.

Lisa rode in first and came out smiling, clutching a cup. "I've never won one for jumping before," she said.

"Don't tell them yet, Harriet," said Mummy in my ear. "Let me tell them tonight."

And so the gymkhana continued and I kept my secret, but it spoilt the day for me, because now nothing else mattered in comparison. Lisa won six rosettes in the gymkhana and the cup for the most points.

Kenny was third in the egg and spoon race and Marion was second in the sack race. Sally was against Lisa and all the other twelve and unders, but finally she was third in the consolation race, so they were all happy.

I held Zed all afternoon and spectator after spectator stopped to admire him and I grew tired of saying "He's called Zed" and "No, I don't ride him!"

Later I managed to catch Mummy alone. "Supposing Christine Lightfoot is another kidnapper?" I asked. "It could be another put-up job."

"The hospital is real enough and the bits fit," said Mummy. "Anyway, it's a chance we can't miss."

"There are lots of blonde women," I answered.

"But the children's hair is more than just blonde; it's thick and pale and coarse and hers is the same, apparently," Mummy replied.

By now we had loaded up Jack and Jill. Lisa was hacking Jigsaw home with Sally on Little Bo-Peep. Zed was in the back of the Land Rover. The jumps were down in the ring already and everyone was leaving.

"One has to trust someone and believe in something. And Christine Lightfoot seems a sweetie to me," added Mummy. There she goes again, I thought, believing in people, trusting them when half of them are thieves and liars.

"Don't think evil of everyone, darling," said Mummy, looking at my face as though she had read my thoughts. "It's better to trust than to hate."

"I'm thinking of them," I answered. "They've been let down so many times. It will be awful if the woman isn't their mother after all."

The next day we travelled to London in the Land Rover – Mummy, Ben, Lisa, the three Travers children and myself. It was quite a squash. Ben always goes with the Land Rover because he's the only person who can change a wheel if necessary, and the children wanted Lisa and me for company. They had taken the news very well on the surface, but deep inside themselves they were obviously in turmoil. None of them had eaten breakfast. Kenny talked non-stop, Marion followed Mummy everywhere and Sally held on to Zed as though he was the last straw which would stop her sinking into heaven knows what. None of them dared hope for much, and we were not hopeful either.

It seemed better that way. It was a long way to London, but we had left early, unable to stand the suspense any longer, and arrived two hours ahead of time in the Cromwell Road.

"Let's go to the Natural History Museum," suggested Mummy. "We can't wait in the hospital for two hours, we'll go mad."

"Super," cried Lisa.

"Yes, please," said Kenny.

So we parked in Exhibition Road and filled a meter and toured the Natural History Museum. I don't think the Traverses really saw anything; their minds were too full of what lay ahead – but at least they pretended. Ben spent a long time studying the deep-sea rig and I liked the model horses and stable of long ago. As for Lisa, she rushed from gallery to gallery pressing buttons. Halfway through we lost Kenny completely, but we found him

eventually, going up and down the escalators.

Mummy bought us all ice creams and then we returned to the Land Rover and continued our journey. I think we all felt on edge. Mummy went down a one-way street the wrong way, and Kenny returned to twisting a handkerchief round and round in his hands.

Lisa whispered, "I'm terrified. I feel sick. Supposing it isn't the right person?"

"We must try," I whispered back.

"She may not want us," said Sally unexpectedly.

"Let's jump our fences as we come to them," replied Mummy. "She may not be your mother at all; in fact it's most likely, so don't hope for too much, please. We are only going on a hunch, nothing more."

"We weren't very nice to her, at least I wasn't," continued Sally.

"She won't hold that against you. Mothers love you whatever you do," said Mummy.

London was full of cars and people and endless traffic jams, when buses seemed to block every junction, and people drooped at bus stops in the heat and swarmed out of Underground stations like swarms of bees coming out of a hive.

Mummy took three wrong turnings, but we were still early when we reached the hospital. The Travers children looked very white, and even Lisa was silent. Mummy went straight to Reception and presently Sister Lightfoot came to meet us. She took us along endless corridors and, as we walked, the Travers children seemed to grow smaller and smaller and whiter and whiter, until when at last we stopped they looked more zombie than human. Christine Lightfoot had hot cups of coffee waiting for us and biscuits.

"I know this is an ordeal for you all," she said, handing round the biscuits. "I think the little boy should

366

come with me first, just me and him – all right?"

"But I'm the eldest," argued Sally.

"But the little boy just the same," said Christine Lightfoot with a firm smile. "He's the youngest, isn't he? And today we are going to do everything the wrong way round."

A minute later she disappeared with Kenny, while Marion and Sally dashed to the Ladies.

The next five minutes were fearsome. None of us could sit still and there was nothing to see outside but the backs of buildings and a small chunk of sky. And I found myself longing for the country, for the clean smell of horses and hay and new-mown grass. I thought of Lorraine unridden for two days, of Windfall growing larger every day without us really noticing, and I wondered what I was doing here in a great city which I hated. I felt shut in, like a wild pony must feel suddenly enclosed in a loose box after the freedom of the moors.

Then Christine Lightfoot came back with her thumbs up, saying, "The other two can come in now."

Mummy asked, "It's all right, then?" in tones of great joy.

And Ben said, "We'll be paid now."

I didn't say anything because what I felt was too deep for words and my eyes were suddenly full of silly, sentimental tears. It was as though we had been climbing a steep hill for a long time and now we had reached the top and there were all the things we wanted on the other side.

Afterwards Lisa told me at that moment she had felt just the same, but later she had hated the Traverses for keeping her at the hospital when she might have been riding at home.

Presently Ben grew impatient too, and Mummy said, "Do stop fidgeting, they won't be much longer."

The minutes seemed like hours and Lisa wailed, "I want to be at home. I hate it here."

"If only there was something to read," said Ben.

"Or see," I added.

Then at last Sister Lightfoot came back with all three children. "I would like to see you in the office, please, Mrs Pemberton," she said.

Ben raised his eyes to the ceiling, muttering, "Another hour of waiting. I can't bear it."

The three Travers children sat down quietly and Sally said, "It is Mummy. She's very ill, of course."

368

And Kenny said, "It's lovely, isn't it? Just like a fairy tale."

They didn't jump for joy or scream with delight, as I might have done. Perhaps being brought up by a nanny makes you like that, or perhaps they were simply dazed.

"Do you think she'll take us miles away to live?" asked Kenny after a time. "We don't want to leave you, and we don't want to lose the ponies, just when we're getting on and winning rosettes."

"Exactly," agreed Sally in a firm voice.

And I thought: They've been bitten by the bug, the horsy bug. How unexpected.

"I couldn't live without the ponies," said Marion.

"And there's Zed too. Mummy may not like him," added Sally. "I've never liked anything as much as I like riding, and I love Jill, though I think she's got a silly name. Can we change it?"

"Of course," said Ben. "They've all got awful names if you ask me, they're so jolly babyish."

"Exactly," agreed Sally.

"You could call them bird names," suggested Lisa thoughtfully. "Things like Curlew and Kestrel and Starling."

A meal was being brought in now for the patients. It smelled delicious and my mouth started watering, but the Traverses hardly noticed.

"I hate changes," said Sally. "I was quite happy with Daddy. Now I don't want to move again."

"I like the country," announced Marion.

"Pavements are ugh!" said Kenny.

Mummy returned at last. "Home," she said. "You can see your mum again the day after tomorrow, so don't worry. The time will soon pass and she'll soon be better and then you will all be home again. It's like a miracle, isn't it?"

"We haven't got a home," replied Kenny.

"Well, somewhere anyway," answered Mummy, leading the way down the stairs.

"What did your mother say?" asked Lisa as we climbed into the Land Rover.

"She cried a lot and kept saying it was like a jigsaw and there were only a few pieces left," replied Sally.

"She'll need nursing for a little time yet," said Mummy. "The Social Services people will be taking you up to see her so not to worry. She's not herself yet but she's going to make a complete recovery, the worst is over now."

"And Daddy?" asked Sally.

"That's our next hurdle. But don't worry, darling, we'll sort it out with time."

We were all half asleep when we reached home.

The house looked dreamy and romantic in the dusk. Our horses were waiting to be fed. Mrs Mills and James had cooked supper. Colonel Hunter was already sitting in the dining-room sipping sherry. Dad was putting garden chairs away.

"Well, what happened?" he called.

"We've found her," called Mummy. "Isn't it marvellous? Now, with time, they can be together again."

"Which calls for a celebration," cried Daddy. "Because I may have landed a job too."

Thirteen

Another job

It was nearly September now and suddenly the rain came and the grass started to grow again and the trees sprouted new leaves and the pond filled up. It was like a second spring. The Travers children were collected in a large car driven by the girl from Social Services and taken to see their mother in hospital. While they were away, the police called. Mummy and Dad talked to them in the dining-room. We were not allowed in and though Lisa listened at the keyhole and was caught by Mrs Mills, she heard nothing of importance. Mummy and Dad would tell us nothing of the visit. "When the picture is complete, you'll know all, but not before," said Dad.

"The police have to see Mrs Travers," Mummy added.

"But when are the children going? It's school in less than a week now. Are they coming with me or what?" cried Lisa, who can never wait for news, food, or anything else.

"I've seen your head teacher," replied Mummy.

"Why didn't you tell me?" cried Lisa.

Our stud of horses was getting fatter. We stopped feeding hay. Windfall coughed no more and the Travers's ponies looked more beautiful every day. Zed continued to steal things off the kitchen table, and the

Travers's bill grew bigger and bigger with no sign of payment from anyone. Dad had been able to find a part-time job, managing the timetable of a fleet of lorries. We started to get our clothes ready for school. I needed new plimsolls, a new winter coat and socks.

Lisa needed a skirt, but Mummy said we had to wait until the Traverses paid their bill.

Ben wanted trousers because his were now above his ankles. "I can't wear them. I shall be the laughing-stock of the whole school," he cried.

Suddenly we started to hate the Traverses because they were the cause of our poverty. "Can't you sue them?" cried Ben.

"They should go to prison," said James. "I must have a decent jacket for the Sixth Form College. I can't go in my old blazer."

"And what about the horses?" cried Ben. "The vet's bill has just come again in red. I wish they had never come."

But they seemed oblivious of our feelings.

When they were not visiting their mother, they rode. I took them for endless marathon rides, down old railway tracks, over hills, through miles of woods. We took picnics and maps in our pockets and they loved it. Their faces were brown, their thin arms sprouted muscles. Mummy said that they must be kept occupied and exercised because they were going through a difficult time, but they looked all right to me.

Everything was rain-swept and beautiful now. Dashing clouds scurried across a blue sky. The nights felt warm and limp.

It was a mad time; the seasons seemed to have changed places. Nothing seemed certain any more. Dad was overcome with spring fever and bought a huge quantity of paint and started to decorate the house in

the evenings. Mrs Mills started gardening again and Colonel Hunter went for long walks, while Mike continued to work on the farm, returning home late in the evening with dead rabbits, which made Lisa scream.

We were all longing for the end of it all, for the final pieces to be fitted into the jigsaw of the Traverses lives. We wanted a final solution. We wanted their fate decided one way or another. "How can we decide how much hay to order if we don't know whether their ponies are staying or not?" asked Ben.

"Supposing some more guests want to come, what then?" asked James.

"I don't know what to tell my friends," complained Lisa.

"It's so infuriating. It's like a book without an ending. I want an end," I complained.

"We are just beginning the last chapter," said Mummy. "Tomorrow is the day."

"The day for what?" cried Lisa.

"For telling all."

"I don't believe you. You're making it up," cried Lisa. "It's the last day before school."

"Their mother comes tomorrow."

"What, here?" I asked.

"To stay?" cried Lisa.

"Yes, with a nurse. I'm afraid you will have to move out of your room again, Harriet," Mummy said.

I looked out of the window at the green grass. I didn't want to move again.

"Where am I to sleep then?" I asked.

"In the attic."

"Why is she coming?" asked Lisa.

"To convalesce, and to work out their future," replied Mummy.

"What about their father?"

"He's not coming for the time being."

"Then what about the bills they've run up?" asked Ben.

"Not to worry. We will know all tomorrow," repeated Mummy, starting to dance around the kitchen.

Lisa cried, "Stop it. Be sensible, Mummy. Is it really happening?"

Later the Travers children returned from hospital, bursting into the house, laughing. "Mummy's coming tomorrow," cried Marion. "She's coming to live here."

"And we can keep the ponies for ever and ever," shouted Kenny. "She's much, much better. She can remember how it all happened. How she walked out, but meant to come back."

"She was knocked down by something and left at the side of the road," said Sally.

"And someone took her rings, her rings off her fingers and her bracelet," added Kenny. "She never meant to leave us. I knew it all the time. She hadn't a boyfriend at all."

The next day the Traverses rose early and started to watch the drive for a car or ambulance, their faces shining with anticipation. At intervals they rushed down to the paddock to throw their arms round their ponies' necks and cry "Mummy's coming!" Zed bounded everywhere after them.

Later, when the heat drove them into the house, he followed them, leaving dirty paw marks everywhere. Mummy sang in the kitchen. Ben wandered about saying, "And supposing she can't pay either?"

"Don't be silly," said Mummy sharply. "Stop thinking of money. Of course she can pay. Why don't you trust people?"

"Here we go again," said Ben.

Lisa was practising for an approaching gymkhana.

"I've put my name down for the Prince Philip B Team," she said, putting up bending poles. "I intend to go to Wembley."

I started to give Windfall leading lessons. She had filled out again and the awful hollows and wrinkles in her quarters had gone.

I hated the thought of school tomorrow, of banging desks and scuffles in the corridors and everyone pushing at lunch-time. I decided I would take packed lunches and eat them outside under a tree. Then I saw an ambulance coming up the drive and suddenly I was running towards the house crying, "She's coming, she's here," and Sally was flinging open the front door and Zed was barking, sounding like the hound of the Baskervilles.

And I knew suddenly that this was the end of the chapter; that whatever happened now and in spite of the pain and grief, we had succeeded. It was a wonderful warm feeling, better than winning a prize or being top of the class at school.

Mrs Travers wore her straw-coloured hair in a ponytail. She had a distinguished nose and beautiful eyes and dimples when she smiled. Her nurse was called Betty and was red-headed with freckles.

Betty said, "Straight to bed, Mrs Travers. We'll do a little more tomorrow," and Mummy led the way into the house.

The children followed at a distance and their mother kept smiling at them over her shoulder. Later we met her properly, sitting in our best spare room. She sat propped up by pillows and said, "I don't know how to thank you all for everything, you have been marvellous. But first of all I want to pay my debts and then I want you to look for a cottage for me – something pretty with an orchard for the ponies and wistaria round the windows, you know what I mean – four bedrooms, because we'll want one for you when you come to stay. And a stable too, and a big kitchen."

"It will cost a great deal," replied Ben from the doorway.

"What is a great deal?" asked Mrs Travers, whom we would later call Sheila.

"Two hundred thousand pounds."

"That's all right. Our old house was sold to an Arab sheikh for a quarter of a million and since it was in my name the money is mine, so not to worry," she replied, smiling. "Now let me write a cheque while I'm still compos mentis. How much do I owe you?"

So the mystery of the Travers's lives was almost solved; and there was only one secret left – the reason for Mick Travers changing his family name and disappearing – and that we never really solved. Ben insisted that the taxmen were after him, while James was sure that he had robbed a bank and escaped with all the money. "The men who tried to take the children from us were his accomplices; they wanted their share," he said.

Mummy and Dad wouldn't talk about it. And Sheila Travers said, "Handsome is as handsome does; we're better off without him."

So one way or another, your guess is as good as mine. Personally I think he was in love with someone else because, if he had loved Sheila, he would have stayed to find her, dead or alive.

The holidays were over now and the future looked as calm as the calmest sea. Then by the next day's post a letter came addressed to me and Ben, which was to start us on another wave of endeavour and excitement.

The letter went like this:

Dear Ben and Harriet Pemberton,

I am writing to ask your help. You have been highly recommended to me as champion horse-breakers, and I have a fifteen hand gelding who needs training. He is not an easy case. His name is Hillingdon Prince (his dam was Hillingdon Princess) but we call him Bronco, which explains a lot. At the moment he is lame from a hock injury, but can you have him in December? I would expect to pay at least fifty pounds a week, plus a bonus of two hundred pounds if you manage to make him rideable in six weeks. You are my last hope. He is very beautiful, a real champion, and he can jump anything. If you can't help, it will mean the knacker's yard for him.

Yours sincerely,
Jean Nuttal

      ✳   *✳*   *✳*

"Whoever recommended us? They must be loony," exclaimed Ben.

"We must have him," I said. "We can't let him go to the knacker's."

"And we'll need the money for hay and oats and hunting caps," added Ben.

"It's a challenge," I said. "Like a glove thrown down in olden times. Let's answer right away."

And so began another battle, equine this time, but how we fought it and whether we won or lost belongs to another book.

Now you must leave us: the Travers children and their mother still with us, Lisa making plans for future gymkhanas, James putting his books together for the Sixth Form College and Ben and I writing:

Dear Mrs Nuttal,
Thank you for your letter. We will be delighted to train your fifteen hand gelding Bronco . . .

Never imagining the chaos he would cause. Blundering into another job without stopping to think. But then that's us . . . we're like Mummy, just plain reckless.